THE RISE OF LADY JUSTICE

A Novel

Alicia Sienne Voltmer

ISBN-13: 9781733425919 (paperback)

ACKNOWLEDGMENTS

This novel is the product of four years of writing, rewriting, revising, and editing all accomplished in the scraps of time outside of my full-time career as a practicing labor and employment law litigator. Whether at my dining room table in Texas or Wyoming, in a hotel room wherever I was, or in airports or coffee shops, I wrote in the early morning hours before work, in the middle of the night when I couldn't sleep, and on weekends and holidays. Fortunately, I had help and wish to recognize and thank the following:

My family, John and Carole Voltmer, Chever Voltmer, and Sabra V. Matovsky for being brave enough to read an early draft and provide feedback.

Nick Matovsky, for giving feedback on the cover art.

Ben Finley, for beta reading and educating me about cycling gear and terminology.

My husband, Jeff Ecker, for the ongoing tutorial on all-things related to firearms and for reminding me to periodically backup my hard drive to avoid losing the work.

Juanici (Nicie) Pratt, a kindred writing spirit who has made me a better lawyer and inspired me to write this novel.

Tilly Dorsey, for her friendship and encouragement.

Terry Trauner, for her kindness, grammatical feedback, and willingness to be a beta reader.

Danielle Sobol, the gifted photographer responsible for my jacket cover photo.

Tiki Engel, the talented stylist who makes me look good even when I feel otherwise.

Marg (Margarita) Shadid, for her mentoring, encouragement, unwavering support, substantive and critical feedback, willingness to critique multiple drafts, enthusiasm, and friendship. And for introducing me to the "Marg" cocktail.

The Kids, who kept me company during all the odd writing hours.

†

My big toe itched.

Body check. It wasn't the first time I'd found myself in a prone position wondering if and how I was injured, usually due to my own carelessness, but something about this time was different. My brain felt soggy and struggled to connect with the rest of my body to make sure it was all still there. After mentally confirming the existence of ten fingers and ten toes, my eyes snapped open as they frequently did during my insomnia-infested attempts at sleep.

I was on my back in a bed staring at an unfamiliar ceiling. I peeked under the covers and saw an oversized gift tag hanging off of my right big toe. Using my left big toe, I dislodged the scratchy thing and kicked it off the end of the bed.

My eyes swept the unfamiliar yet oddly comforting room and settled on my favorite dusty, well-worn pair of hiking boots lying on their side near the closet. They were soaking wet, as were the thick hiking socks strewn haphazardly across them, which was odd considering I hadn't been hiking in a long time.

Where the hell was I?

The light reflecting off the puddle of water under the boots drew my attention to the rays streaming in from the doorway. I wanted to investigate their source but wasn't sure if I could due to the dull ache that thumped in my chest like the metronome app I used on my iPod when I ran. The guy at the running store had convinced me to download it to improve my cadence. My brain associated that particular sound with shin splints and a sore Achilles tendon. It was uncomfortable, and I didn't like it.

Instinct told me that sitting upright would be unpleasant, but I needed to figure out why I felt as if I'd been hit in the chest with a baseball bat. I forced my body up, swung my feet off the bed, and hit the oak wood floor with an involuntary grunt. I padded into the adjoining bathroom to find my faded-blue, palm tree-covered bathrobe hanging on the back of the door and the green charging light from my electric toothbrush winking at me from the corner of the vanity. The bowl-shaped sink was smeared with old makeup and dried toothpaste, just the way I remember I'd left it at home. But this wasn't home.

I doubt you'll want to hear this, but that wasn't a gift tag on your toe. I think it was a morgue tag, so now is as good a time as any to confront the bad facts, Lawyer Brain said. *Isn't that what every good trial lawyer would do?* Lawyer Brain was the name I'd given to one of several of the voices in my head, and although it occupied a modest amount of space in my gray matter real estate, it undeniably had some of the best views.

Unable to argue with Lawyer Brain's logic, I turned my gaze to the mirror above the sink. The image that stared back at me was a slightly different version of my former self. My dark auburn hair and pasty skin color hadn't changed, but the menacing, indigo circles that had taken up permanent residence under my eyes during the last twelve months had disappeared. My right shoulder moved effortlessly as I jostled the ball and socket, but the continuous burning in my chest brought me back to the reason I'd decided to leave the bed.

There was no other way to do it. I grabbed the bottom edge of my pajama top and yanked it up violently, the same way I always ripped off the Band-Aids that covered my frequent knife mishaps and paper cuts. I shrieked and let go of the fabric when I saw the black flesh of my upper torso punctuated by a partially healed wound through my heart. I turned to the side and noticed an exit wound through my back. I returned to the bedroom and picked up the toe tag I'd kicked onto the floor.

"Adeleine Tanis, female, GSW, g1p1," it read.

I didn't recognize the second acronym, but I did know the first one. *GSW. Gunshot wound.* Considering that everything I knew about them came from watching late-night re-runs of crime-scene dramas, I had no idea what caliber of weapon had made this hole, but I knew the person who wielded it had a compelling motive and a damned-good aim.

The words sank in, and I started hyperventilating. I'd been on the receiving end of some vague threats associated with the high-dollar, high-profile case I'd been defending, the one that would take my trial lawyer career to the next level, but nothing I'd taken seriously. I eased myself onto the floor and stuck my head between my legs.

When my breathing returned to something closer to normal, I cobbled together enough courage to wander out of the bedroom, where I found myself in a large, square room. It was familiar to me not because I'd been here before but because I'd imagined it in thousands of daydreams. It was the home I would've inhabited in my version of a perfect world.

To my left was a floor-to-ceiling wall of glass overlooking a vast stretch of ocean, held at bay by a beach of twinkling, pale-pink sand. The distant horizon revealed no secrets of the world beyond, but the sound of the ebbing tide, clearly audible from where I stood, provided a comforting counter-rhythm to the pain in my chest.

Polished wooden beams traversed the cathedral ceiling, and the electronic blinds were raised to maximize the spectacular views. The tide clock on the wall, which indicated the flow of the water but not the time of day by hour, reminded me of the one in the house where I vacationed as a child, only there was no identification of the body of water to which it belonged.

To the right was another glass wall with a view of jagged, snow-capped peaks unmarred by the vertical lines of ski trails or fire breaks. I saw the electric-green needles on the pine trees that lined the ridges and smelled their fresh scent intermingled with the taste of salt water on my tongue.

A crackling sound diverted my attention to the opposite end of the room where a wood fire burned in a large, rough-hewn stone hearth. Perched atop the mantle like roosting birds were photographs in frames of different shapes and sizes. They were the same pictures that occupied that position of importance in my home, and nestled behind the protective glass barriers were the faces I loved—my parents, my little brother Christopher, my best friend Liz, and my feisty Abyssinian cat, Maverick.

My eyes lingered the longest on the last one, a picture of my boyfriend Rynner and me, standing at the Death Canyon trailhead in Grand Teton National Park. Rynner grinned at the camera as if he'd just won the lottery and looked like an outdoor guide ready to film an expedition segment. The cream-colored, linen envelope resting against that photo was addressed to me, and the note tucked inside was written in mercilessly efficient block print, the kind I associated with engineers and number crunchers, the type with no wasted curls or grandiose flourishes.

"Welcome. Get some rest. We've got a lot to discuss," it read. I didn't recognize the handwriting. The hair on my arms stood at attention. I needed something more than a few familiar belongings to use as an anchor point before I lost it in a complete meltdown.

A device that resembled a laptop with a keyboard was centered on the bow-front desk facing the water. I used the fumes from the courage I'd summoned to make it to the desk chair, where I sat down and hit the return key. In response to my keystroke, the screen lit up with an Internet search browser. I stared at it for a while wondering what to do next, until it became clear to me that I couldn't remember anything that preceded my presence here. I typed in my name, thinking it was plain stupid to run a search on myself for the thousandth time but did it anyway.

Every hit on that first search result page told the story of my end. Another sharp pain arced across my chest as I scrolled through the headlines.

"Lawyer murdered during opening statement in TSC trial."

"FBI launches investigation into fatal shooting in historic courthouse."

The first story featured a black-and-white photograph of the familiar state courtroom in Dallas where I'd spent a good deal of time earning my paycheck, with a close-up of the wooden lectern, the sides framing the surface worn smooth and discolored by the thousands of lawyers' hands that had gripped it in both triumph and defeat, where I'd stood to deliver my opening statement in the most significant case I'd defended to date.

I opened another, salacious-looking story and rocked back in the chair from the shock of the cover photo. The photographer had zoomed in on my legal pad covered in dark splotches. I could just make out the only words on the page, scribbled in my familiar hand, that read, "YOU, THE JURY, ARE THE SOLE DECISION-MAKERS REGARDING THE FACTS OF THIS CASE, AND MUST DECIDE…"

I stopped reading. When I jotted down that one line on the morning of my opening statement, I was on the cusp of making partner with the boutique defense firm of Philmore, Grace, and Rhein, and had been hand-picked for the daunting task of defending TSC, formally known as TriStateCorp. TSC was the largest oil and gas company in the South and had been sued in a multi-plaintiff lawsuit for personal injuries allegedly related to its hydraulic fracturing activities, or fracking, in a small town outside of Dallas called Radiant.

Winning this case would not only be the equivalent of my Southern Debut but would also result in my name on the letter-head and a few extra decimal places in my paycheck.

Five years prior, during the worst recession in modern history, TSC's engineers had discovered an extensive natural gas reserve within the town limits of Radiant, a podunk, unattractive, blue-collar dump that had been home to an automobile assembly plant that employed several thousand people until the mid-1990s, when the company's owners moved the work overseas for cheaper labor.

The sprawling, decrepit facility, surrounded by a fence topped with razor wire and punctuated by "DO NOT ENTER" signs, was a monolith to the global economy where foreign workers could produce the same vehicles at a fraction of the cost. The town was as depressed as it was depressing, which made it an attractive opportunity and high-value target for my newest and most significant client.

TSC's comprehensive engineering surveys revealed that Radiant sat directly over dense, natural gas deposits which, in the right market, could be worth hundreds of millions of dollars. Tessa Carter, TSC's President and CEO, recognized the potential to make a killing through a kind of delayed gratification and conscripted her crack team of advisors, described by insiders as the Dust to Dividends, or D2D Team, to assist with a plan to turn the dirt into dollars.

†

A light scratching sound at the front door startled me, spreading goosebumps down my legs. *Now someone was trying to get in?* My fear was raw, fueled by the adrenaline of the fight-or-flight twins. The lovely room had no apparent weapons. The only viable flight path was through the front door. I was trapped.

"*I know you're scared. I won't hurt you. Please open the door for me,*" said a voice in my head, and not one of the ones I recognized.

The panic level at full throttle, I slid off the chair and hid under the desk.

"Get out of here. Leave me alone," I screamed as loudly as I could.

"*Addie, it's me, Peter. Your Peter. Don't you remember the day we met at the pet adoption?*"

It's okay to open the door. There's no boogeyman on the other side, Sixth Sense said. Sixth Sense was one of the voices I did recognize in my head, and I trusted it because it had never led me astray. Yet.

I pulled myself off of the floor, shaking uncontrollably, walked over to the door and flung it open. I blinked several times to adjust my eyes to the bright sunlight, but no one was there. A scuffling sound redirected me to the ground at my feet, where I stared into the melting-chocolate-brown eyes of my beloved Peter, a fluffy, black-and-white, floppy-eared bunny with a pink satin ribbon tied loosely around his neck. I recognized the distinctive black ring around his left eye because it was that same mark that made my five-year-old self throw an epic tantrum at the pet adoption center until I convinced my dad to let me take him home.

Peter had lived a pampered life as my first pet and died at the ripe old age of ten. His was the first family death I'd experienced, considering that both sets of my grandparents had, to my current knowledge, survived me. And now, here he was on the doorstep of my mountain beach house. The image of *Alice in Wonderland* flashed through my mind, and I wondered if Peter would speak out loud, but he didn't. He turned his head away and then back to me.

"Thank you for opening the door. I've waited a long time to see you again. You'll be okay, but right now, I need you to follow me," said the unfamiliar voice in my noggin that I figured out was Peter's.

Peter wasn't the type of anchor point I'd had in mind to keep me from losing it, but the sight of him, fifteen years after the last time I saw him, made my eyes well up. Before I took another step, I leaned down, scooped him into my arms, and planted tear-soaked kisses on his pink, freckled nose. He briefly indulged me and then squirmed to be released. I followed him down the powdery beach to the only structure along the shore, a two-story, clapboard house with a wrap-around deck on the second floor. We entered through an open door on the bottom floor and found ourselves in an ample, open living space.

Linen-covered sofas and chairs decorated with throw pillows in varying shades of blue surrounded a square, glass coffee table. A vase full of seashells sat in the middle of the table surrounded by a circular-shaped, wooden planter filled with Arabic jasmine. Prisms danced around the room from the light reflecting off of the stained-glass windows set high up in the walls. We crossed through the room and simultaneously stopped at a wooden staircase that led to the second floor.

"Go on up," Peter said in my head. *"I'll wait down here."*

I broke out in a nervous sweat as I climbed the staircase alone, telling myself there was no reason my childhood pet would cause me more harm than I'd already suffered. When I reached the second floor, the sliding glass doors to the deck were open, and two, strappy beach chairs faced the water. One chair was already occupied. The other was waiting for me.

As I stepped onto the deck and eased into the empty chair, I instinctively repositioned myself for a better view of the figure seated beside me, who was a woman of nearly indiscernible age. If I had to guess, I'd say She was somewhere north of twenty and south of sixty. Her fiery red hair, several shades brighter than my own, was tied back from Her face with a green velvet ribbon, and an over-sized pair of black sunglasses peeked out from the brim of Her white sun visor.

In Her left hand, a sunrise-colored cocktail sweated in a tall glass, and in Her right hand, She held what looked like a computer tablet. Her skin gave off subtle pulses of light that ran the length of Her body and ended at Her studded, wedge sandals.

A highball glass filled with clear liquid sat on the mosaic table next to my chair. The familiar smell of gin wafted past my nose on the ocean breeze, tempting me for a taste. When She turned toward me, I knew that although I'd never seen Her before, I'd known Her my entire life.

Admittedly, I'd cursed Her, confided in Her, thanked Her, asked for favors, and begged for Her forgiveness. From the deepest and most private part of my soul, I knew She was the living embodiment of my personal vision of the Almighty.

"Your opening statement would've set the stage for a spectacular victory if you'd had the chance to complete it," She said in a voice that was authoritatively soothing.

"Who are you? What happened to me, and why am I here?" I blurted out, distracted by Her orange toenails, each of which was adorned with a perfectly painted yellow sun.

"Am I dead?" I added meekly, almost as an afterthought. She gave me the same look my mother gave me when I asked a stupid question.

"You know who I am. I must say I do enjoy this look. It's far more comfortable than many others. The answer to your question is that I'm known by hundreds and maybe even thousands of names, including *God, He, She, the Almighty, the Alpha, the Omega, the Divine,* and *the Creator.* It shouldn't surprise you that I appear to each person I meet as they truly see me. From the Burning Bush to the Bright White Light, I've found it helps with the transition. As to what happened to you, I know you've figured out that you were murdered by a sniper during your opening statement to the jury at the TSC trial. That wasn't your original destiny, but intervening events required an alteration in your fate. Fortunately, it just so happens that the course correction was, and pardon the pun, a godsend because I need you, Adeleine, and earlier than planned."

The cold sweat that had drenched my pajamas evaporated. I settled back into the chair as She took a long sip from the straw in her drink. Her words were unsettling, but I wasn't sure what disturbed me more—that I was dead or that the Divine needed me.

I don't want to be here, I thought.

"My judgment is final. You need to accept it," She replied out loud. My inner voice was no longer private.

"You're telling me that I have a purpose here? What on earth is it? Why couldn't it wait?"

"You do have a purpose here, but that's a discussion for a different time." I opened my mouth to protest, but she pulled her sunglasses a few inches down her nose and stared at me with eyes that looked and moved like a kaleidoscope. I was unable to form any words. She'd effectively tongue-tied me.

Understanding we were done with that topic for the moment, I switched subjects.

"Why Peter?"

"The Rule of Firsts. Every soul's first encounter here must be with a close relation, usually a deceased family member. In your case, you're survived by your entire immediate family, including your cat, Maverick. Brilliant cat, by the way. Peter was the closest living thing to family who passed before you, so naturally, he was your Greeter."

She adjusted the brim of her hat to deflect the rays of the setting sun and drained the remnants of Her cocktail. I had so many questions to ask, but Her body language told me we were done for now.

"You have other business to address, as do I. We'll speak again soon."

I found Peter waiting for me at the bottom of the staircase, and we meandered along the beach until I could see my dream house down the coastline. When the pain in my chest increased from aching to searing, I took a break and sat down on the sand to rest. I extended my arms to Peter, who raised one ear in an expression of mock disdain before climbing into my lap to watch the sun journey below the horizon.

As terrifying as this all was, and setting aside the physical pain I was experiencing and the emotional pain I was blocking, I was confused by Her words and the jumble of conflicting emotions. During the past year, I'd lost count of the number of new lows I'd hit and wasn't sure I recognized or even liked the weak-willed person I'd become. *That* person didn't deserve to be *Here*.

Lawyer Brain needled at me for answers. *You weren't randomly selected for that shot, it was intended for you, which means someone planned your death. We've got intent, so what's the motive? I'm betting it has something to do with the role you're supposed to play here. Figure it out.* I leaned back with my elbows planted in the sand to meditate on the rising tide.

✝

Thoughts crept into my head as the water inched up the beach. I couldn't deny things began to change less than twelve months ago when TSC decided to retain me as lead counsel, and I decided I'd do anything to secure a stunning victory to earn the title of the youngest and most successful female litigator in the city's testosterone-filled legal profession.

Had I gone too far?

It was an otherwise unremarkable Monday morning in early September when a massive explosion leveled the town of Radiant. Within minutes of the town's destruction, local media from the surrounding areas converged on Radiant's perimeter, immediately secured by Homeland Security and FBI teams, to be the first on the scene to capture and broadcast the Hiroshima-like devastation. Preliminary estimates put the death toll at close to 6,000 people, and by the time FEMA and the EPA showed up, Radiant was an alphabet soup of Feds.

At the time of the blast, I was in my office in downtown Dallas staring out at a distinctive bend in the road several blocks away while taking a break from drafting a legal brief. My window looked out over the Grassy Knoll where President John F. Kennedy was assassinated, and sometimes I stared at that gentle curve of the street and the innocuous mound of grass wondering whether the conspiracy theories were true.

The only reason I knew about the explosion was that the background music from the radio station I was streaming was interrupted by the breaking news story. David Philmore, whose name was the first to grace the law firm door and consequently the signature line of my paycheck, stopped by my office during the announcement.

"TSC will be here in fifteen minutes for a meeting in Main. They've specifically requested your attendance, so come prepared."

This had to be important because Main was our most technologically advanced conference room equipped with the latest wireless gadgets and doodads and reserved exclusively for our largest clients with "bet the farm" cases. TSC had never before engaged the firm, but all of us knew that representing a client like that was better than owning a platinum mine.

I changed into my tried-and-true red power suit and five-inch heels I kept in the office for emergency court dates and last-minute meetings, swiped on the *I mean business* Chanel lipstick, and headed for Main. Inside the conference room, Philmore, Edward Grace, and Jürgen Rhein, the firm's founding members, assembled stiffly around the far end of the burl oak conference table that seated forty.

From the neck down, they were nearly indistinguishable in their tailored, dark-blue suits, except for the different colored silk ties each sported. All three wore white, Italian-made dress shirts with monogrammed cuff links and leather loafers buffed to a high gloss. Three of the six wrists among them featured a different version of the Rolex Mariner.

As soon as I crossed the threshold into Main, I felt a change in the room's energy. All eyes were on me.

"Do we know why they're coming?" I asked.

"Not yet," replied Grace, "but we heard Wiley walked out of a meeting with his favorite New York City defense firm to fly to Dallas to meet us."

I heard TSC's AugustaWestland VVIP helicopter approach the building's helipad before I saw it through the windows overlooking downtown. The majestic, thirty-seat bird was one of several I'd heard TSC owned and was painted metallic black with TSC's red and yellow triangular logo emblazoned on the side and tail. The color scheme reminded me of snakes.

Weren't the poisonous ones black with red and yellow rings?

We seated ourselves in the usual pecking order along the side of the table with our backs to the window, meaning I, as the youngest of the foursome, was closest to the conference room door and farthest from the center of the legal business universe. Within minutes, Tessa, who barely crested five feet in her stilettos, and her entourage filed into the room and curtly introduced themselves. Four of the members were bodyguards.

Like most groups, this one had its own dynamic tension that manifested itself through body language cues and tones of voice. In an unexpected move, Tessa took the seat directly opposite from me and with nothing more than a nod directed the remainder of her team to sit opposite my partners.

I'd never met her before, but unidentified tabloid sources described Tessa Carter as a member of that elite tribe of successful but soulless female mercenaries who viewed kindness and empathy as weaknesses inherent in the XX chromosomal scheme. If she had a personal life, no one kissed and told. Regardless of whether she controlled the media or her security detail managed the Paparazzi, there were rarely unauthorized photographs of or articles about her published in any medium.

The backbone of her D2D team consisted of Goddard "Gator" Beaudoin, TSC's Senior Vice President of Engineering, Carlos Guerrera, Senior Vice President of Operations, and Reyna Malone, Director of Marketing.

Benton Wiley, the company's General Counsel, served as the legal skin that covered this beast. Wiley was a legend among in-house lawyers due to his knack for bending straightforward legal precedent and government regulations into pretzel shapes and balloon animals.

To avoid unwanted attention by the regulators, competitors, concerned citizens, and anyone else who might have an interest in or concern about the profits, politics, or collateral damage of D2D, Wiley created a mind-boggling number of shell companies through which Guerrera's team purchased or otherwise acquired the slurry blenders, high-pressure, high-volume fracturing pumps, storage tanks, proppant, cement, and other equipment and materials necessary to develop dividends from dust.

During Wiley's twenty-two-year reign over TSC's legal department, the company had never paid a dime in regulatory fines despite its questionable drilling and reclamation practices and had never been found liable by a jury in any court across the country. If the D2D team had a chief wrangler, it was Wiley, and his invisible lasso was fashioned out of his knowledge of each team member's closet skeletons. Those familiar with the inner workings of TSC knew there was no amount of discord a private discussion with Wiley couldn't quell.

Immediately upon taking his seat, Guerrera pushed his chair away from the table and leaned back, arms crossed over his chest and legs splayed. Judging by the look in his grey-green eyes, he was testing me for a reaction. Afraid I would blush if I stared too long, I redirected my gaze toward Gator, who sat close to the table with his hands calculatingly folded to cover the three missing fingers on his right hand.

Wiley, whose face was kind but unreadable, sat across from Philmore clutching several files he'd brought with him. Philmore was the first to speak, but before he could finish his warning about the need to remove the bodyguards from the room to protect the attorney-client-privileged conversation we were about to have, Tessa cut him off.

"Skip the bullshit, David. They stay, and for purposes of any and all future conversations, they were never here."

"Of course, Ms. Carter. We understand."

The familiarity with the way she addressed Philmore and his immediate and uncharacteristic submissiveness to her ethically questionable request was unexpected, but I had no time to dwell on it because the next thing I knew, Wiley pulled the roadkill out of the bag.

He slid a file across the table to me.

"We've got a problem in Radiant," he said, so casually you might've thought he was talking about the weather.

I opened the file to find a number of pictures of TSC's pre-explosion drill pads in Radiant, along with satellite photos of the blast site wasteland that had to have been taken within the hour.

"The explosion occurred near one of our drill sites, and we received a tip that parasites from Budd Frantsen's law firm will file a lawsuit this evening," Wiley continued.

"*Ga lee, what a De'pouille,*" Gator muttered in Cajun. *Wow, what a mess.*

"English, please," Tessa snapped.

I caught the menacing look Gator shot her, but it never reached its intended target because her eyes were locked on me.

"This will be your only case, Ms. Tanis, and I expect nothing less than a victory."

My partners leaned forward in their chairs and stared down the table at Tessa, but no one objected to her unlikely selection of lead trial counsel. Lawyer Brain, filterless as always, piped up. *Not the choice I'd expect her to make. You're capable but not the logical candidate for this assignment.*

I don't trust her, Sixth Sense added.

My internal voices were rational, but I wasn't in a position to question my new client's decision or ask about her motives. Wiley told us he'd send over some additional files and photographs, and with that, the entire group maneuvered out of the room like a tactical team with the trifecta of law partners traipsing along behind them.

I lingered in the conference room to watch the helicopter's ascent and wondered how that very different group of people functioned as a team. Following the obligatory huddle with the partners, I returned to my office to find a large, sealed envelope marked "private and confidential" on my chair. Someone from the TSC team must've had it delivered during the meeting.

Inside the envelope was a modified copy of our firm's client engagement agreement, executed by Tessa in the cerulean blue ink of a fountain pen to distinguish it from the two copies clipped behind it. In scanning through the document, I noticed my billable rate had vaulted from $450 per hour to $1500 per hour. No one in this town, not even Frantsen, commanded that kind of hourly rate, especially not a senior associate attorney.

When my cell phone rang, it registered an unlisted number. As soon as I answered, I knew it was Tessa.

"Meet the team on the helipad at 5:00 a.m. tomorrow." Click. Dead air.

The last thing I noticed on my desk was the bouquet of sunflowers with an attached card that read, "*Love you, baby. Rynner.*"

✝

Rynner Engel grounded me, and it wasn't just because of the way we'd met two years ago by accident, and by that, I mean, *by accident*. I'd worked late one Friday night and was feeling guilty about orphaning my running shoes. To redeem myself and because my apartment was only a few miles from White Rock Lake, I took a few hours off from my weekend work the next morning to run the entire length of the lakeside path, which was just under ten miles.

I donned my usual garb, doused myself with tropical sunscreen, and found a parking space by the dog park. After clipping my iPod to my waist and tuning into my favorite *one-hit wonders from the 1980s* playlist, I started running as gracefully as a three-legged gazelle. It was early enough that the lake, the only one of its kind in the city, wasn't too crowded.

By the sixth mile, I was barely able to keep pace with the metronome app ticking in the background of the music when I rounded a blind corner by the spillway.

I glanced down, willing my feet to move faster.

When I looked up, I saw the blur of a cyclist who'd taken the corner too wide from the opposite direction.

The two-wheeled tornado swerved violently to avoid a direct hit.

Despite his effort, he managed to clip me with a handlebar. I sailed several feet in the air until gravity, deciding it had better things to keep aloft, released me from its grip and cast me back to earth.

Already a highly decorated veteran of falls during running usually caused by my lazy, dragging feet and inattention to things like slightly askew manhole covers in my path, I knew precisely how to take a digger without breaking any major bones. This one was different, though, because I was falling backward, not forward, but I did succeed in ensuring that my body, not my head, made the first contact with the asphalt.

It happened so fast it knocked the wind out of me. I didn't even have time to scream and instead, hit the ground like a sack of sand.

For a moment, I couldn't move. A body check told me I hadn't broken anything, but I felt the small, sharp prick of metal on the waistband of my running shorts. My real injury was the child-ish embarrassment I felt imagining how I looked to passersby, sprawled out flat on my back on the pavement like an idiot.

"Oh my God, are you alright?"

I peeked through the slits of my eyes hidden behind my wrap-around, polarized sunglasses just as the cyclist jumped off of his well-ridden bike and tossed it, his helmet, and his sunglasses into the grass beside the path. A small crowd formed around us.

"Get her some water," a voice in the crowd said.

"Stabilize her neck," another one added.

In the moment before my *She-Attitude* formed the expletives I planned to unleash on the cyclist for ruining my workout, he kneeled beside me and stuck out an arm to keep the onlookers at bay.

"Give her space."

He peeled off his cycling gloves and positioned his middle and index fingers on my wrist to check for a pulse.

"If you can hear me, please stay still. I'm calling 911 now. I promise I won't leave you." He dug around in his biking jersey and pulled out a cell phone.

I eased myself up onto my bloody elbows and said the first thing that came to mind.

"I think you broke my iPod." His head jerked back, and his cornflower-blue eyes widened in surprise.

Only after the words tumbled out did I realize how ridiculous it must've sounded to a man who thought he'd broken my neck.

"No need for an ambulance, just give me a minute," I added, hoping to soften my initial, sharper-than-intended reaction.

"That was a hard fall. You really should get checked out by a doctor."

"No, really, I'm fine," I said, gritting my teeth as I struggled to stand up.

Apologizing profusely, he helped me to my feet, inspecting my bare arms and legs for signs of damage. The crowd dispersed while my mind obsessed about how frightening I must've looked and smelled in my sweat-drenched running clothes with my stringy, wet ponytail, bare face, and bloody elbows. Primarily due to my personal mortification, I declined his offers to drive me to the hospital or escort me to my car.

"Listen, in light of what happened here last year, I have to know that you don't die during the night from internal bleeding or some other type of traumatic brain injury. Can we at least meet tomorrow afternoon for coffee?" I understood his reference to the bizarre tragedy that occurred not far from this spot where a female jogger was struck and killed by a speeding cyclist.

I accepted his invitation and invited him to meet me for coffee the next day at the local coffee shop by my apartment.

"I'm Rynner, by the way," he said after I'd turned around and started limping the long six miles back to the car. Almost two hours later, I made it home for a shower and a bottle of wine I drank through a straw.

I woke up the next day barely able to walk thanks to the massive bruise on my rear end, which had taken the brunt of the fall. The fresh scabs on my elbows oozed and my palms burned from the rawness of the road rash. I considered being a no-show, but my Southern-born-and-raised mother taught me better manners than that. I dressed in my favorite miniskirt, added a black top, and slid my feet into a pair of platform sandals that put me a few inches above six feet.

I arrived at the coffee shop half an hour earlier than our meeting time to find a good table and eat a late breakfast. Rynner walked in right on time by my watch, which earned him silent praise for punctuality. In his hand was an unwrapped, hot pink iPod, one model newer than yesterday's casualty. Dressed in worn but clean jeans and a white button-down shirt that was ironed but not starched, he was trying, but not too hard.

"See, I made it through the night," I said when he arrived at the table. I hoped he wouldn't notice how slowly I moved or how angry my asphalt-dimpled arms looked.

He apologized again and asked if he could buy me lunch. We spent the next three hours doing what few people actually did anymore. Not talking or texting but engaging in the old-fashioned art of conversation.

"When you're not busy flying around Dallas like a speed demon on your bike, what do you do?" I asked.

"I'm finishing up my Ph.D. in Environmental Science. Several years back, the Centers for Disease Control identified cancer clusters in a swath of land along the Texas-Louisiana border, not far from long-abandoned drill sites. My research team has been conducting extensive soil and groundwater testing to determine the existence of any biological or chemical contaminants. Shortly before I ran you over at the lake, I'd spent close to two weeks in Louisiana researching permits and ownership documents and collecting additional soil samples from the area, but the unrelenting humidity sapped my energy and hastened my return home four days earlier than planned."

"Is cycling a hobby, a passion, or both?"

Rynner shifted in his chair and stared beyond me for a moment.

"Cycling is a personal form of meditation I developed as a coping mechanism for my life in foster care, where I was often nothing more than a reason to collect government subsidies."

I'd read the horror stories about children who'd disappeared from the foster system, or worse, who were murdered by their foster parents. He must've been a resilient kid to survive the experience.

"I'm familiar with the foster agency's dismal history. What was it like for you?"

"It's hard to pick an adjective to describe the experience. I never knew my parents and still know nothing about them. During my younger years, all of the clothes I owned could fit into a plastic shopping bag with plenty of room left over for my toy collection, which consisted of two Matchbox cars. Desperate for a means of escape, I scoured neighborhood trash piles and back alley dumpsters for months until I found what I'd been longing for."

"What was it you wanted so badly?" I asked, intrigued by what would cause a little boy to become a professional dumpster diver.

"A bicycle like all the other kids had. The one I found was so rusted that its original color was indiscernible. The front wheel was bent at a ninety-degree angle, the gears didn't work, and there were tattered tassels of various lengths glued onto the handlebars, but none of that mattered to me. I spent days at the public library reading books on bike maintenance until I'd taught myself how to fix the gears. I couldn't afford to replace the bent wheel, but my foster care caseworker was impressed enough by my determination that she found me a used one to make the bike rideable."

His voice took on a tinge of nostalgia when he explained how he'd used a broken razor knife to remove the handlebar tassels and found a can of black spray paint in his foster parent's garage to transform the piece of junk into the first real, working bicycle he ever owned, something that gave him a sense of freedom and independence.

On one occasion, he'd biked more than 100 miles away from a foster dad whose belt was too small to hold up his pants but large enough to use as a switch when he'd had too much to drink. The police officer who'd found him lectured him about his misbehavior but experienced a change of heart when Rynner told him why he'd fled so far. The officer loaded Rynner and the bike into the squad car, bought Rynner an ice cream cone, and returned him to the foster family with an explanation that the little boy had merely gotten lost.

"Here she is," Rynner said as he pulled a photograph of the old bike from his wallet and showed it to me with what had to be as much pride as he'd felt on the day he'd finished repairing it.

"What happened when you aged out of the foster care system?"

"I put myself through college and decided to go to graduate school and study something that could make the world a better place."

His story of perseverance and humility touched me. I also liked the way he leaned in with his thumb under his chin and his index finger on his cheek when he listened, and the way the lines around his eyes softened when he smiled.

We parted with an exchange of phone numbers. I knew before I left the coffee shop that from an outsider's perspective, we'd make a contradictory couple. I didn't care and was willing to see where this thing went. The day after our non-first date, he sent a bouquet of Birds of Paradise to my office with a card that read, *"Sorry I nearly killed you. Hope I earned a real first date."*

†

Tessa didn't join us when the helicopter arrived on the roof of my office building to whisk me, Gator, Wiley, Reyna, TSC's top engineers, and a team of photographers to the blast site the day after my first meeting with the D2D group. As soon as I climbed the stairs into the main cabin, Wiley gestured to an aisle seat toward the back while he and the rest of TSC's team took the window seats where the shades were already closed. Once we were airborne for the short hop to Radiant, Gator handed out dust masks, Kevlar gloves, safety vests and glasses, and TSC lanyards with identification badges that would allow us to get past the Feds.

Reyna blanched and held up her pair of yellow safety glasses as if it were a dead rat.

"I'm not wearing these," she announced when she handed them back to Wiley. She grabbed her Birkin bag, pulled out a pair of designer shades embellished with rhinestones, and slid them on. Gator said something unflattering-sounding in Cajun, but Wiley smiled and tucked the extra pair of glasses in his shirt pocket.

We landed on a private helipad where Gator took charge of the initial investigation and navigated us through the government blockade for an extensive tour of the blast site. We spent hours picking our way through and examining the still-smoking debris in the area where TSC's fracking activities had taken place. The outer perimeter of the property was littered with twisted metal, engine parts, human remains, pieces of tools, and other scraps I couldn't identify.

The closer we got to the primary drilling areas, the smaller the pieces became until the ground was covered in nothing more than dust the consistency of powdered sugar. At the end of a ten-hour day, coated in grime, sweat, and Lord knows what else, I was delivered back to the helipad at the office,

In need of decompression time before I headed home, I called Rynner and asked him to meet me at my favorite bar for a beer. Known for its peanut-shell-covered floor and sizable outdoor patio, Milo's was a place I'd frequented since college except for the brief hiatus management forced me to take after I'd set the bar on fire while demonstrating the flammability properties of grain alcohol.

All but two of the bar stools were occupied, and the eight television screens mounted above the glass shelves of liquor behind the bartender delivered a steady stream of stomach-churning images of the devastated town of Radiant interlaced with talking heads offering nothing more than rank speculation and conspiracy theories as to the cause of the disaster.

Milo's patrons that night included a mixture of professionals, alumni, and college kids trying out their fake licenses. Rynner was already there, seated in a corner booth with his back to the wall.

I slid into the booth opposite Rynner and tried to unwind, but couldn't wrap my mind around the thought that I'd just walked around in a place where thousands of people were now nothing more than particles on the wind. I didn't feel like talking, and Rynner didn't press me for details. I was glad when he broke the silence and said he had his own news to share. Sparing me the scientific minutiae, he told me he'd made significant progress on his analysis of the groundwater samples and believed he'd identified the chemical signatures of the contaminants at the site he was investigating.

Unfortunately, his day ended early when the University's computer network crashed from an apparent hacker attack. No one knew whether it was a data heist or a prank by bored computer geeks. What the University did know, but didn't publicize, was that the perpetrators were sophisticated and took significant measures to conceal their digital tracks. It could take weeks, if not months, to figure out who they were, how they got in, and what they were after.

"How long will it take you to recreate the results?" I knew the research had already consumed several years of his time and energy. Rynner pulled the tiny flash drive from his pocket and handed it to me.

"It's all there. Luck favors the prepared. You can never have too many back-ups."

I'd stopped counting how many times he'd reminded me to back-up my files.

"Can you take it home for me? You know how I always forget to take stuff out of my pockets before I do the laundry. Wouldn't want anything to happen to that."

I took the flash drive, stuffed it into the back pocket of my jeans, and stared at my untouched beer.

"Looks like you've had enough for one day." Rynner threw a twenty on the table, stood up, and walked me toward the door.

I felt slightly possessive when I saw he'd caught the undivided attention of two pretty, young co-eds sitting at the bar. As we exited and headed for the parking lot a block away, Rynner draped his arm protectively around my waist and took his usual position to my left, closest to the road. Although I hadn't parked that far from him, he insisted on escorting me to my car. It was a chivalrous act for which I was especially grateful because the sidewalk seemed unusually dark.

A quick look upward confirmed that several streetlights were out.

Tap. Tap. Tap.

I recognized the staccato of a runner's footsteps approaching from behind. Evening runners weren't unusual in this part of town, which was also home to expensive townhomes coveted by young professionals.

Rynner tilted his head down, kissed my forehead, and whispered, "I love you now and forever."

At that moment, time simultaneously stopped and accelerated when the runner slammed into Rynner, severing our physical connection and shoving Rynner into the road.

The momentum sent me tumbling forward until the sidewalk broke my fall, causing my right shoulder to crack upon contact with the pavement. White dots of pain filled my vision like fireflies.

Thunk, thunk.

I heard the sound of a car flying over a speed bump but couldn't see any headlights. I thought I heard another *thunk,* and the darkness got darker.

†

Another body check. My feet were trapped. Why couldn't they escape?

I kicked harder and harder to free them from the end of the bedsheet but stopped when I heard a familiar voice.

"Honey? Honey? Are you awake?" It was my mother's voice, in the tone reserved strictly for emergencies and tragedies.

Someone un-tucked the bedsheet.

Everything was wrong. I never tucked in my sheets, which meant I wasn't in my own bed. And for that matter, my mother usually didn't show up unannounced at my house to inquire about my sleeping habits. Especially not using *that* voice. And why did it feel as if someone were boring a hole through my temple with a pickaxe?

It took several silent commands for my eyelids, which felt oddly weighted, to open. The room was dim and smelled like antiseptic. Mom was seated next to me, looking anxious. Dad was at the foot of the bed where he'd just freed my feet. Vases of flowers occupied every flat surface in the room.

"Sweetie, you've been in an accident, and you're in the hospital. You have a dislocated shoulder and a serious concussion, but the doctors say you'll be fine. Thank heavens you didn't crack your skull open."

"Good thing our family's so hard-headed," Dad added. Misdirected humor was his coping mechanism for all things medical, especially when they were family-related.

"Where's Rynner?"

Silence.

"Where's Rynner?"

The heart rate monitor spiked, and an alarm sounded. A stern-faced nurse scurried in and silenced the racket.

"No excitement," she snapped and stuck a needle into my IV port.

The medicine coursing through my veins stopped the pick-axe, and I melted away into the nothingness of narcotic-induced sleep. I awoke again and saw a tired-looking nurse reviewing my chart. My parents must've taken a break because my mother's purse sat on the guest chair, but she and my father were gone.

My last thought was now my first.

"Is Rynner Engel here? He's family," I fibbed. Despite my dulled senses, I noticed the nano-expression of apprehension cross her face.

"He's still in the ICU in a coma. The hit-and-run severed his spine and caused massive head trauma..." She continued to speak, but my mind processed nothing but nonsense.

God, please don't take him from me, I pleaded silently.

I needed to see him and tell him, as he'd once told me, that I would stay with him and everything would be okay.

"Lower the fucking safety rails on this bed, or I swear I'll kick it to pieces."

The nurse's eyes widened, and the bed rails lowered.

"Where's the ICU?"

"Second Floor. Mr. Engel's in room 214."

I felt a cold sting when I yanked the IV needle out of my arm and tossed the line out of my way so I could roll onto my left side and angle my feet toward the floor. I flopped out of bed and landed on unsteady legs.

"You aren't cleared to walk unattended yet," the nurse said, sounding slightly more concerned.

I interpreted what she said as more of an observation than a directive to stay put. Someone barked at me from the nursing station. I told myself that if anyone wanted me back in that bed, they'd have to tackle and sedate me.

My head was throbbing by the time I made it to the ICU. The door to 214 stood before me.

✝

The incoming tide washed away the rest of the flashback. The sun was setting, and Peter was gone. I made my way back up the beach to my place, enjoying the feel of the cooling sand between my toes. A few Land Crabs scurried across my path, and clam holes bubbled exposing the whereabouts of their occupants. When I opened the door to my new home, I realized I had my first visitor.

Perched with his sandal-clad feet on my living room sofa was a Tween engrossed in a gaming console. His curly, black hair fell into his eyes as he focused on the small gadget in his hand, and from what I could see, his build and features were that of a boy on a permanently interrupted path to manhood. Peter dozed on his lap, oblivious to the boy's inability to remain still.

When the boy turned to greet me, his face, dominated by large, charcoal eyes, lit up in a smile radiating a combination of charm and mischief common to boys of that age. He reminded me of my little brother.

"My name is Caleb, and I am your Guide. I'm here to start you through the process of acceptance."

I wasn't ready to accept *this* yet, but I didn't see that I had a choice.

I couldn't place his accent, and as skeptical as I was about his offer of assistance, I accepted the fact I was in a position of unequal bargaining power and sat down next to him. He waited for me to speak, and when I did, I asked one of the many questions that had been knocking around in my head since my arrival.

"Why were my hiking boots wet? I wasn't wearing them in the courtroom when I…"

My brain vetoed my mouth's attempt to form the word "*died.*"

"You needed them for your passage. Everyone arrives here through a portal of their own design, which appears when it's needed, or in some cases when it's wanted."

He explained to me that his portal was a shaded path through an ancient grove of olive trees owned by his family for generations until extremists occupied their land. Eager to instill fear in the locals, they hacked down each precious tree with their machetes until there was nothing left but a large patch of fertile, tinder-covered soil. When the occupiers reduced the last tree to sticks, they turned their blades on him and his family.

We shared the common theme of a violent death, but at least I'd reached adulthood and experienced many of life's expected milestones. Caleb hadn't made it through grade school. "Can we go back?"

"Yes and no. Your ability to return and what you can do when you're there depends on many things I can't explain."

"I want to go now," I demanded like the petulant three-year-old I once was and sometimes could still be.

"I know. Put on your hiking boots, and I'll meet you there."

I walked into the bedroom thinking about what it would be like, knowing I had exited their world, to see my family and friends again. I had no idea what to expect when I stuffed my feet into a pair of dry socks, pulled the still-damp boots over them, and began the familiar crisscross lacing process.

Caleb leaned against the door jamb watching me. I stopped mid-lace and looked up at him.

"How will I know where to go?"

"Don't worry. I'll make sure you get there."

The instant I finished tying the knot on the second boot, the bedroom and the house around it dissolved into tiny, shimmering particles, as if they, like the beach outside, were made of diamond dust. Transfixed, I watched them rearrange themselves into an enormous waterfall flowing from a source beyond my sight.

Heavy drops of mist sprayed my face as my ears adjusted to the roar of the water. Broad stone steps materialized at the far edge of the downpour, and up I went. The climb was steep, but I wasn't winded. Three hundred twenty-seven steps later, I arrived on a sidewalk in front of the church I'd attended with my family for as long as I could remember. Without a sound, Caleb appeared at my side.

The church bells tolled as men, women, couples, children, and families, all dressed in variations of navy, gray and black, walked past us in the direction of the nave. The massive organ that rattled the windows during Sunday services sat silent. We fell in step behind them and entered the church. No one looked at us or otherwise acknowledged our presence.

"We're invisible, aren't we?" I don't know why I asked him because I already knew the answer.

"At this point, yes."

"What are we doing here?"

"We're attending a funeral."

A chilling thought occurred to me. *Had someone else in my family just died?* If that were the case, I would've been the Greeter.

Mourners filled the pews and lined the aisles to the chancel. The smells of various perfumes mixed with the scents of lilies and roses to give the church a sadly sweet smell. I knew these faces. Philmore was seated near Rhein and his wife in a middle pew. My law school study group buddies clustered in the back, exactly where I'd expect them to be, with colleagues and acquaintances interspersed among them.

The TSC elite, minus Guerrera, along with the obligatory security escort, occupied pews closer to the front. Every one of them had eyes downcast not in solemn reflection, but on their cell phones. The first two rows on either side of the aisle were empty.

Pastor John, whom I'm told baptized me and then suffered through my endless questions in Confirmation class, entered the sanctuary through a side door followed by my parents, brother, Liz, and two sets of grandparents. They filed into the pews closest to the pulpit as Pastor John paused, made the sign of the cross, and opened his Bible.

"We are here to celebrate the life of Adeleine Tanis, daughter, granddaughter, sister, friend, colleague and confidante, and ask the Lord Almighty to bless her, take her into His fold, and watch over her in the Kingdom of Heaven."

One of the better photographs of me appeared on a large, overhead screen, followed by several others. I swore silently thinking that as an attorney, I should've had the foresight to prepare a will with instructions that I didn't want a slide show at my funeral, but I'd never gotten around to it.

I walked up to Pastor John, turned and faced the congregation, and watched the reactions unfold. It felt repulsively mesmerizing to be a voyeur at my funeral service. Some cried while others sat stoically. Liz, tears washing a stream of black mascara down her face, smiled at the photos on the screen, oblivious to the mountain of used tissues covering her lap.

My father stroked my mother's shoulder, and all four of my grandparents sat motionless, looking shell-shocked. My brother never looked at the pictures, preferring instead to keep his gaze focused on his shoes.

The service proceeded as most funerals do, with readings from Bible passages, blessings, and prayers. Thankfully, there were no speeches or embarrassing stories, and the Pastor kept it short and straightforward. Following the service, an intimate group made its way to the cemetery next door where my ashes would be interred.

Caleb and I followed them and watched the assembly form a few feet away from an open marble box. A simple urn rested on a small pillow of blue satin in an otherwise unadorned niche.

†

Whether it was planned or spontaneous, I'll never know, but one-by-one, each person approached the opening to say a personal goodbye. I stood next to the niche while Caleb kept his distance behind my family.

My mother was first. She inhaled deeply, her body stiffening as if she expected a physical blow, and cupped her hands around the urn.

"This wasn't part of the plan, Pumpkin. There's so much we didn't get to share with you, and now we'll never know if you're where and what you're supposed to be. Pastor John says that God works with purpose, but I can't make a damned bit of sense out of it."

She paused and then placed a small, red box on the satin pillow.

"Before the accident, Rynner asked us for our blessing to propose to you. He was so worried you'd find the ring that he asked us to keep it in your father's gun safe until the time was right. We don't know if he'll ever recover but are certain he'd want you to have this, and now you do. He loved you so much. We all do too."

The pang of remorse stung. Rynner and I had talked about marriage, but I'd been adamant that I wanted to establish myself in my career before taking the marital plunge.

My father joined her and shook so hard he had to brace himself on the surrounding stones to keep from collapsing.

"I don't know what to say," he said in a voice so low I had to strain to hear him. "I should've protected you. That's what fathers do, and I failed you. I failed you."

His body sagged from the weight of his guilt. Unable to speak another word, he grasped my mother's hand and allowed himself to be led back to the group.

My brother was next and delivered his goodbye with his characteristic candor.

"I love you Big Sis, but I don't understand any of this shit. God help the bastard responsible. I'll kill him myself if I ever find him."

He kissed his fingers and tapped them twice on the urn.

Liz followed him and rested a photo of the two of us, a copy of the one on my mantle, next to the urn. On the back, written with her signature purple Sharpie, was a note that read, "Come what may. Love, Liz."

It was a good thing the sniper's bullet already shredded my heart because if it hadn't, I would've collapsed from the emotional weight of the farewells.

With Pastor John's final blessing, they departed, leaving the niche open until the groundskeeper could affix the temporary cover. Caleb joined me, and we studied the small square that housed all that remained of my physical self. My entire life, my memories, and experiences were reduced to a cup of dust and bone fragments. Cliché after cliché scrolled through my head like a ticker tape.

"Ashes to ashes, dust to dust…."

"The Lord is my Shepherd; I shall not want…"

Two men in brown coveralls approached us and maneuvered the temporary cover stone into place. At that moment, I knew the purpose of this task was to accept the loss of my life and embrace the knowledge of transcendence.

That life was over. The Afterlife was just beginning.

The cemetery fell away into tiny specks, replaced by the waterfall with its ascending steps. I climbed them alone to find myself back where I started. My face was wet but not from the mist.

Everything was as I had left it except that clenched in my hand was the small red box my mother had placed in the niche. Unsure whether it was really there or just an illusion, I closed my eyes and flipped open the lid.

†

My hands were empty when I opened my eyes and found myself at the door to Rynner's room in the ICU. I hesitated before I swung it open, and entered the dark room occupied from corner to corner with the marvels of modern medicine.

A ventilator *whooshed* rhythmically as red, blue and green lights blinked from various panels, and a heart monitor pinged with each faint pulse.

Rynner lay motionless in the center of the mechanical chaos, almost unrecognizable due to the bandages and tubes that traversed around and through his body. His eyes were covered with medical gauze, and his arms and legs were strapped to the bed. A whiteboard on the wall identified the attending nurse and ER physician. A medical chart rested on the unused tray table attached to the bed railing. I gave a silent prayer of thanks that this hospital hadn't already made the switch from hard copy to electronic medical records.

Sitting on the edge of the bed, I flipped through the lengthy notes desperate for something, anything that would tell me he would regain consciousness.

"Acute trauma. Spinal cord injury at C-2. Brain swelling." I wasn't a doctor but understood the severity of his injuries.

How could you do this to me? I asked Her from my heart. As usual, there was no answer.

I didn't realize I was screaming until two orderlies rushed through the door and began interrogating me about my presence in the restricted ICU room. Through my tear-choked responses, they determined I belonged on the floor below and escorted me back to the room where my parents and the surly nurse were waiting. Fortunately for me, the nurse's lecture about my wandering around the hospital without a medical escort was offset by my mother's reassuring words and my father's announcement that during my absence, they'd completed the discharge papers allowing me to return home.

After a clean change of clothes courtesy of my parents, I collected the hospital bag filled with my battle-damaged garb and became a reluctant passenger in a wheelchair piloted by my father. Groggy from the narcotics, I didn't pay much attention to anything on the way home.

Home was the quaint and quirky, Robin's egg blue, Tudor-style house in a Dallas neighborhood known as the "M Streets" that Rynner and I had purchased a few months after we'd met. Boasting a completion date of 1938 etched into a stone on the front pavement, it was the oldest house in the neighborhood by at least seven years. Although it lacked modern conveniences such as an attached garage and occasionally lost power due to a blown transformer, the original and still-functional shutters and yellow oak floors gave it plenty of character. There wasn't a right angle in the entire structure, but every room captured just the right amount of natural light to provide the place with a cheerful vibe.

Mom's prattle about the discharge instructions and her admonishment to follow the doctor's orders filled the abyss of time and space during the drive between the hospital and the house. Dad pulled into the driveway and helped me out of the car. I told them I could get situated by myself because I needed to be alone, process the last two days, and figure out how to coordinate Rynner's care.

As he usually did, Maverick met me at the door with the tandem expressions of excitement and indifference only a cat can master. I walked in ignoring the fact it appeared someone, probably my mother, had scrubbed the place clean, and meandered into the bedroom. Not ready to deal with its contents, I threw the hospital bag into the back of the closet, an area Rynner referred to as "No Man's Land."

After several frustrating minutes spent prying the child-proof cap off of the bottle of painkillers, I poured a few into my mouth and pulled a beer from the refrigerator. I maneuvered myself onto the couch, careful not to disturb my tender shoulder, and let the beer wash the pills down my throat.

Four hours later, I awoke to the throbbing indication that the pain pills had worn off and the familiar sensation of Maverick resting on my head with his tail swishing back and forth across my face. I found my cell phone at the bottom of my purse and called my work voice mail to see what I'd missed. There was only one message from that same day, and it was from Tessa.

"Team strategy meeting at 10:00 a.m. tomorrow at your office," she said in her clipped, authoritative tone.

"Crap, crap, crap," I swore aloud.

I threw my phone back into my purse and thought about my to-do list, which was growing by the minute. Once I finished reviewing the snail mail, I flipped open my laptop and began researching long-term care facilities with the expertise to care for Rynner. He would need the best, and I'd do everything in my power to ensure he got it. After several hours of research and multiple e-mail exchanges with friends, I developed a short list of possible locations that specialized in caring for patients with head and spine trauma. I would start contacting them tomorrow.

Next, I logged into my work e-mail to play catch-up. Somehow, 581 new e-mails had staged a hostile takeover of my inbox. After deleting the junk, I reduced the number to a mere 311 messages. I was sure it was a new record. Knowing I couldn't review them all that night, I segregated the ones dealing with Radiant and reviewed them in preparation for tomorrow's meeting.

Reyna had sent me a set of press release drafts and a proposed publication schedule for my review. Wiley sent at least a dozen e-mails with suggestions for subject matter experts he wanted me to interview, and Tessa wanted to discuss our litigation strategy.

Several e-mails were from various governmental agencies demanding, under threat of subpoena, information on TSC's operations in Radiant. As I scrolled down the screen, one e-mail caught my eye. It was from Rynner, and the time stamp indicated he'd sent it early in the evening on the date of the accident during the time I was driving to the bar to meet him. I opened it and saw two simple lines:

"'Carrying your heart with me. Waiting for you at Milo's."

The sobs welled up from deep within and racked my diaphragm so hard that I slid off the couch and onto the floor, where I cried until the returning pain in my shoulder convinced me of the need to down a few more narcotics. I choked down three more pills, dragged myself into the bedroom, and sat propped up against the maple headboard.

I prayed the drugs would work quickly to deaden my senses because every one of them was measuring a magnitude number of Rynner like a Richter Scale. His pillow released a microscopic cloud of his *Hanae Mori* cologne when I used it to prop up my elbow. His Luminox watch, which sat idly on his nightstand, reflected a dot of light onto the opposite wall. His nightshirt hung off the top of the bedpost like a flag with no wind.

Christ, why? I thought.

I awoke at 3:32 a.m. from the void only drug-induced sleep can produce. It was a time that would otherwise have been meaningless except for the fact that since that night, I would awaken at that same time every morning for the rest of my natural life. It didn't matter how much I drank, how late I worked, how many sleeping pills I took, or how much exercise I had before I climbed into bed each night. I was physically and mentally incapable of sleeping beyond 3:32 a.m.

✝

My first shower since the accident was complicated by the fact I had to wash my hair with one hand while trying to keep the arm sling dry. Failing miserably, I got shampoo in my eyes and tripped on the shower door ledge as I tried to pivot toward the faucet spray for relief. I tumbled out of the shower and grasped for the edge of the vanity with my good arm to keep from cracking the bathroom tile with my skull.

When my heart stopped racing, I straightened myself and came face-to-face with a stranger in the vanity mirror.

I'd had some rough nights in my life, but the accident had been transformative. The continuous crying over the past few days had left my grotesquely puffy eyes crisscrossed with webs of broken blood vessels. The fluorescent lights gave my complexion a yellow tone, and my lips were pursed in a sour lemon expression. No amount of make-up or concealer could hide this, much less fix it.

I gazed at the bathroom ceiling. *Really? What else, God? Haven't I suffered enough?* She declined to respond to my simpering.

I applied two coats of foundation as if it were wall spackle and swiped on several layers of black mascara. It took a full five minutes to shimmy into a gray sheath dress and another ten to figure out how to zip it up with one hand. Once I'd done so, I fed Maverick, crammed my laptop and my care facility notes into my briefcase, and headed for my detached garage.

By 5:15 a.m., I was sitting at my desk staring at a large pile of paper in my inbox and the vase of wilted sunflowers from Rynner. The next time I looked at the clock, it was 9:55 a.m. and time to head to Main for the TSC meeting. At precisely 10:00 a.m., the TSC team filed into the conference room followed by a nameless bodyguard-slash-personal assistant carrying two large leather briefcases. He deposited them on the table in front of me, along with a meeting agenda, and retreated to his post beside the door. As they had before, the guards stood vigil in each corner of the room. Tessa and Wiley took the seats to my right and left while Guerrera, Gator and Reyna sat across from us. Tessa spoke first.

"You look like shit, but we have six months until you have to face a jury. No settlement."

Due in part to the level of publicity the case had generated, the judge had placed us on a rocket docket, which meant that the usual time to prepare for trial was reduced by about sixty percent. We'd drawn the Honorable Ronald Katzenburg, a yellow dog Democrat who'd been on the bench for longer than I'd been alive.

Judge Katzenburg was a strange bird who carried on a public love affair with the life-sized statue of a blindfolded and bare-breasted Lady Justice standing guard in the corner of his courtroom, with her foot on a serpent, a sword in one hand, and the scales of justice in the other hand. The judge was a living legend for his witticisms, including one he rolled out when he disliked a lawyer's argument. Pointing to his beloved idol, he'd say, "*Counselor, see that ol' gal there? Lady Justice may be blind, but she's armed, and she sure as hell ain't stupid. Your motion is denied.*"

I bit my tongue to stifle a flippant retort to Tessa's comment and turned to Wiley.

"What have you got for me?"

Right on cue, he flipped open the first briefcase and withdrew a large stack of documents.

"Preliminary expert packets with CVs, prior deposition transcripts, and fee schedules."

Finding the right experts was critical to the success of a case like this. Each would have to possess a perfectly balanced mixture of scientific credentials, theatrics, and personality to gain the jury's trust and explain why TSC was not liable for the explosion.

An imbalance of any of these necessary ingredients could be disastrous. Too much cockiness or dramatic flair could alienate a jury, just as an excess of scholarly preaching could bore them to tears and cause them to tune out completely.

"I'll have my selections to you tomorrow. What's next?"

Reyna, characteristically glassy-eyed but coiffed to perfection, opened the second briefcase and removed two manila folders. The first contained a proof of the branding for TSC's Victim Relief Campaign. The cover shot was breathtaking. Reyna's team had captured the first rays of the morning sun reflecting off of the defiant cross on the steeple rising above the charred remains of Radiant's First Baptist Church. The caption read:

RADIANT'S LIGHT SHINES ON
"The people who sat in darkness saw great light, and to them who sat in the shadow of death light is sprung."

I had to admit that Reyna's skill was worth every drug-infused dime Tessa spent on her. Tessa knew it too, despite her disdain for her own sex, and realized the value of such an asset following a deadly chemical fire that killed dozens of pharmaceutical research scientists. Working at the time for a PR firm, Reyna recast the horrific accident as the genesis of a promising new cancer-fighting drug. Never mind the fact that the researchers had made little progress in their work or that a malfunctioning fire suppression system caused the casualties. What mattered most was that Reyna's client emerged unscathed and with its venture capital funding intact. As the woman who manipulated the masses from behind the curtain, Reyna had earned the sobriquet of "Oz." Tessa had lured Reyna to TSC with a seven-figure paycheck, a limitless supply of the amphetamines on which Reyna was hooked, and around-the-clock access to the country's top-rated plastic surgeons to keep Reyna looking her best at all times. Tessa's job offer was a drug-addicted narcissist's dream.

The second folder contained a press release about the Victim Relief Campaign, and I approved both in short order.

"I meet with the jury consultants next Monday and will provide a report by Tuesday morning," I advised the group. "Is there anything else we need to address?"

Tessa was already at the door.

"Not at this time." She never looked back at me.

Guerrera winked at me as he passed with a noticeable bulge in the front of his slacks.

Back at my desk, I spent the next four hours reviewing the expert dossiers. Before day's end, I'd selected the interviewees, sent Wiley my list of candidates, and tasked my assistant, Kathy, with scheduling the meetings. With the billable work completed, I turned my attention to the list of long-term care facility options for Rynner. I called the Facility Administrator of my first choice, introduced myself, and told her what I needed.

"Do you have proof of marriage or legal guardianship?"

"No, but…"

"Then I'm afraid I can't help you."

"Is there any information you can provide me to help me navigate through this?" I pleaded, my voice cracking.

"If the individual has no medical directives, will, or living family members to make decisions on his behalf, then he becomes a ward of the state. That's all I can tell you right now."

I thanked her for her time and hung up the phone. Another quick call to the state agency responsible for disabled adults confirmed that the information she provided was correct.

So that was it. Rynner had come full circle and was now involuntarily committed to the same nameless, faceless state system from which he'd freed himself. I had neither control nor influence over his care, which more than likely meant he'd be lucky if he received the bare minimum.

I raked my good arm through my hair, waiting for the flood gates to open. Nothing happened. My primitive survival instinct ensured that my heart thudded on like the metronome app, but on some level, I knew I'd just experienced the mental equivalent of a bleed out. My emotional reservoir was tapped out and bone-dry.

Thunder cracked, and the deafening noise bounced off of the downtown skyscrapers like ping-pong balls. Sheets of rain pelted my office window, and elongated zigzags of lightning streaked across the black sky. I locked my office door, kicked off my shoes, and popped a few painkillers. Confident I wouldn't be bothered, I propped my feet on the desk and drifted out of consciousness.

A light knock roused me.

"Are you in there?" purred a silky Latin voice.

I heard the click of the door lock, and Guerrera stepped in carrying a bottle of gin and two coffee mugs from the office kitchen.

"I know you've been working hard and thought you might need a drink." He leaned over the desk and set the bottle and mugs down in front of me, casually but intentionally brushing my thigh in the process.

I shouldn't have liked the feeling, but I did.

The office light dimmed as another lightning flash lit up every corner of the room.

I couldn't identify his cologne, but it had a seductive quality about it that evoked visions of swarthy men engaging in dangerous activities. He filled the two cups with gin and placed one in my good hand. It was almost 9:30 p.m.

I took the drink, knowing that spending time alone with him *could* be a dangerous activity. My legal wits were focused, but the sadness and loneliness I felt every day without Rynner dulled everything else. I told myself I needed a harmless distraction, and this was nothing more than a drink with a client.

By the time he poured our second cups of gin, Guerrera had moved from my guest chair to a position where his long legs had straddled the corner of my desk. He spoke in his accented clip about his childhood and belief that his penchant for mischief sent his mother to an early grave. I threw in several well-timed exclamations and nods and enjoyed the attention while the alcohol worked its magic on my painkiller-infused bloodstream.

An hour later, the gin bottle was empty, and I was plowed. I slipped my feet back into my shoes and managed to stand upright but only because the wall was supporting my full weight.

"You should get home," my sober-sounding new friend said.

I agreed but teetered on my heels when I tried to put one foot in front of the other. With flawless timing, Guerrera caught me around the waist and steadied my balance. I struggled to focus on him but saw nothing more than a hazy shape that smelled really, really good.

"You can't drive like this. Where's your car?"

"In the Uber. I'll take a garage."

He mumbled something I didn't catch, pulled my purse from a drawer in my desk, and located my car key fob with a single-handed search. With his arm secured around my waist for support, mine, not his, he guided me to the parking garage where he identified my gold Tesla. Just as Rynner always did, Guerrera opened the passenger door for me and closed it when he had me securely situated with my seat belt fastened.

He eased himself into the driver's seat, adjusted it to accommodate his long legs, and tuned the radio to Rynner's favorite jazz station. I thought I heard him speaking softly on his cell phone but was unable to concentrate on anything he said. The last thing I remembered with any clarity was being lifted out of the car by well-defined arms. The rest of the night was lost in a filmy, sometimes spinning haze.

At the usual, ungodly hour the next morning, I found myself in bed, naked, with my dress, bra, panties, and arm sling in a heap on the floor by the bed. Body check time. My neck was sore, I'd collected a new bruise on the top of my left hand, and I felt queasy. Guerrera's scent was all over me, and my mouth tasted faintly of cinnamon. No matter how much my shoulder hurt, that was the last time I'd wear the arm sling.

Rynner's side of the bed was neatly made with no head impressions in his pillow, which I interpreted as a sign that *thank God*, Guerrera hadn't spent the night. I absentmindedly scratched an itchy spot on my hip while I let the nausea pass. Wondering if a spider had bitten me, I pulled back the covers and saw several deep indentations where Guerrera's teeth had broken the skin.

At that moment, I didn't want to know why his mouth had been anywhere near my bare hip.

After confirming I was alone except for Maverick, who was thoroughly pissed off that Guerrera had locked him out of the bedroom the night before, I rubbed my stiff neck and headed to the kitchen. When I found the bottle I wanted from the refrigerator, I swallowed the last of my pain pills, which were supposed to last another week, and pondered this new low.

The man I'd hoped to marry someday was in a vegetative state from which he would likely never recover, and I could do nothing but watch from the sidelines as his body slowly decomposed. In a moment of weakness, I'd allowed Guerrera's purely physical attention to seduce me into whatever weird thing this was that involved large quantities of alcohol and possessive wounds. Disappointed by my lack of judgment, *bad judgment*, Lawyer Brain corrected, I threw the empty pill bottle across the table to the trashcan and noticed that my house keys and car key fob were on the counter by my purse.

I unlocked the front door and poked my head out to verify that my car had made it back into my driveway. With a press of the button on the key fob, I noticed that he'd even remembered to lock the doors. There were no signs that Guerrera had ever been here. He'd left as covertly as he'd arrived at my office last night.

A call to Liz, who was currently consulting with a large accounting firm in Chicago, confirmed I was a complete idiot who needed to get her head back in the game. Concerned that I was barely holding it together, but intrigued by my description of Guerrera, Liz promised to fly down the next weekend to straighten me out.

This too shall pass, I said to myself after the call ended. I showered away the external layer of shame and got ready to visit Rynner. It was already after lunch by the time I pulled into the visitor parking lot at Evergreen, the long-term care facility that had recently admitted Rynner. With no chance he could wander off, he was assigned to the third floor of the old building that reeked of bleach and mothballs.

I checked in at the nursing station and climbed the stairs to the third level. I pushed his door open, ready to make a confession of the conscience, but once again found myself in a different place.

†

Barefoot with sand-crusted feet, I stood in the entryway of the beach house dressed in a pale-blue, cotton t-shirt and tan miniskirt. Peter appeared to be sleeping on my desk until one ear crooked lazily in acknowledgment of my return. As I walked over to scratch his head, I noticed a Post-It note, in Her handwriting, stuck to the desk.

"Swing by when you're ready."

The back and forth from past to present left me tired and irritable. I crumpled up the note, threw it on the floor, and worked my way back down the beach. I had no idea how much time had passed since I'd arrived here. So far, the only constants were the ebb and flow of the tide and the rising and setting of the sun.

Her house was in the same place it had been on my previous visit, but except for the location of the ocean-facing deck, it looked completely different. As I approached the open front door, I noticed that the clapboard façade I'd first encountered had been replaced with tabby, a concrete mixture made from sand, lime and oyster shells common in historic buildings along the coasts of Florida and Georgia.

The interior of the house had also changed from its previously modern appointment of art and furniture. The great room floor was now covered with a colorful, hand-braided rug, and in one corner of the room, four distressed-leather chairs encircled a splintered steamer trunk doubling as a coffee table. Spread over the makeshift coffee table was a yellowed nautical map anchored by a sextant. A faded-green rocking chair sat motionless in the corner.

A formidable wooden table cluttered with leather-bound books, quills, and inkpots dominated the middle of the room. The only artwork on the wall was an enormous ship's wheel.

I walked up the metal, lighthouse-like spiral staircase and stepped out onto the porch where I'd first met Her. This time, three chairs were facing the ocean, two of which were occupied. Judging by the tone of the voices I heard when I climbed the stairs, She appeared to be engaged in a serious discussion with her current guest. I paused before stepping onto the deck.

"Adeleine, glad you could join us." The tone of her voice was now lighter than the one She'd just been using.

The other visitor stood up, removed his hat, and helped me angle the empty chair toward his. I didn't recognize his face but based on the style of his dress, including the old-fashioned, brown tweed trousers and spectacles teetering on the bridge of his nose, he looked like a scholar from another era.

Trying not to stare, I stole a glance at Her. Today She wore a white sundress patterned with pink flamingos and a pair of sparkly flip-flops. Her straw, broad-brimmed hat hid all but a few wisps of her red hair and covered a large, dark pair of sunglasses. Nothing, however, obscured the pulsing light dancing along her exposed skin.

The elderly gentlemen bowed and extended his hand in greeting. "Andrew Cornelius, I look forward to working with you."

"Andrew will be your full-time assistant and mentor. He's had plenty of experience deciding important matters and will provide you with anything you need."

His name bounced around between my ears until a single word came into my head.

Acorn.

In my second year of law school, my Constitutional Law professor always included extra credit questions on her exams about the identities of long-dead United States Supreme Court Justices. I'd reduced most of the names I'd memorized into clever shortcuts. "Acorn" was short for Andrew Elias Cornelius IV, the Chief Justice who'd served on the Court in the late 1800s. The name seemed funny then but not so much now that this great legal mind was not only standing in front of me but would be working for me.

"What could I possibly be doing that would require Acor— Justice Cornelius to assist me?"

"Housekeeping. Maintaining order. Making decisions."

"What exactly will I be deciding?"

"Many things, chief among them, Fate."

Come again? Lawyer Brain chimed in. Sixth Sense was taking it all in.

"You are an *X Triplici*," She continued. "You've known your destiny for a long time. You'll be administering justice by deciding the fate of souls."

Now I felt as though I were plummeting toward the earth at terminal velocity. What was once my stomach was now firmly lodged in my right foot. Recognizing the signs of oxygen deprivation, I doubled over in my chair, dropped my head between my legs, and concentrated on not passing out.

But that's Her job, Lawyer Brain challenged.

I forgot She could hear it too.

"It is, but I need help, and I've entrusted certain individuals with this responsibility and authority," She said aloud.

Being a lawyer had been hard enough. Acting as a judge, jury, executioner, and savior to and for the masses was unfathomable.

But what does it mean? I thought as I stared at the wooden planks on the deck and struggled to breathe.

Her words frittered around the back of my mind until an acrid smell snapped my head back to its upright position. My nose burned, and my eyes watered.

Acorn rolled a small vial between his fingers.

"Smelling salts. Always carry it for the ladies."

I refocused my eyes.

"The blackouts and the flashbacks are perfectly normal," She said in a voice that reminded me of my mother. "They fade with knowledge." I noticed She didn't use the word "time."

She smiled and tilted Her head back just as a fearsome-looking man in black tactical gear appeared at the sliding door. In addition to the oversized and ornate gold seal ring on his right index finger, the newcomer had outfitted himself with a small armory. His thigh rig included a 9mm pistol and a large knife in a separate holster. His vest was crammed with gear, including fragmentation and concussion grenades, carabiners, rope, and extra ammunition. Topping off his ensemble was the M24 rifle secured to his body by a three-point shoulder harness. Other than a noticeable dilation of his pupils when he locked eyes with mine, he stood silently.

She looked at the visitor and then back at us.

"I'm needed elsewhere. You're in good hands with Andrew."

Acorn stood up, tipped his hat again, and told me to proceed across the street to the chalet for my first briefing when I was ready. To date, I'd seen neither street nor chalet but knew that meant nothing.

She dematerialized into thin air with the commanding visitor at her side. Acorn turned his back and descended the stairs as sprightly as a child. Relishing the tranquility, I remained on the deck to survey the view from Her vantage point, which was something I'd neglected to do on my last visit here.

I'd been so self-absorbed when I first met Her that I hadn't noticed that the beach was both crowded with sunbathers, surfers and boaters, and as empty as it was the first time I dug my feet into the sand. Scanning the horizon, I noticed that houses of all shapes and sizes were present and absent at alternating intervals.

The inhabitants here existed in a multi-dimensional space connected in a way I didn't yet comprehend. The theory could undoubtedly explain how souls from different ages could adjust to eternity in a timeless universe. With this thought, I too descended the stairs and lingered a while longer admiring the map and playing with the sextant.

Acorn was long gone by the time I stepped back out onto the beach, and I saw no footprints to indicate the path he'd taken. I began the journey back to my Cabin, as I now called it, mindful of the fact that as I walked, I was interacting with thousands of people in phantom forms.

My mind began to wander as a squadron of pelicans soared overhead.

†

Time moved again, and I was back at Rynner's door at Evergreen, where I slipped unseen into his room. At some point between my last visit and now, someone had moved another bed into the room, indicating it wouldn't be long before Rynner had a roommate.

The brick-sized window, the only one in the room, provided a weak stream of natural light that was overpowered by the buzzing fluorescent lights overhead. I sat on the edge of Rynner's narrow bed and took in his debility.

His eyes were no longer covered with gauze pads, and the arm and leg restraints were gone, but the machines and other noisy equipment remained in place, ensuring he received food, fluids, and each successive breath. I studied his face but detected no movements. His eyelids didn't flutter as they used to do when he slept deeply, and his body was uncharacteristically still.

The old lights hummed above, enhancing the already unnatural gray tinge to his skin, and his fingernails had grown much longer than he usually kept them. I pulled out a nail clipper and trimmed them for him.

I ran my fingers through his hair several times before massaging his scalp and ears. These were among his favorite forms of physical contact, but they elicited no response from him, not even a muscle spasm. Although I knew I was violating several laws, I opened his medical chart attached to the end of his bed and read the most recent entries.

His prognosis hadn't changed. It was a near certainty that he would never regain consciousness. He'd now require continuous care until his body surrendered. I remained emotionally detached as I flipped through the rest of the chart until I reached one short entry occupying its own line.

"NNK."

I'd reviewed enough medical charts in my work to know it meant "No next of kin." That one line opened the floodgate holding back the pent-up anger directed at everyone and everything I could think of except, of course, myself. *I* was supposed to be his next of kin. He should've proposed before the accident. She should've been watching over him. The doctors should've tried harder to keep him out of a coma.

To dissipate the rising rage, I stroked his hand, careful not to disturb the IV line, and kissed his cool forehead.

"*Forgive me*," I whispered in his ear. "*I love you.*"

I left a picture of the two of us on the whiteboard where the staff posted its shift notes and skipped the elevator in favor of the stairs to the first floor. My next stop was the local liquor store where I picked up a few bottles of spirits and proceeded home to test the *Hair of the Dog* theory on a bottle of gin.

My mother called in the early evening to tell me she'd stop by the next day to check on me. She reluctantly agreed to pick up a refill of my pain medicine when I told her my shoulder wouldn't stop hurting, which was a half-truth at best. Maverick, still acting strangely since Guerrera's appearance in my house, disappeared into the back of the bedroom closet to emerge only when I filled his bowl for dinner.

Just after 9:00 a.m. on Sunday, my parents arrived at my house, arms laden with containers of my favorite meals, bags of groceries, and a small sack from the pharmacy. After I put the food away, Mom started cleaning the kitchen, and Dad paced the floor and fidgeted, anxious to return home to settle in for a Texas ritual of twelve hours of back-to-back football games. They were gone in less than an hour. With pantry and pill bottle fully restocked, I prepared for the next week of meetings, hoping my contact with Guerrera would be minimal.

To fully understand the fracking process, its lingo, and the science of what could and couldn't go wrong, I spent the next four days woodshedded back in Radiant with Dr. Kevin Baker, the consulting expert I'd hand-selected to give me the crash course in all things fracking. From dawn to dusk, we sat in TSC's mobile response unit, plush by most standards, equipped with a galley kitchen, conference table, and bathroom, reviewing government reports, survey results, satellite photos, schematics and various scientific analyses collected both before and after the blast. Armed with this knowledge, I'd be able to translate the technical information into language a jury could understand, as well as cross-examine the plaintiffs' expert.

Wiley and Gator insisted on joining me under the guise of overseeing my preparation work but spent most of the time reviewing e-mails or taking calls outside of the trailer. I spent my evenings holed up in a local motel in the next town over studying the materials and reports Dr. Baker had provided me while Wiley and Gator slept in their own beds at night courtesy of the private helicopter trips to and from Radiant.

Dr. Baker was all business until our last day together when we had a chance to dine alone for lunch.

"How well do you know Gator?" he asked, wiping burger grease from his fingers.

"Not well. Is there something specific I need to know?"

"He's quite a character. Have you heard the story about his fingers and his boots?" I'd noticed Gator's exotic boots but hadn't given them much thought.

"No, no one's shared that one with me."

"It's a good one. Gator grew up in the bayous of Louisiana and lost those three fingers on his right hand to a fourteen-foot alligator while hauling in a crawfish trap for his daddy. The sonofabitch was so determined to get 'em back, regardless of their condition, that he tracked and killed the offending reptile and had the skin made into those boots he wears to drilling sites."

"I had no idea but can appreciate his tenacity."

"Ms. Tanis, make no mistake about him. Gator operates in the shadows and has friends in the highest and lowest of places. He knows how to find things, but no matter how much you need something, don't ever ask him to do you a favor."

We wrapped up our work on Thursday evening, and instead of staying one more night in the motel, I opted to make the two-hour drive home to get ready for Liz's weekend visit. The neighborhood was quiet when I pulled into my driveway and schlepped my suitcase into the house. Maverick, tail twitching in agitation, sat on the sofa table in anticipation of my arrival. When I picked him up to greet him, I noticed he smelled faintly like Guerrera's cologne.

I picked up another unusual scent as I moved toward the bedroom and found its source the moment I walked across the threshold. On my nightstand were the shards of a small crystal vase. The floor below was dotted with water droplets and shredded petals of a *Flor de Mayo.* I couldn't find an accompanying note, and Maverick jumped up onto my side of the bed and emitted a long, low growl as I cleaned up the mess.

"Crazy cat, that flower could've killed you if you'd eaten it," I said to him.

Guerrera had been here, although how he'd gained access to my locked house and why he'd come remained mysteries. I thought about calling and confronting him about his breaking and entering behavior but decided I'd address it in person the next time I saw him. Exhausted and battling cramps, I kicked off my shoes and fell into a dreamless sleep where I felt as if I were drowning. Every time I tried to sit up and open my eyes, an invisible assailant pulled me back below the murky surface.

†

I pried my lids open to find myself on the couch in front of the fireplace at the Cabin. The surf was high, and the waves roared onto the shore, littering the beach with seaweed, sand dollars, conch shells, and writhing jellyfish. From the opposite window, I watched the Aspen leaves shimmer in the wind and snow flurries dust the upper peaks of the mountains in the distance. Peter jumped up onto the couch and told me it was time to go. Acorn's directions to the chalet were simple.

"*Cross the street*," he'd said.

I slipped on a pair of flip-flops and walked out the door, where an unpaved, two-lane street was barely visible above the sand dune to the left of the Cabin's front door. I slogged up it to find, just across the road as described, an Austrian-style, stone ski chalet decorated with brightly painted and overflowing window flower boxes. Acorn met me in the lobby and walked me to a conference room where another man was seated at a table.

"John West," the man said without standing up or providing any additional information about why he was there. His faded jeans and polo-style shirt belied his former occupation as a member of the Army's elite Delta Force. The crew cut and tattoo on his bicep gave it away.

"We've got a situation at hand."

Having grown up in more polite company, Acorn pulled out a chair for me and took a seat.

"As you already know, I'm Andrew, and yes, you can call me Acorn. I lived a full life to the age of seventy-four and passed from natural causes when it was my time to go. My job is to answer questions, provide advice, and school you on a number of important subjects, including the powers you possess and the hazards of this job."

"Hazards? What kind of hazards?"

"Examine your palms," Acorn continued. "Those matching Xs aren't there by accident. They mark you as one with the power to maintain justice in the universe by passing judgment on others. Everything about your Human Experience, every setback and success, as well as every doubt and failure, prepared you for your role here."

As a litigator, I was comfortable with my role as an advocate. Nothing, *nothing* in my life had prepared me to act as judge, jury, and executioner. The air buzzed with static electricity. My palms started to itch as the Xs lit up like a silver road map. No matter where I placed them, whether it was palms down on the table or in my pockets, the light refused to be suppressed. Unsure of what to do, I sat on my hands, causing an eye roll with a soft snort from John.

She'd told me I'd known about this. What was I forgetting? The thought niggled at the back of my mind.

"Well, first things first," Acorn said. "I believe you already know that as you are now, you are virtually invisible to the living. Humans can see you but will have no memory of you, and those who knew you won't recognize you. A human Seer like the palm reader you met when you were younger can always identify an *X Triplici* by sight alone and knows how to reveal the light hidden within."

As if it were a subliminal tripwire, the words *palm reader* triggered a mental *click* that unlocked the memory of my first and only visit to a chiromancer, a memory I'd long ago relegated to the cerebral recycle bin.

It happened at the Texas State Fair on my sixteenth birthday. Liz and I had spent the latter part of the afternoon meandering down Grease Alley, that part of the fairway reserved for the award-winning vendors who'd mastered the art of deep frying everything from butter to beer, until we reached the opposite end crowded with rides that twirled, dipped, and spun.

"Time for your present," Liz had announced as she steered us away from the smell of hot grease toward the far north corner of the expansive fairgrounds. We followed the blacktop for at least half a mile until it tapered to a dirt path that led straight in the direction of the large, metal perimeter fence.

The dusty trail ended at the door of a structure that had reminded me of a weathered barn. Attached with rusty metal hooks to an eve above the door was a splintered wooden sign with the word "*Chiromancy*" outlined in white, cursive lettering.

"Chiromancy? What is that?" I'd asked Liz as she dragged me through the entrance.

"It's palm reading. Don't you want to know your future?"

She'd reached into her purse with one hand for the reading fee while expertly balancing her whipped-cream-topped funnel cake and phone in her other hand. The attendant took the money and instructed us to wait for our turn in the small antechamber. Skeptical as I was, I did want to know my future in the same way as most girls of my age.

As a senior in high school, younger than most in my grade, I measured my future in increments of hours and days, not years.

"Next," the attendant had announced after we'd wasted a few minutes fidgeting. Seeing the sign that read "No Bystanders During Readings," Liz had plunged her face into the crispy, fried dough and shoved me through the thick layers of tapestry separating us from what my mind pictured as the gypsy's lair.

The space I stumbled into was poorly lit and sparsely furnished with a rickety wooden table and two folding metal chairs atop a peeling linoleum floor. I took a seat in one of the two battered chairs and surveyed my surroundings for cameras, speakers, projectors, or any other mechanisms that could provide illusions of magic.

A woman who could've been close to my age entered through an inconspicuous doorway on the opposite end of the room and sat backward in the seat across from me, folding her arms over the back of the chair. Her dark-washed jeans and white t-shirt made her look more like a teenager than a master fortune-teller.

She didn't greet me and instead stared at me with her amber eyes for what felt like an uncomfortably long time before gesturing with a nod for me to put my hands on the table. I presented them, palms up, expecting the reading to begin, but she ignored them.

"Are you sure you want to know your fate? A prophecy revealed is the doorway to destiny." The modulation of her voice indicated an omen, and she studied my face for a reaction.

Thinking this was part of the charade, I gazed back at her with a look of feigned seriousness. "Of course, I do. Why else would I be here?"

She placed her smaller hands over mine. Her eyes fluttered and then closed. My hands prickled at the connection with her skin and grew warmer under hers.

Before I could react, she applied enough pressure to my wrists to clamp them to the table. Her eyes opened, their caramel color now replaced with the red and orange hues in a blazing fire. From the catacombs of my memory, the niggling teased out the long-forgotten words she'd spoken to me that day.

She told me she didn't have to look at my palms to know what I was.

"Made not born, to justice sworn," she'd said in a singsong voice, followed by several verses of what sounded like nonsense—

The hands of time
have etched the lines
as if they were in stone
thrice across each palm they stretch
with tendrils to the bone
across the lines

a seam defines
three Xs mark your fate
to fulfill your destiny
'til death you'll have to wait

She released my wrists, and with a few quick strokes of her index finger across my skin, she'd traced the three, perfectly spaced Xs in my palm prints which now glowed iridescent in the candlelight. When she lifted my hands off the table and moved my thumbs slightly toward one another, I saw the mirror images of the lines she'd outlined. Out of the corner of my eye, I saw the Eye of Horus tattoos, one on the inside of each of her wrists, wink at me while the flames danced within her firelit eyes.

A feeling of complete disorientation hit me at the moment she removed her hands from mine, causing me to lean forward and put my head between my legs to avoid fainting or vomiting, whichever came first. When I finally raised my head and felt steady enough to stand up, she was gone.

Weak-kneed, I staggered back toward the curtains through which I'd entered. As I lifted my hands to part the dense layers of fabric, I noticed the silver lines and Xs were gone. Liz was waiting outside with a super-sized soda and a heaping plate of now-cold, ketchup-smothered waffle fries. Before I could say anything to her, I involuntarily donated the contents of my stomach to the fairground.

"Adeleine? Adeleine? Are you still with me?" Acorn asked. "I was talking about Seers and seemed to have lost you."

"I'm sorry, I got hung up on something you said," I replied. I didn't know how long I'd tuned him out. "Please continue."

Acorn explained that Seers were neutral observers in life, and I would easily recognize them by their Fire Eyes, which matured in adulthood. As he spoke, my mind conjured up the image of the palm reader's fiery eyes. What I thought was a trick of the eye had been real.

"Your light also gives you the power to reveal members of the Pellico but not without revealing your own identity in turn," Acorn said.

"What's the Pellico?"

John gave Acorn a smug look, clasped his hands together, and rested his chin on the steeple he'd formed with his index fingers.

"They're a radical faction of those who've been denied entry to the Hereafter and for the time being, *Below,* who spend their time on earth influencing human behavior for their amusement. They walk among and are indistinguishable from the living. They cannot, however, distinguish you from other living beings unless another Pellico member identifies you or they make physical contact with you. If they do, they reveal their identity, as well as yours," Acorn explained.

The fact that modern earth did double-duty as Purgatory didn't escape me.

"Is their light like mine?"

"No. When the energy from your light makes initial contact with one of them, the result is an initial flickering of their form, much like a candle flame in a light breeze. To the untrained eye, the effect would be too subtle to notice."

John leaned toward me.

"On earth, the Pellico's best and worst human traits are magnified. Their brilliance can be destructive, their beauty deceptive, and their possessiveness violent. Because they have nothing better to do, they derive great pleasure from creating chaos on earth. Our intelligence shows they're looking for ways to free themselves and destroy the balance of power. To further that goal, they've captured two of your colleagues. Before you can start your Soul Decision Maker training, we need your help to find them."

"I'll give you an updated briefing when I'm ready," John continued on his way out the door.

"What am I supposed to do now, wait around for the end of the world?"

"Get settled in. Tomorrow I need to introduce you to an old friend," Acorn replied.

Tomorrow was a time reference that was difficult to gauge because no one here wore a watch, and there were no clocks that told time. The sun rose and set, but I had no idea whether those events corresponded to time in the human world. As a lawyer, I'd been a slave to the billable hour, which meant I was a captive of time. Without the ability to mark it, my inherent restlessness manifested itself as edginess.

"What is it?" Acorn asked, sensing my subtle mood shift.

"There are a few things I'd like to have right now. How would I go about getting them?"

"For the time being, tell me what you want or need and I'll handle it."

"I'd like a watch and a case of gin."

Acorn grinned. "Easy enough. Ask, and ye shall receive."

The fierce-looking man I'd seen earlier at Her place stalked into the room and stood at the far end of the table. He stared at Acorn, face expressionless, until Acorn stood up, patted my shoulder, and walked out the door beside the visitor. I followed behind and watched as they faded away into the Aspens.

The first thing I noticed back at the Cabin was the wooden crate on my desk with a pair of familiar bunny ears peeking out of the top. The remainder of Peter's head popped up when he heard the front door close. Clasped around his neck was what I thought was a watch.

"Would you mind getting this thing off of me?" he asked. *"So undignified. Collars are for dogs and cats."*

I plucked him out of the box and slid the watch from his plush fur. The band was made of a thin and flexible gold metal, and the round face was the size of a silver dollar. Clouds floated across the dial obscuring the numbers or hash marks if it had any.

"If this is a watch, do you know how to use it?" I asked Peter.

"*No idea. I've never seen one like that before. I'm sure you'll figure it out.*"

With Peter under my arm and a bottle of gin in my hand, I made myself comfortable on the couch to digest this first day of lessons.

Questions outnumbered answers. Chief among them was the subject of what made me any different from the millions and maybe billions of people in the world who, as I once did, made judgment calls in their personal and professional lives every day. Other than a law degree and a few years of the practice of law under my belt, neither of which was in any way remarkable, what separated me from the masses and required me to undertake such responsibilities?

And what about the missing colleagues I'd never met? They'd been taken for an unknown purpose by a dangerous pack of troublemakers. I took a long swig from the bottle and turned my attention to the watch. The clouds passing across the face darkened when I clasped it around my right wrist, but no numbers appeared.

"*Maybe it does something other than telling time,*" Peter offered.

Maybe so, I thought. Coincidentally, the skies above the ocean outside turned a deep gray, and the waves grew larger as they pummeled the shore. I succumbed to the drowsiness and fell asleep.

The next time I opened my eyes, I was standing near the baggage claim area at the airport waiting for Liz to exit the terminal among a sea of commuters. True to her word, she'd flown to Dallas on a late Friday afternoon to keep me company and help reset my moral compass. As a thank you to her, I'd made dinner reservations at an upscale steak house where we could catch up over a leisurely meal.

I grabbed her as she exited the security area. After hugging me tightly, she stepped back and gave me the once-over.

"Damn, woman. You look worse than you sounded. Do you ever sleep?"

On the drive home to drop off her luggage, I filled her in on Rynner's prognosis and my predicament with Guerrera. When she asked me what I saw in Guerrera, I gave her the brutally honest answer.

"I'm lonely, and aside from Rynner, Guerrera's the best-looking man I've ever seen."

"Since when did you park your ass in the shallow end of the pool? You're smart enough to know there's no good ending to this."

She was right, of course. The question was whether I could stop whatever this was before it went any further. Having made her point, she changed subjects and spent the rest of the drive describing the intricacies of the dating scene in Chicago.

When I led her through the front door, I saw pieces of plastic wrap all over the floor leading from the kitchen to my bedroom. Since the time he was a kitten, Maverick had a habit of carrying all sorts of items, from washcloths to wine corks, around the house, but he'd never exhibited destructive tendencies. It took me a few minutes to figure out that my cat had burrowed his way into the depths of my closet, found the hospital bag filled with the clothes I'd worn on the night of the accident, and shredded it.

To make whatever point he was trying to make, he'd scattered the plastic shrapnel throughout the house. He sat on the bedroom floor with a piece of plastic between his paws and although I never would've thought it possible, an undeniably smug look on his face. I waded into the back of the closet and kicked the pile of filthy clothing now freed from the shredded bag into a corner, threw a coat on top of it, and hoped I would forget about it. I still wasn't ready to acknowledge the consequences of the bag's contents.

Liz and I spent another hour primping before grabbing a ride to the restaurant. After checking in with the hostess, we took the last two seats at the swanky bar and ordered a round of Flaming Dr. Peppers. As we always did, we turned to one another, held our glasses high while the flames burned out, and made our favorite toast.

"Come what may," Liz said.

"Amen," I replied.

We'd barely had time to set the empty glasses down on the bar when the hostess approached us.

"This way please, your table has been waiting."

Instead of seating us in the main dining room, she led us through the maze of tables and past the portraits of nameless but important-looking people to a private room in the back I didn't know existed. My stomach lurched when she slid back the pocket door, revealing more than just the strains of soft Latin jazz.

Seated at a table for six and facing the door was Guerrera flanked by three, nearly equally-handsome and virile-looking men cut from the same cloth.

A magnum of expensive champagne provided the centerpiece for the table already littered with bottles of wine in various stages of consumption and dozens of empty wine glasses. Liz, who'd been standing behind me, moved to my side so our shoulders were touching, and leaned toward my ear.

"Do you know these people?"

I nodded my head slightly. "It's Guerrera," I whispered back. "With friends."

One side of Guerrera's mouth curled up.

The four men studied us until Guerrera broke the silence.

"The owner is a friend of mine and mentioned that you had a reservation tonight. I thought you might like to join us."

"That's very thoughtful of you, but we wouldn't want to intrude," I replied. Liz gave my back a quick flick with her finger. She wanted to stay.

"I insist. And this must be the mysterious Liz?"

His use of her name caught me off guard. How did he know it? I couldn't recall ever discussing Liz with Guerrera, and I'd made the reservation under my name, not hers. He knew what I looked like naked, but he sure as hell shouldn't know the name of my best friend.

But he did.

"You must be Guerrera. I've heard all about you," Liz said, her voice far more confident than how I felt.

Amused by her implication, Guerrera flashed her a mischievous smile and beckoned us to sit while he introduced his friends as "Pietro," "Tomás," and "Mateo." Guerrera made a few remarks in Spanish, but the only word I understood was *Abogada,* or *attorney.* Tomás responded with a short quip of his own. Guerrera might've known Liz's name, but I was sure that neither he nor his friends knew she spoke fluent Spanish.

Liz ensconced herself between Pietro and Tomás while I took the seat farthest away from Guerrera. Making extra room for Liz, Mateo shifted in his chair, revealing a shoulder holster under his navy suit coat. His weapon of choice, recognizable by the width of the magazine, was a .45 caliber Grizzly, preferred by those with more than a cursory knowledge of firearms. Mateo was packing serious heat, and it wouldn't surprise me if the others were too.

Pietro inched his chair toward Liz. When his hands weren't engaged in the task of topping off her wine glass, his fingers were busy playing with her thick curls. The next time I looked at Liz, Pietro, who knew I was watching, leaned into her, nipped her ear lobe, and said something to her in Spanish that made her face flush. I flared my nostrils in response.

Guerrera reached for a bottle of Cherry Pie Pinot Noir, my favorite, and poured two glasses for Liz and me. From the hundreds of bottles of wine the restaurant offered, he'd managed to select the one I would've ordered for a girls' night out. I didn't know whether his choice was calculated or coincidental.

Probably the latter, Lawyer Brain quipped.

His and his companions' glasses were already filled with a dark-brown liquid. Feigning a recently acquired allergy to sulfites, I ordered a vodka tonic from the server. After it arrived, I assessed the threat level in the room, decided it was high, and promised myself that in this den of wolves, I'd remain vigilant. And sober. It was the least I could do for Liz, and in any case, I owed her one for the visit.

I felt a brief wave of nausea, which seemed to be on the rise from the stress, and used the trip to the restroom as an opportunity to intercept our server and let him know that for the remainder of the evening, he was to refill my vodka tonic with nothing more than soda water and lime.

After a few dry heaves and a swig of mouthwash, I felt well enough to return to the soiree and keep tabs on Liz. Guerrera and his friends drank like sailors but never appeared intoxicated. The group conversation was upbeat but light, and Pietro took every opportunity to shower Liz with compliments. When Tomás asked me how I liked working for Tessa and Pietro, and Mateo groaned in response, I knew they all had a connection to TSC. I dodged an answer by telling Tomás that I preferred not to talk shop and would rather debate the pros and cons of the best Fútbol team in Venezuela.

As I suspected, the topic of soccer proved to be a wise choice and consumed the remainder of the evening, just as Liz consumed the rest of the ornate bottle of wine sitting in front of her. Guerrera added his opinion about the best players, but even when my attention was diverted elsewhere, I could sense he was observing me like a hunter in a blind, stealthily stalking his prey.

I checked my watch. Midnight had come and gone, and my energy was waning. Liz's face was flushed, and her neck had trouble supporting her head.

"It's getting late, and I really should get Liz home," I announced during a pause in the conversation.

"Our driver is waiting out front. As gentlemen, we must be allowed to escort you home safely," Guerrera said.

I agreed because I knew that even if I could stuff Liz into an Uber, there was no way I'd be able to get her out of it. Pietro maneuvered an inebriated Liz through the now-empty restaurant and into the Bentley limousine parked at the front door. Guerrera and I followed and climbed in after them. Mateo and Tomás left together in a white Aston Martin Vanquish parked on the other side of the restaurant's *porte cochère*.

Liz passed out in Pietro's arms on the ride home. With her legs stretched out over the seat, I was forced to sit next to Guerrera. I spent the entire trip squished up against the side of the door to create as much space between us as possible, and he spent the time chatting in Spanish with his accomplice.

When the chauffeur pulled into my driveway, I jumped out to unlock the front door with Pietro in tow carrying Liz. He was kind enough to deposit her on the bed in my guest room and put her purse on the nightstand. He bid me goodbye with a kiss on both cheeks and returned to the waiting limousine. I forced Liz awake long enough to get a glass of water down her throat and pull off her shoes, and then tucked her in for the night.

When I doubled back down the dark hallway to lock the front door after Pietro, I was ambushed.

Leading with his chest, Guerrera used his weight and momentum to push my back against the closest wall. He pressed his body against mine and slid his right thigh between my legs, forcing them apart. He planted his hands on the wall above my head, leaving my body pinned, but my arms free.

"*Shhhh,*" he whispered, pressing a finger to my lips.

I squeezed my right hand into a fist to punch him. In anticipation of my move, he shifted his body and pinned the arm to the wall.

"Let me go," I hissed.

He leaned in, pressing me harder into the sheetrock, and replaced the finger with his soft lips, starting with a light nibble before committing to a full, sensuous lip-lock. My fist unfurled and my muscles relaxed as my body, craving physical contact, kicked my brain out of the driver's seat. Guerrera cupped my face with his hands as his lips traveled across my cheeks to tease my nose and eyelids.

Not. A. Good. Idea. Sixth Sense protested. I responded with the mental equivalent of sticking my fingers in my ears to block it out.

Fight and flight, the fraternal twins, had abandoned me. All that mattered was that Guerrera not stop. I slid my hands around his backside grazing the long barrel of the gun tucked into his waistband, pressed him hard against me, and sent a message with my own lips that I was all in.

He murmured approvingly in Spanish while he repositioned his legs, so there was no doubt of his commitment.

"Give yourself to me." It was a direct and straightforward request that bordered on a demand. He exhaled slowly as he slid my skirt up past my waist.

He parted my lips with two fingers, pulled them away, and slipped them inside my panties, where he found what he wanted and deftly applied just the right amount of pressure with circular, pulsing motions. With his free hand, he cradled the back of my head to protect it from the wall and engaged his tongue to converse with mine.

A mix of heat and adrenaline coursed through my body and my pelvic muscles tensed involuntarily as he increased the speed and pressure until I gasped, overwhelmed by the nerve-tingling climax. I grabbed his waist for support when my knees buckled and tasted blood when he bit down hard on my lower lip.

"*Otra vez*," he commanded. *Again.*

His magical fingers began working a new pattern.

My hushed pleas only increased his focus and intensity. I placed my hands on his stomach and tried to push him back toward the couch in the living room.

"*Todavia no.*" *Not yet.*

His self-discipline was remarkable. Judging by the fact that I was melting into the wall, mine was non-existent. I moved my hands inside his sweater and braced against his chest for the next round.

"Don't stop," I murmured, barely able to get the two words out of my mouth.

An ear-piercing screech caused him to jerk away from me, swearing in two languages. I moved a few feet down the hall and flipped on the light to find that Maverick had attached himself with all four sets of claws to Guerrera's back and was yowling like a tomcat. I disentangled him from Guerrera's cashmere sweater, leaving a long gash in the back of it and ran through the house to lock my psychotic feline in the master bathroom.

Once Maverick was sequestered, I splashed cold water on my face to quell the endorphins Guerrera had unleashed, smoothed my skirt, and returned to the hallway.

Guerrera was gone. Even though he didn't have my house key, he'd somehow locked the front door behind him. He'd fled so fast that he'd left his sport coat draped over the back of the sofa. In flagrant disregard for the rules of etiquette my mother had drilled into me, I picked up the jacket and rifled through the pockets to see what kind of items a man like Guerrera would want at his fingertips. The money clip filled with crisp Benjamin Franklins, the box of cinnamon Altoids, and the condoms didn't surprise me. The miniature, surgical-looking sewing kit, on the other hand, was puzzling.

✝

I hoped the older woman was wrong, but I wasn't in the mood to dwell on that right now. All the pieces had fit into place, and Adeleine was mine, willingly, until that damned cat ruined everything. I wanted this to work the easy way but doubted I'd have another opportunity.

I'd performed hundreds of similar types of procedures on my patients and could do it in my sleep but never on an unwilling woman without her consent. This wouldn't be the worst thing I'd ever done, so the guilt-like feeling confused me.

I made no excuses for myself. The Indian pronounced my sentence and I landed here, *nec supra, nec infra. Neither above nor below.* Fate offered me more than one chance, and I fucked up each one worse than the last. The rough start I had didn't help.

My mother never graduated from grade school and became pregnant with me when she was twelve. Just after she turned thirteen, she gave birth to me in the *barrios* of Caracas. She told me my father was a married, low-level bureaucrat, three times her age, who refused to acknowledge me and publicly denounced her as being nothing more than a common street whore. The one-room shack we inhabited with my grandparents on the eastern slope of the hillside a few miles from the city center was made from scraps of corrugated metal and cardboard fastened together with chicken wire and string. With no running water or electricity and no financial assistance from my father, I spent the first four years of my life in unimaginable squalor.

I slept on top of a wooden crate elevated off of the floor by a crumbling stack of bricks. The only other furniture we had consisted of a table made from a small piece of plywood supported by plastic milk crates and half of an appliance box repurposed as a cabinet that held all of our material possessions. The stench from the raw sewage that ran through the shallow trench past our front door permeated the flimsy walls and was occasionally diverted into our living area, necessitating the elevated sleeping arrangements.

Every year, our shanty, along with our neighbors' shacks, slid down the hillside during the rainy season and ended up in an enormous pile of mud-covered refuse, the remains of which were fought over during the ensuing rebuilding process.

Our two meager sources of income came from my grandparent's efforts to scavenge for recyclables to trade for cash and my mother's work as a courier for a small-time drug runner. Every Sunday, my grandparents hauled me down the hillside to attend Mass at a small Catholic church a few miles from our shantytown. Because it didn't require attendees to trek through the city to get there, it attracted worshippers from neighboring *barrios*. My mother, who'd lost interest in me when she realized the work it took to raise a child, refused to go, reasoning that she could earn more money if she worked seven days a week. We had no money to buy books, paper, or pencils, which wasn't a problem because there were no schools for kids like me to attend.

Although they were illiterate, my grandparents memorized most of the prayers and hymns in the church books and were devout in their faith. When I turned seven, they convinced the resident Priest, Father Antonio Eduardo Davila, to allow me to apprentice as an Altar Boy until I received my first Communion. That same year, my mother disappeared for several months. My grandparents, who made no secret of their disapproval of her life-style and her Godless ways, explained she was away for work, and they weren't sure if and when she'd return.

She never came back, and a local official arrived at the door one evening with an envelope full of black and white photographs. With privacy a luxury we couldn't afford, I stood behind my grandparents when the man notified them that the police had found my mother's body stuffed inside the trunk of an abandoned car. Based on the ligature marks around her neck, visible from the photographs he showed us, the authorities concluded someone had strangled her. The official didn't say it, but my grandparents knew the police wouldn't waste their time investigating her death. Instead, she'd join the thousands of other expendable women who faced violent ends to their short and miserable lives.

My grandparents showed little emotion and with the assistance of neighbors, managed to scrape together enough money for a simple but proper Catholic burial. She'd been absent so long, both emotionally and physically, that I strained to recall the details of my mother's face when I learned she was dead.

With nothing positive or productive to fill my days on the hillside, I spent more and more of my time at the church, where Father Davila became my mentor and surrogate father. My grandparents didn't mind because they had one less thing to worry about and one less mouth to feed. Father Davila had rummaged through the lost-and-found box to find me a clean outfit consisting of a pair of jeans, a long-sleeved shirt, and a pair of sneakers. I never had underwear because, as Father Davila explained, no one ever left any behind at the church.

In his free time, Father Davila instructed me in a wide range of subjects, including reading and writing in Spanish, Latin, and English. He also taught me how to sew and explained that the ability to make perfect stitches wasn't just a woman's work. Later in life, I'd learn how right he was on that point.

As do most good things in life, his patience and paternal instruction came with a price. He was, as I soon learned, a pedophile with such perverse predilections that even now, I couldn't think of him without feeling dirty and ashamed of the things he'd done to me and forced me to do to him. Trust was his weapon, and once he knew he had mine, he began making requests, simple ones at first, that drew me further into his web.

I saw no harm in shining his shoes or washing and pressing his chasuble, alb, and cincture. His praise meant the world to me, and the more he heaped on me, the harder I worked to please him.

In turn, he rewarded me with greater responsibilities, and as those increased in number and complexity, so did the type and extent of the physical contact. Out of naiveté and fearful of losing the only father figure I had, I agreed to do anything he asked of me. He was a Priest and would never, I thought, harm me or betray our faith. I also agreed to his request to keep our physical relationship a secret from the world.

"*It's our Sacred Covenant,*" he'd said to me in the same tone he used when delivering Mass.

No one suspected anything was amiss because a gutter rat like me was as good as invisible, and no one questioned a starched white collar.

My language skills improved to the point where I could converse fluently, with few mistakes, in all three languages. I'd also been born with the gift of steady-handedness, which I used to stitch intricate patterns for the altar decorations.

I lost my grandparents when I was eight. I returned home from an afternoon of studying with Father Davila to find them cold and slack-jawed on the damp dirt floor. We had no doctors on the hillside, and no one would care enough to order autopsies. Looking back, and considering the symptoms I remembered, I think they both succumbed to a bacterial infection they'd probably picked up from the human, animal, and other waste and chemicals that impregnated the ground below and the air above the hillside.

I bid them goodbye and made the long walk back to the church, where Father Davila consoled me and arranged for their funerals. He also took me in as his full-time *Inamorato*. He fed and clothed me and continued with my lessons, including those in pain and pleasure. By the time I was eleven years old, I knew more about sex than most grown men.

✝

My unhealthy routine took an unforeseen turn one afternoon when my daily chore of cleaning and polishing the pews was interrupted by an unexpected traveler. The heavy church door in need of a proper oiling groaned, pushed open by an elderly man shuffling forward with the help of a painted wooden walking stick. The green coat that hung mid-calf and the similarly colored, three-cornered felt hat he wore instantly marked him as a foreigner.

He made his way to the altar, used his cane for balance, and lowered himself into a kneeling position. Once situated, he began incanting in a language I didn't recognize.

Trying hard not to disturb him, I moved from pew to pew as quietly as I could. His hearing rivaled that of a bat judging by his reaction when I accidentally dropped my cleaning rag. The sound the threadbare cloth made upon contact with the worn stone floor was barely audible, but he stopped, mid-sentence, and cocked his head toward me.

"*Wer ist das?*" *Who is that?*

I popped my head up but didn't respond because I didn't understand him.

"*Knabe, komm her!*" *Boy, come here!*

I'd learned the importance of obeying my elders. To my young ears, a command in any language sounded the same, so when I heard this one, I walked up to the man and waited for him to speak again. He started babbling in what I later learned was German.

With the hope he could understand my native tongue, I told him my name and asked if he needed help. He looked at me with a puzzled expression and shook his head from side to side, which I took to mean that Spanish wasn't a language in his repertoire.

He paused momentarily and restarted his questioning in Latin. He was pleased when I responded in kind and held my own in our conversation.

His name was Herr Bauer, and he was born in Salzburg, Austria. He immigrated to Venezuela after the Second World War and was visiting from his adopted hometown of San Cristóbal by the Colombian border. When I asked him what he was doing here, he told me he was searching for forgiveness. My suggestion that confession might help brought tears to his already watery blue eyes and a declaration that God knew well what tortured him. He told me that a lifetime of repentance could never be enough.

I helped him to his feet as Father Davila returned from his errands. He and Father Davila traded greetings in Latin, and I felt a swell of pride when my new friend complimented my good manners and Latin proficiency. Father Davila said the recent and unexpected rainfall had sickened many of his flock, requiring more time away from the church, and invited Herr Bauer to stop by anytime to practice Latin with me.

For the next two weeks, Herr Bauer visited me daily, although he avoided confession with Father Davila, and provided a break from my daily routine. He brought me books on Latin and German grammar and a book in English about a bull that hated fighting, preferring instead to sit under a tree and smell the flowers. Unlike the grammar books, the storybook was filled with colorful pictures that had nothing to do with religion.

Herr Bauer's platonic attention didn't go unnoticed by Father Davila, whose warped sense of reality misinterpreted what was nothing more than Herr Bauer's grandfatherly benefaction. One evening when he returned to the church reeking of alcohol, Father Davila whipped himself into a jealous rage and accused me of ungodly relations with Herr Bauer.

My steadfast denial of the accusations that Herr Bauer was making physical advances toward me fell on deaf ears. Father Davila called me a liar, backfisted me across the face several times, and told me I would burn in Hell. It was the first time he'd laid his hands on me in anger. He left the church and didn't return by nightfall. I slept curled up in a ball under the altar, praying that God would forgive whatever sins I'd committed.

Alarmed by my appearance the following day, Herr Bauer grilled me about my black eye and bruised cheek. Scared if I said anything but terrified about what Father Davila might do next, I broke the *Sacred Covenant* and divulged the details of my relationship with Father Davila. I had trouble explaining some of the activities because I didn't know the Latin words for specific body parts or sexual interactions. Herr Bauer asked me simple questions using words I knew and pointed to various body parts to confirm what I was trying to convey.

"Have you told me everything?"

"Yes," I replied through the tears.

Herr Bauer closed his eyes and recited the Lord's Prayer in German. When he'd finished, he told me he needed to take care of some business but would be back the next day. Father Davila locked me out of his small bedroom that night, so I slept on the stone floor between two pews.

As promised, Herr Bauer returned in the morning carrying a stained and bulging paper sack in his hand and requested a private audience with Father Davila, who hadn't spoken to me since he'd struck me. They weren't alone in Father Davila's office for long when Herr Bauer emerged from the meeting without the sack and told me we were leaving the church and wouldn't return.

Father Davila stayed hidden in his office. I never saw him again.

Herr Bauer held my hand when we walked to his car.

"You are now my ward, and I promise you I will spend the rest of my life educating and raising you to be a good, honest man."

"Herr Bauer, what was in the paper sack you brought to Father Davila?"

"*Libertatum,*" he replied. *Your freedom.*

☦

You were blind if you didn't notice how different Herr Bauer's neighborhood in San Cristóbal looked and felt from the rest of the city. The houses were of sturdy, wooden construction with slanted roofs and windows that opened both outward and sideways. Short fences surrounded garden plots in most of the front yards, and every driveway had at least one car parked in it.

"A place for everything and everything in its place," Herr Bauer said when I commented on how neat and orderly everything looked.

For the first time in my life, I had my own bedroom with real furniture and a closet filled with toys, books, and more than one change of clothes. The house rules were simple: cleanliness, Godliness, respect, honesty, thriftiness, modesty, and hard work. Herr Bauer never said it, but he included love on that list.

As was the case at Father Davila's church, I had assigned chores and was expected to keep my room clean and pick up after myself. Herr Bauer's housekeeper, a local woman named Daniela, worked six days per week cooking, doing laundry, cleaning, shopping, and fussing over Herr Bauer. Daniela spoke enough passable German to perform her job, and I was able to connect with her through our common language.

It wasn't long before she became my surrogate mother who counseled me about my personal hygiene, manners, and clothing choices. Her devotion to Herr Bauer quickly extended to me, and within months, the few memories of my birth mother faded out of existence.

Daniela said she had a daughter a few years older than me who attended school in another city and would introduce us over a school break. I spent the rest of that year safe and sequestered in the homogenous community, meeting Herr Bauer's close-knit group of friends, all of whom were German or Austrian, learning and practicing language skills and studying history, math, and science. Sewing socks, punch pictures, and anything else Herr Bauer or Daniela provided me was a welcome break from the academics.

Regardless of the weather, we walked to Mass every Sunday evening. I went through the motions in deference to my adopted father but didn't have the heart to tell him that Father Davila had stripped me of my faith.

At the beginning of December, Herr Bauer gave me a traditional German *Adventskalendar* with tiny pieces of chocolate tucked behind every paper window that covered each day of the month. He mounted it on the wall in the kitchen to prevent me from being tempted to eat all the candy at once.

Every morning before breakfast, Herr Bauer and Daniela watched as I opened the little door corresponding to the day, popped the chocolate into my mouth, and in German counted down the days until Christmas. We bought a real Christmas tree, my first, which I decorated with chains of garland I'd made from colored construction paper and ornaments I'd sewn together from patterns I'd seen in Daniela's lady magazines. When I finished wrapping the tree, Herr Bauer disappeared into his bedroom closet and emerged with a dusty cardboard box.

"These and my wedding ring are the only objects I have from Mrs. Bauer," Herr Bauer said as he began unwrapping the contents.

Herr Bauer removed two dozen balls of colored silk, decorated with beads of gold and silver glass that were held in place by pearl-topped stick pins, from their paper cocoons. All of the delicate ornaments had been handmade by Herr Bauer's wife before the War. Daniela and I were careful to treat the mementos with great respect and used them to finish trimming the tree.

On Christmas Day, and after I opened my presents of an ivory-handled pocket knife, an anatomy book, and a set of sewing needles, Herr Bauer told me I'd surpassed his expectations, and as my reward, he'd enrolled me in a private school for a proper education. His connections helped him secure a new birth certificate for me, along with identification papers that confirmed his status as my legal guardian.

The all-boys' Catholic school required that I take placement tests because I had no formal academic record. To my surprise, I tested two grade levels above my age group and was allowed to start in the middle of the term provided I made up the work I'd missed.

The learning part of school proved easy for me, thanks to Father Davila and Herr Bauer's earlier tutelage. I did, however, find it difficult to befriend other boys because of their obsession with girls and sex. The only sex education in my life had come from a perverted priest, and I didn't know if men and women engaged in the same types of acts that Father Davila and I had. I didn't dare ask anyone, and my classmates teased me for never having kissed a girl. Some even suggested I might be gay.

Tatiana, Daniela's daughter, resolved that issue. Tatiana, two years older than I was, came to visit that spring while on holiday. Every day, she accompanied her mother to our house, and read and watched television while Daniela worked. Tatiana was well-developed for her age and initially ignored me until the day her mother went grocery shopping and left us together, unsupervised. Herr Bauer was out visiting with friends, and I was in my room studying when she walked in without knocking. Tatiana told me I was cute and wanted to know if I'd ever been with a woman. When I told her I hadn't, she told me it was time I learned.

She undressed in front of me and tossed her clothes on the floor. I'd never seen a naked woman before and was intimidated by the physiology so different from my own. Tatiana wasted no time with foreplay. She climbed on top of me while I sat at my desk and began kissing me on the mouth. It didn't take long for the bulge in my clothes to appear. When she saw it, she took off my pants and showed me what went where. She rocked up and down and back and forth, and as the pressure inside me mounted, she rolled off of me and helped me reposition myself on top of her.

The act was different from anything Father Davila ever did and was beyond any feeling I could've imagined. When we'd finished, she showed me how to tidy up and leave no evidence for her mother or Herr Bauer to find. No longer a virgin, I joined in my classmates' obsessions and was finally able to make new friends.

My discrete sexual relationship with Tatiana continued through most of my schooling. She was the first in a long line of women I used for pleasure and discarded. Due to my earlier experiences with sex, I didn't connect the physical act with a positive emotional attachment, or any romantic commitment. That chain remained irreparably broken throughout my life.

☦

College was a blur of studying and a steady diet of short-term girlfriends and trysts. I'd decided I wanted to go to medical school and didn't want the burden of a long-term relationship to weigh me down. A gradual decline in Herr Bauer's health didn't stop him from encouraging me and sharing in my success. When I was accepted into medical school, he insisted on paying for all of it. He established a bank account in my name and generously funded it with more than enough money to pay the tuition and other expenses.

I graduated from medical school near the top of my class and chose emergency medicine as my specialty. I passed my medical examinations, finished my residency in Colombia's most prestigious hospital, and moved back to San Cristóbal to help Daniela care for Herr Bauer, who'd already suffered two strokes. He died in his sleep weeks after I returned to be with him, and his was one of only two deaths I would, in this life and the next, ever mourn.

While his body was at the mortuary, I had time to start sorting through his belongings. On the desk in his study was a large envelope sealed with a wax stamp of two eagle heads. Inside it was a copy of his will and a letter addressed to me, handwritten nostalgically in Latin, the language that had brought us together. His soul-bearing confession brought tears to my eyes:

My son Carlos,

There are many things I couldn't share with you during my life for fear that you would know and shun me for the monster I am. On the day I met you, you suggested that I attend confession to soothe my soul, and I told you that God already knew what haunted me. Now it's time that you know too. I am a vile man. As a member of the German *Schutzstaffel* during the War, I was personally responsible for the deaths of thousands of innocent men, women, and children at the *Mauthausen-Gusen* Concentration Camp. Young and power-hungry, I felt no remorse and carried out my death orders with pride and satisfaction. When the War ended, my staff and I fled like cowards to Venezuela to avoid prosecution for our unspeakable crimes. Without my beloved wife Erika, who died in an Allied bombing raid before my escape, I've had years to reflect on the genocide I'd committed, the families I'd ripped apart, and the terror I caused people who'd never lifted a finger against me. I believe it was God's will that we met all those years ago. You represented the youth and hopefulness I stole from so many and gave me the chance to prove, to myself and to you, not only that I could change but that I had enough goodness left in me to mold you into an honorable man. We both know that I am not your real father, but you must know that you have always been my beloved son and the only good thing to come from my life. Other than a generous stipend for Daniela, who has served us both like family, I've left my estate and all of my possessions to you with the hope that you will forgive me and become everything that I couldn't and wasn't. And for my final confession, on the day I took you away from Caracas, you asked me what was in the bag I gave to Father Davila. I told you the truth, but not all of it. It was a human head with the eyes and mouth sewn shut. I told Father Davila that I would add his to the bag then and there if he didn't agree to release you from his sadistic captivity. Pray for me and my tortured soul.

Your loving Father, Herr Heinrich Bauer.

I read and re-read the letter, grappling with the duality of the man who, despite having murdered so many, saved me, raised me, and loved me. Every night for the next month, I lit a candle in his honor and prayed to his God for redemption.

Just as God was absent from my life, He was absent from Herr Bauer's. According to my father's instructions, I arranged for his funeral Mass and buried him in the plot he'd purchased long before I met him. For the top of his headstone, I chose the following inscription:

"At Spes Non Fracta." But hope is not broken.

From the day we'd met until the day he died, we'd had hope for one another. It's a good thing he's gone because it would've broken his heart to find out that his legacy was the antithesis of a decent, honest man.

†

In the posture he took when he was mad, Maverick sat on the bathroom vanity with his back to me while I inspected the small bruise forming around Guerrera's bite mark on my lip. When I reached out to pet him, Maverick slinked further down the counter knocking over Rynner's cologne bottle. After stripping off my clothes, I brushed my teeth and rinsed with mouthwash to cover the lingering taste of cinnamon before falling into bed to chase a few precious hours of shut-eye before the 3:32 a.m. witching hour.

With the covers pulled up around my chin, I thought about how close to the edge I'd been with Guerrera. If it hadn't been for Maverick, I would've crossed a hard, red line. I covered my face with my pillow and screamed into it until I was out of breath.

It was still dark outside when I awoke, a time I now referred to as the *crack of ass.* On the bright side, at least I didn't have a hangover. Knowing Liz wouldn't stir until at least 11:00 a.m., I got up, showered, and spent the next seven hours reviewing the notes I'd taken during my week with Dr. Baker and refining my expert deposition outline.

Sparing no expense, Budd Frantsen had retained the expert witness services of Dr. Richard Perryman, an outspoken critic of fracking known for venting his strong opinions and referring to himself publicly as "Fracking's Greatest Foe." Few scientists dared to make guest appearances on shows when Dr. Perryman was scheduled because he was known for shouting down and belittling anyone with a competing viewpoint. I doubted Dr. Perryman had digested the thousands of pages of government investigation reports that Dr. Baker and I had, which made his opinions highly susceptible to attack.

I had enough scientific ammunition to discredit his theory that TSC's fracking had caused the blast in Radiant and a silver bullet to ensure that once I'd taken him out, he couldn't be rehabilitated. The bullet was a gift from Gator who, just days earlier when he and Wiley departed from our meeting in Radiant, had handed me an unmarked package. Inside the package was proof positive that Dr. Perryman had plagiarized most of his doctoral dissertation. Why no one else had discovered the fraud to date, and how Gator had located it so quickly, were questions for another day. Or maybe never.

Because I'd use the evidence to impeach the good doctor, I wasn't required to produce it to Frantsen in discovery. Instead, I would spring the revelation on him like a trap during the deposition. I'd waited until the day the expert designation deadline expired to take this deposition, knowing that once I'd disqualified Dr. Perryman, Frantsen would be out of time to designate a new expert for trial.

I was so engrossed in my work that I didn't hear Liz shuffle up behind me around noon. She plunked the empty water glass down in front of me and smacked her cottonmouth several times for effect.

"I need some Mexican food," she croaked. "Chips, salsa, margaritas. By the way, was I dreaming last night or was somebody screaming bloody murder?"

"Grab a shower, throw on some clothes, and I'll tell you about it."

Within the hour, we were sitting in a booth on the patio of our favorite Mexican restaurant nursing our sangria-swirl margaritas. Aviator sunglasses obscured Liz's face, and the server refilled her water glass twice before she spoke.

"Now I understand your attraction to what I thought was the shallow end of the pool," Liz admitted. "We were lured into dangerous territory by four male sirens. I knew better, but they somehow disarmed me."

"So, I saw. I practically had to scrape you off of Pietro to get you home."

Liz's phone buzzed with a text message.

"It's from Pietro. He asked how I'm feeling this morning." She typed a short reply and slid her phone back into her purse.

"This is going to sound crazy, Liz, but something about last night felt off to me. I didn't tell anyone about your visit or our dinner plans. I feel like I'm being watched."

"Maybe your client wants to make sure you keep your nose clean before the trial."

"That's possible, but it doesn't explain how Guerrera knows so many details about my personal life. By the way, before I forget to ask, what did Guerrera say to his friends when we arrived?" I added.

"I meant to ask you about that. After Guerrera told them you were the attorney, he said he'd gotten some strange results and was still running tests. Mateo's response was to tell Guerrera to cut the bullshit and stick to the plan. Any idea what they meant?"

"No clue. Maybe I'm overreacting."

"I've known you for a long time. You've always had a killer instinct. Trust your gut."

We spent the remainder of the day window-shopping at a mall located in the high-end rent district in Dallas. Liz continued to trade text messages with Pietro, and when we returned home, she announced that he wanted to take her out for some late-night clubbing. I declined her offer to join them to avoid being the third wheel. Liz napped for the remainder of the afternoon while I continued to work.

Pietro pulled up just after 10:00 p.m. in a black Mercedes and slid out of the driver's side through the gull-wing door. Leaning against the doorway waiting for Liz to emerge from the back of the house, he could've been mistaken for a model posing in a shoot. I caught Liz as she passed me, slipped her an extra house key and several packets of condoms, and told her to be careful. If anything happened to her, Guerrera would have hell to pay.

On my way back to the bedroom I noticed that Guerrera's coat was gone from the back of the sofa where he'd left it the night before, which meant he'd broken into my house again while Liz and I had been out for the day. Too tired to care at that point, I crawled under my covers and fell asleep. I was relieved to find Liz safely in bed, alone, when I awoke at my usual time a few hours later.

We had brunch with my parents on Sunday and made a final stop at Evergreen to see Rynner before I had to return Liz to the airport. During the hour we spent in Rynner's room, Liz had a lively, one-sided conversation with him and told him all about her work in Chicago and her current love interests. Neither one of us knew whether he could hear her, but on the off chance he could, he'd be caught up with her social life.

During the drive to the airport, we planned the dream trip we'd take after the trial, narrowing down the choices to Nepal or Ireland. Inside the terminal, Liz wrapped her arms around me.

"Be smart, brave, and fearless, my friend. Keep Guerrera at arm's length and focus on the trial. Remember who you are and who loves you." She disappeared into the long security line.

†

Now prepared for Dr. Perryman's deposition looming just one week away, I turned my attention to the plaintiffs in the case. Their claims ranged from personal injuries to property damage, with plenty of emotional distress allegations thrown in for good measure.

The week flew by with minimal interruptions from Wiley and no contact from Tessa. I busied myself reviewing stacks of reports on each plaintiff compiled by Gator's team. Most of them included high-resolution, color photographs of various plaintiffs in compromising positions, arrest, conviction, and bankruptcy records, and fact sheets that read more like rap sheets.

Bucking my and Wiley's advice, Tessa had made the controversial decision to skip the critical step of deposing the plaintiffs before trial. Without each plaintiff's testimony committed under oath, I'd have to be prepared with every fact available to tease out the information I needed from them on the witness stand.

At the end of the week, I received an invitation to meet Reyna for happy hour at her private residence. I accepted the chance to get to know her better, and at just after 5:30 p.m., a white limousine picked me up outside of my office and ferried me to her high-rise on the northern edge of downtown. Her driver pulled into a restricted access garage and directed me to her personal elevator that opened into her penthouse suite, where the messy interior belied the vanity of its owner.

Strewn among the stacks of gossip magazines on the floor were at least a dozen empty prescription pill bottles and a few broken wine glasses. The breeze from the open balcony door created a mini-cyclone of white powder atop her glass coffee table and blew a partially-rolled, one-hundred-dollar bill onto a pile of empty take-out cartons.

Oblivious to the loss of what was probably several thousand dollars' worth of cocaine, heroin, or some other illegal narcotic, Reyna stood on the patio with her back to me, hands resting against the fleur-de-lis-topped, wrought iron balustrade surrounding the 360-degree view. She turned her head when she heard me enter and gave me an elevator stare through her saucer-shaped pupils.

"I've been wondering what makes you so fuckable," she slurred.

I wasn't sure I'd heard her correctly but was certain she was already a few sheets, if not an entire linen closet, to the wind. Without a further invitation from her to join her on the patio or anywhere else, I stood anchored just inside her doorway.

"I'm sorry, what did you say?" She was the highest functioning drug addict I'd ever met.

Ignoring me, she grabbed a glass of wine from her patio bar and finished it in one swallow. She stepped back into the penthouse and found a space on the suede couch that was an arm's reach away from another open bottle of wine. She turned sideways to face me.

"Tell me about Rynner," she said, switching gears without a trace of interest in her voice. "He was analyzing groundwater or something, wasn't he?" With her left hand next to her face, she repeatedly tapped her middle finger against her jawline.

She was the only person from TSC who'd ever mentioned his name to me, and I'd never spoken to anyone about him or his research. Careful not to reveal any intimate details, I told her how we'd met and about his passion for science. I ended with a brief description of the accident and mentioned he had a long road to recovery.

She flipped through several pages of the fashion magazine she'd collected from the coffee table and tossed back her second glass of wine.

"What happened to his research?" Her eyes never left the page in front of her.

"I haven't thought about that. The University must have it."

She dropped her magazine on the floor in response.

She picked up her empty glass by the stem and turned it in her fingers. When she reached the bright-red lipstick stain on the rim, she glowered at me and hurled the crystal at my head with as much force as her Cartier-clad arm could muster. Even though I ducked as it whizzed past my ear and struck the doorframe beside me, a fragment of glass ricocheted off the wood and lodged itself in the outside corner of my right eye. The stinging prick I felt was followed by a bead of blood that slid down my cheek.

"I don't know what the hell you said or did to Guerrera to make him lose interest in me, but if you don't back off and stay away from him, I'll make you regret it."

Her fury receded as quickly as it had emerged. She turned back toward the open patio door, pulled her cell phone from a hidden pocket in her pantsuit, and started texting. I wanted to bitch-slap her but reminded myself that she was still a member of the client's inner circle. I ignored her threat, backed out of the doorway leaving a bloody finger smudge on the doorframe, and hustled to the lobby to find a ride home.

✝

Dr. Perryman's deposition was now two days away, and a solid scab had formed over the crescent-shaped cut by my eye. Feeling I was already well prepared, I took the weekend off and locked myself in the house with plenty of junk food and two seasons of my favorite cable show to binge-watch.

Monday morning was showtime. Dr. Perryman's deposition started at 9:00 a.m. in Frantsen's office in the heart of downtown Dallas. Although I'd never been there, I'd heard the inspiration for the garish décor came from a painting in his home depicting a Confederate States Army General in his command post. That description proved to be reasonably accurate.

Upon arrival at Frantsen's office, an assistant escorted me through the dark, Mahogany-accented lobby past a stack of vintage cannonballs and several glass display cases featuring pistols and muskets. A long rack of rifles fitted with rusty bayonets stood like sentinels at attention on the far side of the room. The walls were covered in gilded-framed Civil War letters from miserable, homesick soldiers.

The conference room was unremarkable except for the wall-dwarfing Confederate flag covering the entire south wall. Battered regiment flags adorned the remaining walls, along with other relics, including belt buckles and badges. Nothing about this display surprised me considering that Frantsen embodied everything I disliked about the practice of law. He was ostentatious and favored theatrics over facts. He was rude to men, nasty to women, and dishonest in court. I'd heard from many of my more-seasoned colleagues that the only thing that could eclipse his obese body was his insatiable ego.

The court reporter and the videographer had arrived before I had and were already setting up their equipment. Wiley had also arrived early and was seated at the conference room table with his back to the Confederate flag. He'd previously advised me that Tessa never attended depositions, so I took the seat closest to the witness chair and arranged my exhibits, careful to obscure them from view behind a stack of rule books. Like many lawyers, I'd learned through experience how to read upside-down from across the table and didn't want to risk exposing anything to Frantsen if he too possessed this skill.

At 9:25 a.m., a panel on the north wall opened and Frantsen, in a three-piece suit, followed by Dr. Perryman and several junior attorneys carrying Frantsen's notepads and laptop, moseyed in and took their seats. None made eye contact with me or offered even a perfunctory apology for appearing nearly one-half hour late for a deposition in their own office.

With the videotape rolling, I started with baby steps. I began the deposition by asking Dr. Perryman a carefully crafted and non-adversarial series of questions about his educational and professional background. These questions served the dual purpose of collecting background information and setting the trap. Dr. Perryman boasted about his Ivy League education and his award-winning doctoral dissertation, and added, unsolicited, that based on his unparalleled credentials, no attorney in any legal matter had ever succeeded in striking him as an expert witness and preventing him from testifying at trial.

I introduced his doctoral dissertation as a deposition exhibit and had Dr. Perryman walk me through what he described as his original and groundbreaking work. By the time we reached the first break, I knew I'd lulled Frantsen into a false sense of security because from my angle, it had appeared he'd started surfing the internet instead of directing his full attention to the defense of his witness. I could also see that each of his young associates had taken less than a page of notes.

We resumed the deposition, and after another hour, Frantsen perked up when I abruptly switched topics and started challenging

Dr. Perryman's conclusions with hard data. By the time I forced Dr. Perryman to admit that his expert opinion was based on little more than debunked theories and sheer speculation, Frantsen's face had turned crimson, and I could hear him wheezing as if he had trouble catching his breath.

At the lunch break, Frantsen pulled Dr. Perryman out of the room, probably to coach him on how to recover from the blows I'd just inflicted. They returned an hour and forty minutes later, and when I asked, back on the record, if Dr. Perryman had any answers he wished to change before I continued down another line of questioning, he launched into a well-rehearsed speech about ongoing scientific studies related to fracking accidents. I allowed him to drone on until he appeared to lose his train of thought and stopped talking. Even Frantsen had to have realized the damage his expert witness had inflicted on the plaintiffs' case.

And then I sprang the trap. I marked my next deposition exhibit and handed the document to Dr. Perryman for review. He flipped through it, set his reading glasses down on top of it, leaned back in his chair, and crossed his arms in a defensive posture.

"Are you familiar with the research conducted by Dr. Hideo Kurosawa in Japan that he published before you earned your doctorate?" I asked.

"Objection, irrelevant," Frantsen said in a louder than normal voice.

Frantsen's objection was frivolous and meant only to distract me.

"No, never heard of him."

"Are you sure?"

"Objection. Stop badgering my witness." Frantsen's voice was noticeably louder.

I scooted my chair up to the edge of the table and rested my chin in my hands. I made sure I took a longer than natural pause before asking the next question.

"If that's true, Dr. Perryman, then how do you explain the fact that over two-thirds of your dissertation contains text that is identical to the text in Dr. Kurosawa's research article which predates your dissertation by six years?"

Dr. Perryman inhaled deeply, and before he could choke out an answer, Frantsen was on his feet, leaning over the conference table toward me.

"Objection. What the hell is this? Who do you think you are, coming into my office with this bullshit? I'll have you sanctioned and disbarred for pulling this crap."

The color in Frantsen's face had turned from bright red to a purplish hue.

"This deposition is over," he added, ripping Dr. Perryman out of the witness seat and dragging him toward the private exit. Not knowing how to react, Frantsen's associates cleared their side of the table and disappeared behind their more-than-ample mentor.

I looked over at the videographer to confirm we were still on the record. As soon as they were gone, I announced that I was suspending the deposition pending a court ruling on what had just transpired and told the court reporter we were going off the record. Wiley suppressed a grin, told me I'd done excellent work, and excused himself under the pretense that he had a meeting to attend.

I packed up my documents and made a stop in the ladies' room before exiting the building. When I passed through the lobby to the exit, I saw Frantsen standing alone by the elevator doors. I didn't notice that he'd positioned himself in front of the call buttons until I was only a few feet away.

"You fucking bitch," he snarled. "I don't lose to anyone, especially not piss-ant girls like you. I will take you out before this is over."

After the defeat I'd just handed him, I wasn't in the mood to roll over and take his intimidation crap.

"Get out of my way, or I'll call the police. Don't make me ask you twice."

His eyes bulged. After glaring at me for at least a minute, he turned and waddled back to his encampment.

Adrenaline fueled my commute back to the office. Frantsen's was the second threat I'd received in less than three days, and it seemed more serious than the one issued by Reyna. I thought about ways to prepare myself but got lost in the stacks of paper on my desk.

I'd done such a good job tuning out other distractions that I jumped when my cell phone rang. The unlisted number told me it was someone from TSC. When I answered, Wiley's voice filled my ear.

"I wanted to reiterate how great you did today and share with you that Tessa is pleased. I also wanted to apologize for Reyna's little outburst last Friday. The medication she takes can affect her mood. If you incurred any medical bills as a result, I'll take care of them."

"How do you know about that?" If he knew about her threat, then he knew about Guerrera. I hadn't breathed a word about her rant to anyone.

"It's my job to know my team," he said and ended the call with a promise it wouldn't happen again. Reyna seemed manic, but I didn't think she'd boast to her employer's in-house counsel that she threatened me over a man. If my hunch was right, I was under one or more types of surveillance.

I felt an immediate uptick in my paranoia meter.

Late in the afternoon, I met with the partners to update them on the case and discuss strategy. They were ecstatic that the firm had already made a small fortune representing TSC and encouraged me to continue whatever it was I was doing because it was making them even richer than they already were. After work, I drove straight to Evergreen to see Rynner. Nothing about his condition had changed, but he had a new roommate.

The thin curtain that hung from a rod attached to the ceiling but didn't stretch the entire width of the room was all that separated the two roommates, and an extra reclining chair and cheap bedside table, identical in condition to the ones near Rynner's bed, had been added to the new occupant's side of the room. I made just enough noise when I entered to alert the visitors that I was there. A little boy with a mop of curly black hair and light-brown eyes peeked under the curtain at me.

"You're the shiny lady. I knew you'd come. My uncle and me are visiting my Mommy. She's very sick and has been sleeping for a long time. Is that your friend?" he asked, pointing at Rynner.

"Well, hi there," I said, kneeling to be at eye level with the tyke I'd never seen before. "This is my friend Rynner, and he and your mom will be keeping each other company for a while if that's okay with you."

"I think it's okay. She might get lonely at night."

"Jackson, leave the nice lady alone," said a male voice. The face and body that went with it stepped around the curtain and gave me a forced smile. "I'm sorry about that. He just turned five, and this is all very confusing for him. He said he expected you. Have you and Jackson met before?"

"No, we haven't. Maybe he's confused me with someone else he knows."

We introduced ourselves, and I offered to return later to give them privacy. Ray Tipton refused the offer and said they'd been there for several hours past Jackson's naptime. The tiny hand waved goodbye as Jackson trailed after Ray toward the stairs. The name written on the whiteboard on the far side of the room was "Katherine," and she too was being kept alive by machines that whirred, pinged and beeped. I stood next to Rynner's bedside and ran my fingers through his hair.

"You've got company, my love."

I dragged the old recliner to the side of his bed, settled in, and told him about the fireworks at the deposition. I described Maverick's bad behavior, leaving out the part about the fatal attack on Guerrera's sweater, and admitted I was looking forward to the upcoming trial for a final showdown with Frantsen.

When the last of the adrenaline leached out of my body, I nodded off.

✝

I awoke in bed at the Cabin. Peter was asleep on my stomach, and I nearly flung him off the bed when I sat upright.

"Easy tiger. You need to practice on making smoother transitions."

"Sorry, furball. I would if I knew how."

"Ask, and ye shall receive," he said, mimicking Acorn.

"Thanks for reminding me. Acorn said we were taking a trip today, if this is today, although I don't know where we're going."

By the time I'd dressed, Acorn was at the door with instructions for me to put on my hiking boots. I started lacing them up but paused.

"How will I know where I'm going?" It was the same question I'd asked Caleb before I'd attended my funeral.

"Always with the questions. Don't worry. I'll make sure you get there."

He pulled a pocket watch from his vest and disappeared just as my waterfall began to materialize. The number of steps hadn't changed, and it took me precisely 327 of them to reach the top. Based on the position of the downtown skyscrapers, I arrived somewhere in the rougher neighborhoods of south Dallas.

The cracker box houses on the street were in varying states of decay with peeling paint, tarps on roofs, and termite-infested fences. A pack of baying stray dogs, not uncommon in this area of town, ran by me and disappeared into an alley. The road, pock-marked with potholes, looked as if someone had fire-bombed it. Behind me was a walkway overgrown with weeds, which led to a tiny house with bars on every window.

Acorn appeared at my side, and together we walked down the crumbling footpath and stopped at the rusty metal screen door. The door behind it opened before we reached it, and I immediately recognized the woman staring at us. It was the palm reader who'd told my fortune at the fair all those years ago, and she beamed at Acorn, who returned the smile with a tip of his hat. If she'd aged even a day since we first met, it didn't show. She still looked and dressed like a teenager.

"Siara, it's always good to see you."

"Andrew, I'm glad you could come. It's been too long, and we have a lot to discuss." She turned to me and grabbed my hands as tightly as she had during the palm reading session where I'd met her.

"Come inside quickly. I never know who's watching."

Her touch released beams of silver light from my palms. She pulled me over the threshold and slammed the door, locking multiple deadbolts in the process before I could focus on my mental dimmer switch. Once inside, I realized the entire house couldn't be more extensive than four rooms.

The sofa, chairs, and coffee table in the cramped living room, which did double duty as the dining room, were covered with tattered drop cloths. Thick, dusty drapes blocked all light from the windows.

Siara's black-stained hands motioned for us to sit as she moved into the galley kitchen a few steps away and pulled a teapot from the cabinet. Careful not to disturb the closest drop cloth, Acorn sat on the corner of the couch and placed his hat on the table. I followed his lead and took a seat next to him.

"I see you've been busy," he said, scanning the room.

Scattered across the chair and floor below it were pages of charcoal-sketched faces, which explained the sooty condition of her hands. I picked up the large stack next to me and flipped through it. Siara was a good artist whose work was complemented by the exquisite beauty of her subjects. I leaned over and picked up another, much thinner stack of sketches off the floor. These faces were markedly different from those I'd just viewed. They weren't unattractive. They were just real-looking people who were attractive not because they were flawless, but because of their imperfections.

Each male, and all I studied were male, expressed a different emotion. I imagined the only way Siara had captured it was without the subject's knowledge. By the time I reached the final drawing at the bottom of the pile, Siara and Acorn were standing behind me, peering over my shoulder. The last sketch was of a younger me, wide-eyed with terror or wonder, depending on how you interpreted it.

"I did that one the day we met at the fair," Siara said. "That was the look on your face when I revealed your light, shortly before you fainted." I'd forgotten about that part of the reading when her eyes had turned to flames.

"Who are the rest of these people?" I asked, gesturing to the shorter stack of drawings.

"They are the *X Triplici* I've met in my lifetime, minus the one who asked me not to depict him in a drawing. You surprised me because you're the only one I'd ever met in human form and the only female. You're also the last new one I've encountered to date."

Siara placed the teacups on the table. Lawyer Brain was alert. "Where are the others now?"

Siara didn't answer. Acorn, who'd relaxed in the chair, shifted uncomfortably.

"You haven't told her, have you?" Siara asked him in a reproachful voice.

"It wasn't time."

Siara looked up at the ceiling.

"It is now."

Acorn's eyes rolled to the top of his head, and he too gazed upward as if waiting for a sign of contradiction. When nothing happened, which both took as a sign of Divine and tacit approval, Siara took a seat on the floor in front of me.

"Those," she said, pointing to the first and larger pile of drawings, "are the Pellico members I've identified. Their ranks are growing, and their discord with their predicament is at an all-time high. We believe they have plans in the works for a rebellion, although we don't know the details."

"As you know, two *X Triplici* have recently disappeared. We found one of their bodies, but the other is still missing. We need your help to find him. We suspect malcontents in the Pellico captured them and have been conducting medical experiments to see if they can extract and weaponize the light," Acorn said.

"How could the All-Knowing not intervene and fix this?" I asked.

Neither Acorn nor Siara had an answer. Acorn admitted they weren't privy to that type of information, but that didn't change the mission. I tuned out the rest of their conversation and mentally chewed on the implications of the Almighty's refusal to intervene in what sounded like a brewing revolution.

I tuned back in to hear Acorn ask Siara about the new intelligence she'd gathered.

She told him she'd overheard several Pellico members discussing the destruction of an *X Triplici* by a particularly ruthless individual and debating the potential uses of the silver light to disrupt the balance of power.

"It's not idle gossip. The General confirmed it," Acorn said.

"Who's the General?" I asked.

"His name is Marcus, but I've never heard anyone call him that. Legend has it he was a prominent Roman General. He's loyal to a fault and as lethal as they come," Siara answered.

"The silent, imposing commando decked out in black?"

"Yup, can't miss him."

"Is he the Almighty's security guard or something?"

"I wouldn't say that to his face. He does protect the Almighty, but his other roles include confidante, advisor, and Intermediary," Acorn said.

Before I could ask the next question, Siara explained that Marcus's role as an Intermediary involved ferrying messages, information, and souls to and from Below. She was sure he served other purposes but didn't know what they were.

As Siara and Acorn continued their discussion of possible motives for the disappearances of my brethren, the weight of their words settled on my shoulders. Putting aside all of the things I had yet to learn about my role, I was now a target, whose mission was to run toward, and not away from, the shadowy beings who would hunt me down, kill, and dissect me if they knew I existed.

The prickly fear rearranged itself into a surge of energy that raced through my body. Not knowing if or how the beams would emerge, or how to control them if they did, I instinctively threw up my hands, palms out, to shield my face.

Even through my closed eyes, I saw the shadow of the silver light arc across the room, decimating everything it contacted. When the breaking, smashing and exploding sounds ceased, I opened my eyes to find I'd unintentionally destroyed nearly every object in the room except for the area where we were sitting and its inhabitants. Acorn's mouth was agape, and the flames in Siara's eyes burned wildly like an out-of-control forest fire. I examined my palms for signs of damage but saw only the faint outlines of the silver Xs.

"Is—is that normal?"

"No," they snapped in unison.

I apologized to Siara for ruining her home and asked what I could do to fix it.

"I was thinking about redecorating. Now is as good a time as any." I didn't know her well enough to interpret her comment as honest or sarcastic.

She placed her arms around my shoulders and pulled me toward her. This small act was the first human contact I'd had since my departure from the living, and her warmth and human smells of charcoal and fruity shampoo were too much to resist. I wrapped my arms around her and squeezed her tightly.

"I'm terrified," I whispered in her ear.

"You'd be a hell of a fool if you weren't. Remember to trust yourself."

Acorn, whose outward composure hadn't changed, nodded to Siara and said it was time for us to leave. As I entered my portal, I heard Siara's warning through the rushing water.

"Never let anyone follow you back."

With the last step, I was standing on the dune outside the Cabin. Based on the footprints in the sand outside the door, it looked like I had company. Inside, John appeared to be sacked out on the couch snuggling a Barrett M90 rifle as if it were a teddy bear. Peter dozed by his head, oblivious to my arrival. I eased the door closed and tiptoed toward the fireplace seeking comfort from the photos on the mantle.

John's voice startled me.

"I know you're back. I served four tours in a place only Hell could rival. There wasn't a millisecond when I didn't worry I'd be shot, stabbed, gassed, or blown up, and in that world, you develop senses so keen you could hear an ant piss in your sleep."

He hadn't moved, and his eyes weren't open. Peter, on the other hand, was snoring.

"You were assigned to be my Security Detail, weren't you?"

Moving as one with his weapon, John sat up so smoothly that Peter didn't stir. Despite his recent state of repose, John's button-down shirt and khaki pants remained perfectly creased.

"For the record, I voted for early and full disclosure to you but was overruled."

Siara's news about the deepening schism within the Pellico and the extermination of an *X Triplici* had spread quickly. John told me the early consensus was that the Pellico didn't know I existed, which would help with our search for the other *X Triplici*, assuming he too hadn't been destroyed.

"Did you know the individuals who recently vanished?" I asked.

"Yes." John wasn't what I'd call a conversationalist.

"Where do we start?"

"We need to return to Siara's to prepare a plan, but before we go, we need to discuss new movement protocols."

As John put it, although *X Triplici* share particular talents, each has intrinsic powers which are unpredictable and can develop and change over time. He'd already heard about my mishap at Siara's and told me the silver lining was that it hadn't taken me long to stumble upon my first aptitude.

Next, he gave me three rules to follow.

First, he told me never to allow anyone to enter my portal. Mortals couldn't but the Pellico and those he described only as *Others* could. They didn't belong Here and posed a danger to this existence.

The second rule was the importance of remaining anonymous. To do that, I had to control the light in all but the most serious of emergencies. Even though I was all but non-existent to mortals, I wasn't to the Pellico, Seers, and the mysterious *Others* who couldn't distinguish me from a human unless the light escaped or I was identified by someone who'd witnessed the rays. And third, I was to always and without question, follow his instructions.

Peter's eyes opened.

"*What did I miss?*"

"Nothing much. John was just leaving." As it always did, my conversation with Peter took place entirely inside my head.

"*Can I go with him for a visit? He lives on a farm with rabbits.*"

"Peter asked if you'd take him to your farm for a play date with your bunnies," I said to John.

"*Very funny,*" Peter responded for my ears only. "*You will always be my human, but sometimes, a rabbit just needs to be with other rabbits.*"

John cracked a rare smile, picked up Peter, and held him like a football.

"*He likes me way more than he likes you,*" Peter taunted.

"I'll bring him back tomorrow," John said on his way out the door.

It was the first time I'd been alone in the Cabin since the day I arrived. I didn't know if I'd been there six days or six months and not knowing what else to do with myself, I turned my focus back to the watch that didn't tell time.

Today its face was a solid sapphire color with no movement of any kind. Now unable to remove it from my wrist, I decided to try some experiments to see if I could get it to do something. A flick of the wrist didn't affect it, and the verbal commands I gave it were useless. Exposure to direct sunlight and submersion in water were also futile. I gave up for the moment and fell into the spot on the couch still warm from John's body heat.

Thoughts of my last date with Rynner before the accident crept into my mind, leaving my hands idle. Looking for something to do, my left hand wandered over to my right wrist and turned the bezel counterclockwise a few ticks. The face of the watch turned black, and I had the sensation of falling backward even though my body was planted firmly on the couch. I closed my eyes and mentally stabilized my body. When my eyes opened, I was there, standing in the doorway of Milo's as if I were inside a virtual reality game.

It looked exactly as it had on the night of the accident. The television screens were rehashing the Radiant explosion while the bartender mixed drinks below them. I smelled the stale beer and felt the crunch of the peanut shells on the floor as I made my way inside. Rynner sat in a corner booth facing the entrance, back to the wall, but he didn't see me. No one did. Cresting just above the top of the booth opposite him was a head, my once human head, shaking from side to side.

Of all the places to revisit in the past, this one currently ranked last. I didn't want to be forced to watch an encore performance of the real-life horror movie in which I'd already starred. I wanted to leave now, but the memory didn't have any exit signs. Making my way back toward the entryway, I passed two pretty girls in sorority shirts planted at the bar. I vaguely remembered that they'd made me feel possessive about Rynner back then. The girl closest to me made a comment that caused me to pause.

"They're here," she whispered.

She had a tiny microphone in her ear. I heard the voice in the first girl's earbud respond.

"Are you sure it's them?" a male voice asked.

"Fairly sure."

"Describe them."

"They're sitting down so I can't tell how tall they are, but the male has brown hair and is wearing dark jeans and a tan button-down shirt. We don't have a full view of the woman, but from what we see, she matches the description we have."

"Lights out," he replied.

I walked around the bar looking for anyone else who matched the descriptions. The only people were Rynner and me. The girls ordered a round of drinks and talked about the fraternity party they'd attended the night before. I saw Rynner put the twenty-dollar bill on the table when he and I had stood and left the bar.

"Targets are moving. Two minutes tops," the girl with the earpiece said.

Wondering what would happen next from this newly discovered vantage point, I hauled ass out the door and ran a few hundred yards down the sidewalk in the opposite direction Rynner and I had taken to the cars. I turned the corner and saw a man, dressed from head to toe in black, holding a cell phone to the side of his hoodie-covered head.

I heard a car engine start not far from where we were standing and watched the dark shape ease out of the shadows. The driver never turned on the lights.

"You're a go," the faceless voice on the other end of the phone said.

"Roger," he replied, shoving the phone into his pocket, turning the corner, and taking off at a full sprint.

I took off behind him and braced myself for what I knew would happen next. I saw Rynner and myself walking down the dark sidewalk with the runner accelerating toward our backs.

The assailant pulled a Taser out of his left jacket pocket and zapped Rynner just before slamming into him. The runner intentionally pushed Rynner into the street, and I saw myself stumble forward, propelled by the surge of momentum.

I watched as my human body landed on the right side, the impact of bones on concrete audible from my spectator position down the sidewalk.

Rynner lay twitching in the road.

The driver of the car without lights hit the gas and aimed straight for him.

Completely helpless, I watched as the still-accelerating car ran over Rynner and barreled down the street until it pulled into an alleyway several blocks away. Those were the first two of the three thumps I'd heard that night.

Our hitman had stopped immediately ahead of where my body had landed, turned around, and delivered a vicious kick to my head. That was the third and final thump I'd heard that night, the one that had knocked me out and explained the nasty concussion that accompanied my dislocated shoulder.

The runner, with me on his heels, scampered to the waiting car. I got a good look at his face and the faces of the other occupants when he dived into the back seat, and they eased away, disappearing into the night. Sirens wailed in the distance, and minutes later, two police cars and a fire truck had pulled up to the crowd that now gathered around my and Rynner's unconscious bodies.

The three faces in the waiting car were among those captured in Siara's sketches of Pellico members she'd identified. I doubted they could've identified me as an *X Triplici* back then, especially when I knew nothing about that designation, and Rynner, as far as I knew, had nothing to do with the Pellico. I was furious, and bursts of light emerged from my palms like sparklers. Now it was personal.

"Come back now," a male voice bellowed in my head.

I didn't know how to exit the past, so I did the reverse of what I'd done on the couch at the Cabin. I turned the watch bezel clockwise and conjured the image of where I'd been when I left. The watch face turned white, and I felt as if I were falling forward. Within seconds, I returned to the same spot on the couch from which I'd departed.

John stood in front of me in what I guessed was his pissed-off military stance.

"That didn't take you long. I leave you alone for five minutes, and you figure out how to Skip?"

"Skip?"

He muttered something about a bullshit babysitting detail under his breath.

"Let me enlighten you. That thing on your wrist isn't a watch. It's a one-of-a-kind Kairometer that allows you to travel through time to observe but not disturb the past. While you'll never possess the omniscience and omnipresence of the Almighty, you've got close to the next best thing to help you understand the past and make well-informed decisions."

I thought about telling John what I'd seen but opted to keep it quiet for now.

"I need to talk to Siara. It's important."

John followed me into the bedroom, where I kept the hiking boots. For this trip, I was sure I didn't need to ask for directions to arrive at my intended destination. As I crossed into my waterfall, I saw John adjusting a pair of polarized glasses over his eyes. We met again on Siara's porch, where I knew in an instant something terrible had just happened.

The air was thick with smoky soot and the odor of burning chemicals. Someone or something with a great deal of strength had shredded the metal security door, and the front door it guarded was gone. The roof had collapsed into the smoldering frame and what little furniture that remained inside the house after my earlier mishap had melted into indistinguishable blobs. Nothing tangible had survived the fire.

I spoke a silent prayer for Siara's safety and waited for John's instructions on what to do next. John inched closer to me and scanned the wreckage for victims. During his multiple missions overseas and out of sheer necessity, he'd become an expert in identifying human remains. I was relieved when he breathed the word "*negative*" in my ear.

Without warning, John swiveled around to face the street and jammed his knee into the back of mine, dropping me straight to the ground. A metallic-blue BWM sedan with opaque windows jumped the curb and screeched toward us. Before it stopped, John had the car's gas tank in the crosshairs of his rifle.

"Don't move," he growled. He shifted his weight to his front foot and exhaled into the impending shot. Before his lungs cleared, a familiar voice called out to us from a crack in the driver's side window.

"Get in. We can't stay here."

We scrambled for the car, and before we slammed the doors closed, Siara peeled out of the neighborhood.

"Thank God, you identified yourself. I was about to turn your ride into scrap metal with you in it," John said, adjusting his side-view mirror for a better view of anything that might creep up behind us.

"There's a gift for you in the glove box," Siara said, ignoring him.

John pulled out a brushed chrome, .44 Mag Desert Eagle pistol with custom grips and adjustable laser sights. At least twenty loaded magazines spilled out onto the floor between his legs. My father had a similar gun, but I never practiced with it at the gun range because it was too big and bulky for my taste, not to mention the massive recoil.

"Hello, beautiful," John cooed to the four-and-a-half-pound hunk of metal.

He chambered a round and engaged the safety.

"We're not here to kill humans, and the Pellico aren't human. Why do you need the gun?" I asked.

"You're right we can't kill 'em, but we can decelerate their progress."

We entered the freeway heading north. Siara and John sat in silence while I made myself comfortable on the baby-soft leather backseat. The smooth, quiet ride had a soporific effect on me, and I returned to dreamland.

†

When my eyes opened at 3:32 a.m., I was curled up in Rynner's guest chair at Evergreen. Thanks to the wafer-thin cushion and stiff wooden armrests, my neck was kinked, and my shoulders were bound up in knots. I picked at the corners of my eyes to dislodge the crusts from the tears I'd shed in my sleep. Rynner and Katherine were precisely as I'd left them. I kissed Rynner goodbye and greeted the graveyard shift staff on my way to the parking lot. I needed to get home, shower, and get to work.

Knowing as cats do when their owners will arrive, Maverick was lounging in the bay window by the front door when I pulled into my driveway. I fed him and logged into my e-mail account to check messages. Amongst the junk e-mails were several from Liz, my parents, and a few other friends who were touching base. Liz's most recent message was short and to the point.

"*Weak women don't rule the world.*"

Maverick hissed when I opened the master bathroom door and refused to enter while I showered and got dressed. His behavior wasn't improving, and I made a calendar note to get him to the vet for a checkup.

Once again, I was at my office well before 6:00 a.m. to continue prepping for trial. A few hours later, I received an electronic order from the court advising all parties that our case had been reassigned to the Honorable Sharon Cordan, a younger judge whose seat on the bench had been generously underwritten by the campaign contributions of Frantsen's law firm. I, along with every other defense attorney, knew this because elected officials are required to identify their donors. The defense bar knew Judge Cordan regularly socialized with Frantsen, and more than one colleague swore the Judge had use of the Frantsen firm's private jet for weekend getaways.

A call to the court confirmed that Judge Katzenburg had abruptly decided to retire to Florida, requiring the reassignment of his cases among the existing judges.

The change in judges wasn't good news. Wiley had given me his private cell number, and he picked up on the first ring.

"Judge Katzenburg decided to take early retirement. We've just been reassigned to Judge Cordan."

"I'm not surprised. It can't be mere coincidence that the case was transferred to her court this close to the trial, although it doesn't change the facts. Thanks for the update. I'll let the team know."

We were now four weeks from the trial date, and I had our witnesses to prepare. First on my list were our experts. As was typical for Frantsen, he hadn't bothered to depose any of them, even though we'd produced voluminous expert reports. I doubted his side had done much digging, and even if they had, they wouldn't have found anything because long before TSC had hired the two men and two women we'd so carefully selected, Gator had figuratively crawled into, between, and through every inch of the bowels of their personal and professional lives to prevent any surprises. If one of them had ever thrown a piece of gum on the ground, Gator knew about it.

I scheduled a week of preparation meetings and sent a final list of questions to our consulting expert, Dr. Baker. It was crunch time, and the closer we inched to the trial date, the longer the days would become.

I wasn't the only one burning the midnight oil. Reyna's marketing machine was working day and night on image control. Two weeks before the trial date, she planned to launch "Radiant Rally Day," a town-wide fair day organized by a coalition of Baptist churches and entirely but quietly funded by TSC. The company would discretely place its name and logo on water bottles and candy wrappers, first-aid station signs, and on the packaging of every award available, but none of the TSC employees hired to attend the event would wear or display the TSC logo.

Instead, they would dress like locals, circulate among the crowds, and gather intelligence on the community's collective mood about the upcoming trial. Reyna's hand-selected recruits had spent the previous three weeks training on everything from the town's history to the quirky euphemisms used by the natives. They'd even been required to memorize a list of innocuous-sounding questions designed to elicit bias for or against TSC.

A copy of the flyer Reyna crafted and had posted on every available public surface in Radiant lay on the top of my inbox:

Radiant Rally Day. Come worship in celebration of God's love and mercy. Town Square. 1:00 next Sunday.
"They looked to Him and were radiant. And their faces will never be ashamed." Psalm 34:5.

I was sure it would be well-received but not so certain about the feedback Reyna's team would collect. TSC was a big and easy target, and the wounds were still fresh and gaping.

As most days did in the countdown window to trial, these passed quickly. Next week, the court would release the juror questionnaires to the lawyers, and then Gator's shadowy team of nightcrawlers would get to work learning everything possible about each potential venire member to assist with *voir dire,* the process of jury selection. Following a quick workout, I stopped for some Thai take out, with extra containers for the night staff, and went back to Evergreen to say goodnight to Rynner.

After distributing the food to the ever-grateful nurses and techs, I opened the door to the room to find Ray sitting slumped over in his sister's guest chair, hands clasped behind his bowed head. He lifted his head as I entered, revealing his red, puffy eyes and his tear-streaked face. I pulled a tissue from my purse and handed it to him.

"I'm sorry," he murmured.

I busied myself with setting out the meal to give him a moment to compose himself. "I hope you'll join me for some Thai food. I've got a lot here and wouldn't want to waste it."

He dragged his chair over to the small table and peered into one of the take-out containers.

"I've met you twice and done nothing but apologize to you," he said, waiting for me to unwrap the plastic ware. "Let me apologize one more time for an even three. I'm usually not this morose."

"It's new to me too, and it's still overwhelming," I replied, handing him a spork and a paper napkin.

He relaxed as he ate, and I felt comfortable enough with our similar circumstances to tell him how Rynner ended up at Evergreen. He shared with me that their Aunt Alvinia raised him and Katherine after their mother died from a drug overdose. He never knew his father, and Alvinia never talked about her brother.

Before she died, Alvinia made him promise to take care of his younger sister and see to it that they both graduated from college. He kept those promises to her by graduating from Harvard with a degree in Chemical Engineering, helping Katherine get into nursing school, and buying his sister a house right next to his own so he could keep an eye on her and help with Jackson. They were each other's only family.

Katherine had some rocky younger years, of which Jackson was a product, but had done well in her first year of nursing school. She was excited about her new career and taking additional classes to learn how to balance work and family. It all came to a screeching halt the day Katherine had a heart attack while taking her second-year mid-term exams. She never regained consciousness, and the remainder of the class was required to finish the test despite the disruptive presence of the EMTs in the exam room.

Ray had taken a leave of absence from his job with an international oil company, one of TSC's competitors, to get Katherine admitted to a long-term care facility and figure out what to do with his five-year-old nephew. At the time, Evergreen was the only skilled-care facility within fifty miles that had an open bed. I offered to recommend a family law attorney who could help with getting him formal custody of Jackson, and Ray gave me his business card with his cell number scribbled on the back. He cleared away the empty containers, kissed his sister on the forehead, and said he needed to relieve the babysitter. He thanked me for the food and the referral offer and told me he appreciated the support.

I left shortly after he did for another night of dissatisfying sleep. I couldn't find Maverick when I walked in the door and finally located him by the frantic scratching sounds coming from the coat closet in the foyer. He hissed when I let him out and ran under the couch.

It was past midnight by the time I hopped into bed. When I rolled onto my side, I felt something scratchy under the covers. I poked around for it and pulled out a piece of notebook paper.

"Don't make me jealous."

The paper was unsigned, but I knew from its scent that it was from Guerrera. I had no idea why this man who knew so little about me was stalking me and banishing my cat to dark places behind closed doors. I thought about calling Wiley but decided it would be better to handle it myself to avoid giving him the impression I was romantically involved with a TSC executive.

Pretrial materials were due soon. I spent the next few days finalizing the jury charge, motion in limine, and witness and exhibit lists. I'd warned Wiley that regardless of what we included in the motion in limine, the list of topics a party wants the judge to keep out of the ears of the jury, our judge would more than likely deny most if not all of our requests and allow the jury to hear anything Frantsen wanted them to hear. I gave the same warning about the jury charge and predicted that the judge would reject the questions TSC would want to submit to the jury for deliberations.

Over the next few days, Ray and I missed each other during our respective Evergreen visits but corresponded several times by e-mail. I gave him two referrals for family law attorneys, and he let me know he'd found one he liked and retained. He also offered to meet me for a drink as a thank you. I welcomed the opportunity to leave the office for a few hours and unwind.

A few days later, we met at a bar in Uptown known for its bartenders' mixology skills. Ray had arrived early to secure a good table and told me he had a gift for me when I sat down.

"It's from Jackson. I told him you were helping his mom and me, and he asked me to give this to you as a thank you."

Ray took a folded piece of construction paper out of his coat pocket and handed it to me. I opened it to reveal a custom piece of art Jackson had drawn for me in crayon. Green trees with brown trunks spanned from one end of the page to the other, with red and blue birds intermingled in their branches. The rays of a brilliant yellow sun, complemented by clouds of Cornflower Blue, pierced through the greenery to the ground.

"Tell him I love it, and he used all of my favorite colors. I think you have a budding artist."

"Jackson's a strangely perceptive kid who's found an outlet in art. I think he sees a lot more than we realize," Ray responded.

We tried several cocktails and shared information about the prognoses of our loved ones. Before Ray changed topics again, I told him I recognized his ring and asked for details about his college days. His tenure at Harvard overlapped with Rynner's by one year, and they most likely attended some of the same lectures. As scientists, Ray and Rynner shared many personality traits, which is why I'm sure I found his company so comfortable. He wasn't bad-looking either.

It was none of my business, but that never stopped me from asking questions. When I gently eased into the issue of his dating status, Ray told me he hadn't been seeing anyone since Katherine's heart attack. Before that time, he'd been in a steady relationship with a woman who broke up with him to date a professional football player. I felt sorry for him but knew without meeting her that his ex-girlfriend was a fool for releasing such a good catch.

When my phone buzzed from a work e-mail, I knew it was time to go. Like Rynner, Ray insisted on walking me to my car and opened the door for me when I unlocked it. He gave me a quick peck on the cheek and said he'd see me soon.

Back at home, I dug some old magnets out of the junk drawer and carefully mounted my new piece of art in the middle of the refrigerator door. I never made it to the bedroom because I fell asleep on the couch before I finished reading e-mails.

✝

My eyes opened at the usual, ungodly hour, but even before I had time to focus in the dim light, I had the sense that something was off. Maverick, who'd typically be crawling on my head by now for breakfast, was nowhere to be seen or heard. I went to the kitchen to fill his bowl, thinking that the sound of kibbles would prompt an appearance, but it didn't.

And then I learned why. There was a yellow sticky note on Jackson's picture on the refrigerator.

"Consider yourself warned."

The handwriting bore some similarities to what I thought was Guerrera's, but I wasn't a handwriting expert, and there were enough differences to make me wonder if someone else had penned it. I walked around the house to check each door to the outside and found all were locked, which meant someone had entered while I was sleeping. I flinched at the thought of my vulnerability.

Both Reyna and Frantsen had threatened me, albeit for very different reasons, but up until this point, I'd dismissed what I thought was hyperbole from a jealous rival and a threatened opposing counsel. Perhaps I needed to reassess that opinion.

I scoured the house for Maverick and found him crouched under the bed in the guestroom in the one spot we both knew no human arms were capable of reaching him. It took several minutes to coax him out and several more before he ventured into the kitchen to eat. By the time I arrived at the office, I'd devised a new plan to meet my dual objectives of feeling safer and deterring unwanted visitors.

I'd grown up around guns and learned to shoot when I was eleven, which is old by Texas standards. I had my own handgun, a Colt Government .380 pistol that was a gift from my father, but kept it at my parent's house because I never felt unsafe living with

Rynner. I texted my brother to let him know I'd be by the house after work and dived into trial preparation. At 5:30 p.m., my assistant let me know she was leaving for the day. I accompanied her to the parking garage and made a beeline for the closest sporting goods store to stock up on a few extra boxes of ammunition.

The comforting smells of homemade lasagna and garlic bread teased my nose at my parent's door, but it wasn't my mother I found slaving away in the kitchen. To my delight, it was Christopher, whose hipster clothes were appropriately protected by the sauce-splattered *"Kiss the Chef"* apron tied around his waist. He smiled at me as he removed a homemade chocolate cake from the oven.

"I'm duly impressed," I said, hugging him and tousling his spikey, teenage-boy hair.

He set the cake on the counter to cool next to the earlier-made bowl of fudge frosting. Unable to resist, I skimmed a finger along the top of it, avoiding a swat from Christopher with my mother's favorite wooden spoon.

"Get out of there, you'll ruin it," he whined, sounding very much like Mom.

"When did you learn to cook? Last time Mom asked you to help her make dinner, you told her it was uncool, and you'd rather wash the dishes."

"True," he said, "but that was before I met Jayde, and every modern man knows he needs a signature meal to impress a woman. I'm perfecting this one."

A few minutes later, Mom appeared and just as I had, skimmed a finger along the inside of the icing bowl for a taste.

"Needs more vanilla."

She swiped another sample to be sure.

"Stop it, or I won't have enough for the cake," Christopher complained, smacking the wooden spoon on the countertop as Mom had done to us thousands of times.

Dad sneaked in and swiped a hunk of garlic bread from the breadbasket earning a sharp *whack* on the back of his hand from the wooden spoon. His lack of reaction was a testament to the years of spoon beatings he'd endured at the hands of my mother.

"How's it going, Lawyer Warrior?" he asked.

I told them about my dustup with Frantsen, omitting the overt threat, and about the last-minute judge swap. As it usually did, the conversation turned to Rynner. I told them about his new room-mate, Katherine, and her small and fragile support group.

"You need to take them some cake," Mom said definitively. "I'm sure it will make them feel better."

Cake was strong medicine in our house. Chocolate cake with fudge frosting could cure anything. I teased Christopher about his new love interest and got the detailed update on my grand-parents' recent adventures, which included a cruise to Alaska for one set and a big win at the latest Bridge tournament for the other. Sufficiently stuffed and with bags of leftovers in hand and my .380 in its case, I drove back to Evergreen hoping to deliver the hunk of cake to Ray and Jackson before I ate it all myself.

Ray's car was in the parking lot, still warm from his recent arrival. He was in the room with Rynner and Katherine and had pulled back the curtain separating the two sides of the room so he could read them an article from today's newspaper about the uptick in violent crime in the Dallas area. According to the report, a young graduate student named Sterritt Hunt was shot to death in a home invasion. The killer remained at large. I sat quietly until he finished.

"How is she today?"

"She looks better, doesn't she?"

"She looks peaceful," I responded truthfully. "Where's Mini Monet?" I added, referring to Jackson.

"He's with the sitter right now. He was sent home early from preschool for biting one of his classmates. I thought he could use some time to decompress."

"I have just the thing for that. My mother believes it has healing powers, and I confess I've watched it work many miracles."

I presented him with the foil-wrapped chocolate medicament. Ray folded back the silver wrapping and took a deep whiff. As if hypnotized, he closed his eyes and hummed.

"Hmm, Hmm."

He refolded the foil to prevent the icing from sticking to it, and I marveled at his self-restraint. I'd seen Rynner make the same, careful creases to preserve the integrity of cake frosting. It had to be an engineer-thing.

"I want to share it with Jackson and teach him to appreciate kindness from others. Lord knows, there's not enough of that in this world."

I could tell from his voice that he was having a tough day. I walked over to his chair and knelt in front of him. I assured him he was doing all he could for Katherine and Jackson, and it was okay to vent as long as he remembered to take care of himself. He extended his arms and took my hands in his.

"Will you sit with me for a while?"

"Of course."

I sat on the floor between his legs, using the front of his chair for a backrest. He gently massaged my shoulders, causing my head to roll to the side to rest on the inside of his left thigh.

†

A loud *BANG* and a shower of popping safety glass jolted me awake, and for an instant, I wasn't sure if this was past or present. I sat up in the backseat of Siara's BMW and was immediately blinded by my hair whipping around my face, courtesy of the hole blown in the rear window.

"Get down," John yelled as he flicked the safety off the Desert Eagle and turned around in the front passenger seat so he faced the back window.

Siara accelerated, and from my horizontal vantage point, I saw that she'd topped out the speedometer at 170 miles per hour. I covered my ears as John popped off six rounds at whatever was behind us. Tires screeched, accompanied by more gunshots.

Siara unexpectedly careened toward a freeway exit and ran a red light to lose our tail. Wherever we were, it was dark and undeveloped. There were no streetlights, and the stoplight we'd blown through was the only one around for miles. Siara switched off the car's headlights and began maneuvering down unmarked roads. She was either gifted with military-grade night vision or had committed the route to memory.

"We lost 'em," John said.

He swapped out his partially used magazine for a full one. With the full magazine in place, he didn't need to rerack the slide because he'd left a round in the chamber. John was a man who understood the meaning of the term "*combat-ready.*" Next, he filled his pockets with additional magazines.

Luck favors the prepared, I thought. That's what Rynner would've said. I cautiously eased myself back to an upright position and brushed the tiny pieces of glass off of myself and the backseat.

"Why were they shooting at us?" I asked. "They must know that bullets won't kill us."

"Won't kill *you*," Siara corrected. "I am mortal, and they can kill me in any number of ways, fire and bullets included.

I thought about Siara's smoldering house and felt guilty for not apologizing sooner for her loss. No one spoke as the car rocked along a lengthy stretch of unpaved road, crossed over a large cattle guard, and pulled up to a steel gate, which opened without a sound. It took another ten minutes to reach the stone house, which looked more like a fortress visible only by the rays from the full moon.

I caught a glimpse of a turret before we drove through a single-car garage door adjacent to seven others just like it. Siara cut the engine and waited for the door to close before unlocking the car and getting out to assess the damage. Bullet holes riddled the trunk and the back window was gone, but the car was otherwise drivable.

"Those assholes. This is one of my favorite rides."

The garage smelled like a tire store because seven other vehicles shared the space with the wounded luxury sedan. Siara's taste in cars was eclectic. A modern recreational vehicle with a bumper covered by national park stickers anchored the far end of the garage, and its neighbors included an electric car, several SUVs, two expensive sports cars, and a camouflage Hummer that looked like it would be more at home on a desert battlefield than in a garage as someone's weekend joy ride.

John, pockets sagging from the weight of the gun magazines he'd stuffed into them, took note of the motor pool as we followed Siara through several sets of security doors protected by both biometric and numerical locks. The last door opened into a perfectly round living area with stone walls and no windows. Mounted on the walls above the long workstation covered from end to end with computers and banks of monitors were four, projection-size flatscreen televisions that were presently dark. John spun around to view the monitors.

"You've got live feeds?"

"Yes, among other things. I also have a 24/7 rotating fleet of helicopter drones programmed for perimeter runs around the property. They return to base when their batteries drain to a certain level, and the system replaces them with freshly charged units."

"And?"

"Audio surveillance, motion sensors, and good, old-fashioned tripwires," she added.

John sat down in one of the command chairs, pulled a handkerchief from a pocket in his jacket, and dismantled the Desert Eagle to wipe it down. Siara scrolled through the last twenty-four hours of security data and pronounced that all was clear. Whoever was following us had either given up or gotten lost in the darkness.

I didn't know what to do with myself.

"I'm sorry you lost your house," I said to Siara.

"I was sad to see it go, but it wasn't my house. It was one of my art studios."

She told me she'd owned it for several years, and it was where she often went after work to relax. No one in the neighborhood paid any attention to her when she came and went covered in paint or charcoal, and judging by the size and condition of the place, no one thought she had anything worth stealing. In sharp contrast, this stronghold was equipped with cutting-edge technology and security, not to mention the cars, and couldn't be cheap for someone who told fortunes for a living. If she didn't come from money, someone was bankrolling her.

"I'm sure you're wondering how someone in my line of work could afford a place like this." Her sense of timing was uncanny.

She told me that palm reading was one of several trades she pursued to stay connected to the other realities. She chose most of her jobs based on the potential for contact with the Pellico. Her current gig was working the late-night bartender shifts for several trendy hangouts that attracted pretty people with money to burn. A few weekends a month, she also worked at a car wash in Uptown Village that specialized in detailing the exotic cars the Pellico members coveted. My face must've registered some dissatisfaction with her answer because it still didn't account for everything I'd seen.

"I admit I haven't confined my skills to fortune-telling. Between gambling and playing the stock market, which let's face it is just legalized gambling, I've made millions. I started preparing this place and other safe houses when I foresaw the conflict several years ago."

"What conflict?"

"The one you're in."

John finished cleaning the gun, reloaded it, and rolled his chair over to another bank of monitors to play with the complicated security system. This time he left the safety off. Siara walked into an adjoining room and returned with two glasses of red wine and a bottle under her arm. She handed me a glass and took a seat next to me.

"Do you think the fire at your studio was an accident?"

"I know it was intentional. At dusk, I ran out for some supplies, and when I returned, I happened to drive past the front of the house and saw the door wide open. I stopped long enough to see two men ransacking the place. They walked out with my sketches and threw an incendiary device inside. They more than likely left a lookout who recognized your face from the drawing."

"Do you know who they were?"

"They'd become regulars at one of the bars where I've been working the last-call shift from 10:00 p.m. to 2:00 a.m. I only knew them by their first names, Tomás and Mateo. Several nights ago, a third man, whose name I didn't hear but whose face I started sketching on a napkin, joined them."

She pulled a crumpled wad from her pocket and tossed it to me. At some point between then and now, the napkin must've gotten wet, because the ink had bled all over, obscuring what had probably been an accurate likeness. Siara glanced at the inky mess in my hand and sighed.

"It doesn't matter. The stranger's face is one I couldn't forget. He's a tall, gorgeous, South-American who is hands down the best looking Pellico member I've ever seen."

I asked if she could draw him again, but she said that too much time had passed for her to recall enough details to make the sketch useful.

I immediately thought of the night in the restaurant when Guerrera invited Liz and me to join him and his friends, Mateo and Tomás among them, for drinks. Again, I asked myself if it was a chance encounter or a calculated rendezvous. I didn't know if and how they fit into this mess, so I kept it to myself and enjoyed another glass of wine. Pretending to study the wine glass, I cast my glance sideways to observe our hostess, who didn't notice I was watching her because she was busy watching John.

He had temporarily overridden the computer software that controlled one of the drones and was using a joystick to fly it manually. Based on the live feed from the monitor next to him, I knew he was flying a reconnaissance mission around the house to look for weaknesses. John had told me that most Seers were neutrals, but Siara must've been an exception. Her expression told me she loved him, but their relationship would never grow beyond what it already was. Setting aside the fact she was mortal and he wasn't, he still wore a wedding ring, which told me he remained committed to his wife. I didn't doubt that even in death, he'd be faithful to her.

"There's more to this conflict with the Pellico than what you've told me, isn't there?"

John's only reaction was a twitch of his jaw.

"I know they tried to kill Rynner." I knew I'd just baited a hook.

"How would you know that?" Siara asked.

"She figured out how to Skip," John replied.

"I told you I knew she would. She's got the insatiable curiosity of a child."

"It wasn't my decision," John retorted.

I looked at the band on my wrist and saw a full moon reflected on the face.

"Tell me more about the Kairometer."

"There are no instructions for it, and you're the only *X Triplici* who's ever had a chance to wear it. The General objected to your use of it, but the Almighty insisted."

"I don't know exactly how I did it, but I Skipped back to the night of the accident. Walking through that permanent notch in time, I saw how it unfolded and who was responsible. I knew the faces in the car that hit Rynner, only because I'd seen them among the faces in your Pellico sketches. They'll have to answer for what they did."

Siara and John exchanged glances.

"Our immediate mission is to locate and rescue your fellow *X Triplici*, if he still exists, not to exact vengeance," John said.

To Hell with that, I thought. I excused myself and said I needed some fresh air. I followed one of the four hallways out of the control room and meandered from room to room, exploring the fortification. I located four bedrooms on the bottom floor, along with two other rooms with locked doors. The sprawling space included a living room, art studio, and kitchen.

Out of sheer habit, I opened the kitchen pantry door and began rifling through the shelves to see what kind of snacks Siara kept. Not that it mattered, because I no longer required human nourishment, but the desire for food remained hard-wired into me and was difficult to relinquish.

As my arm stretched deeper into the stockpiles of food on the middle shelf, my hand made contact with an unusual indentation embedded in the back wall. When I pressed my finger against it, the shelves parted to reveal a steep set of stairs leading downward. I peered into the darkness and saw what could've been a wine cellar, although basements were unusual in this part of Texas because the high clay content in the soil could cause extensive shifting in the foundation.

Then again, it could've been a torture room or contained a holding cell, but I wasn't in the mood to find out. I found the switch, closed up the hidden entryway, and followed the main staircase to the second floor. I expected to see another half dozen rooms up there, but instead, found a space that housed far more computer equipment and electronics than the control room below.

†

Back in the first-floor command center, John remained planted at one of the consoles, only now he had his feet up on the desk and was playing an interactive video game involving ninja assassins. Siara, wrapped in John's jacket, was sleeping on the floor near him.

"Impressive place, isn't it?" he said without missing a move in his video game character's fight with a six-headed dragon.

"Have you been here before?"

"Not here, but I knew Siara had multiple safe houses."

"There's a basement concealed by a façade in the pantry and a room upstairs that's similar to this one, only much bigger. She seems prepared for Armageddon."

"Don't underestimate her skills or her loyalty. She would die to protect us."

She would die to be with you, I said to myself. I wasn't sure John appreciated the fact that her loyalty to us was based, in whole or in part, on her love for him. If he knew or suspected she had feelings for him, he neither acknowledged them nor encouraged her.

"What's the plan?"

"Traditional reconnaissance will take too long. Siara knows their haunts, and they know your face. Waiting for them to find us leaves us exposed to too many unknown variables. We need to flush a few of them out in a controlled environment and capture at least one for interrogation."

Using me as bait, or more accurately, shark chum, was what he had in mind. He told me that while I'd been rummaging around in Siara's kitchen, they'd been mapping out our next, anticipated encounter with the Pellico. John said he'd devised the most efficient method for getting the big fish into the net. When I asked about my role in the planning, his answer was simple.

"Stick to the instructions we give you and don't improvise. Until then, stay put and don't mess with anything, including the Kairometer."

Preoccupied with the new surroundings, I'd ignored the accessory on my wrist that now displayed bands of lines moving vertically across its face. John noticed my rekindled interest in the Kairometer and frowned.

"No Skipping until we get what we came for."

By the time Siara stirred from her sleep, John had reconfigured the flight path of the drones, written new code to update the security software, and killed every opponent who challenged him in the fight-to-the-death video game. I, on the other hand, had alternated between watching the news and marveling over John's ability to commit mass, online homicide using a computer and a joystick.

Patiently, John waited while Siara went about her human morning rituals. Feeling nostalgic for the days of make-up and preening, I sat on the edge of the tub in her bathroom and giggled along with her as she styled her hair and told stories about her funnier palm- reading sessions.

"It's too bad we were destined for this kind of relationship. In a different time and place, we would've been close friends like you and Liz. She misses you every day."

I missed Liz too. Siara was now the closest thing I had to a friend.

"Does he know how you feel about him?" I asked, referring to John.

She blushed.

"No, and I'd never do anything to interfere with his family. His wife is devoted to his memory and will never remarry. His boys will follow in their father's footsteps and find their purposes in their military careers. Someday they'll all be together again." She made me promise not to share this information with John before we left the bathroom.

Siara spent the rest of her day drawing diagrams of the lay-out of the bar and sharing as much detail as she could about the entrances and exits. John took no notes but questioned her exten-sively about the smallest details, including the number and place-ment of the tables, chairs and sound speakers, and the length of the bar. After 9:00 p.m., Siara, now dressed in her bartending uni-form of form-fitting jeans, navy suede stiletto boots, and a pink, plunging V-neck sweater, along with John in jeans and a leather jacket, and I in a borrowed, silver-sequined outfit from Siara that was far outside my comfort zone, loaded into an older, white SUV fitted with two sets of hand and leg shackles bolted to the floor of the back seat.

Tonight's destination was *Crédit*, located in an old warehouse district called Deep Ellum that was just east of downtown Dallas. It took over an hour to get there, which meant Siara's hideaway wasn't that far from the Oklahoma border.

John briefed me on my assignment during the drive. Siara had reserved a table for me in the VIP area of the bar, where patrons paid $1,500 for the privilege of sitting down and were expected to rack up at least another $3,000 per table in bottle fees.

"Your job is to watch for familiar faces and flirt with any Pellico members who approach you. Don't touch anyone or leave your seat for any reason. If you run into trouble, I'll be feet away in the manager's office monitoring the surveillance feeds," John instructed.

Siara would, as she always did when bartending, continue to eavesdrop on the bar-goers' conversations to see if she could learn anything new about the Pellico's plans. If a target arrived, John would move in and subdue him with a few, sub-sonic rounds of his Desert Eagle, recently modified and fitted with a suppres-sor, and Siara, with the help of the bouncer, would escort the inebriated-looking guest to our mobile holding area in the back of the SUV.

We drove by the front of the bar to access the gated, staff parking area behind the building. A sizeable female bouncer who rivaled in size any heavyweight male bodybuilder guarded the bar's entrance with strict instructions to admit only the wealthiest and best-looking guests, of which there were many in the line that wound around the block.

After parking as close as she could to the staff entrance without blocking the back door, Siara punched in her door code and led us down a hallway past several offices. She entered another set of numbers into a keypad to access the security office and gave John a quick tutorial on the hardware and software before leading me through the back of the bar into the VIP room.

I counted nine tables, excluding my own, rimmed with LED lighting that changed colors every few seconds and two lounge nooks on opposite ends of the room that contained blue velvet sofas covered with animal-print pillows. Horizontal lines of blue and silver lights were embedded into the walls and the bar, constructed of sheets of steel dotted with rivets, was outlined in pink neon. Pretty people occupied seven of the tables when Siara relieved the bartender. Other than a drunk and boisterous bachelorette party, the remainder of the patrons appeared aloof while they silently judged one another's clothing, accessories, and choice of companions.

Euro-trash music, loud enough to drown out conversational tone discussions, pulsed from the floor and wall speakers, and I now understood why Siara preferred working at the bar as opposed to frequenting it. I could've exploded a grenade in this space, and no one would've heard it.

Depending on where she was standing when mixing drinks, Siara was always inches away from the partygoers placing orders or making small talk with her, which was close enough to eavesdrop on any intimate exchanges.

I found my dim corner spot, marked with a "Reserved" placard and a bottle of hand-crafted gin, and made myself as comfortable as I could under the circumstances. I couldn't see any cameras but knew they were there and that John and Siara were watching. Around 1:00 a.m., the bouncer escorted a party of four to one of the lounge areas and dozens of heads, including mine, turned for a view of the parade.

Three pencil-thin women draped in runway couture slinked across the floor followed by their escort, who was none other than the uber-stylish Guerrera. The Pellico women reveled in the attention they openly attracted from the men and begrudgingly extracted from their imaginary competition. When they reached the couch, two of them flanked Guerrera as he sat and the third, in a provocative move, climbed onto his lap and locked her arms around his neck.

Siara had seen him once before but didn't notice his entrance because the soon-to-be bride and her party had commandeered Siara's attention to pour multiple rounds of shots. I knew John didn't know Guerrera's face but had to be smart enough to distinguish Guerrera's drop-dead gorgeous escorts from the local socialites.

Guerrera's placid expression never changed, even when the woman in his lap pulled her fingers through his hair and repeatedly pressed her breasts against his face. Instead, he leaned back and stretched out his arms to rest on the shoulders of his other two companions.

His eyes swept the room with indifference until they rested on me. A casual observer wouldn't have noticed any change in his face, but I saw the momentary look of shock accompanied by the subtle twitch of his jaw. He said something to the woman using him as a seat cushion that made her roll off of him with a sulky expression before he abruptly left the VIP area.

When he returned a few minutes later, he said his goodbyes to his harem, handed the server a wad of bills wrapped around a cocktail napkin with a prompt in her ear, and disappeared. The server pocketed the cash, walked over to me, and laid the still-folded cocktail napkin down on the table in front of me without looking at it, probably as he'd instructed her to do. When I picked it up, I smelled Guerrera's cologne. When I opened it, I saw the barely legible warning.

"*They're waiting for you.*"

Siara made the last-call announcement signaling that the bar would be closing in half an hour. As instructed, I stayed put and didn't leave my table until Siara turned on the house lights at

2:00 a.m. to help the patrons, in various states of inebriation, find their way to the front exit. Once the room was empty, John emerged from the back and came straight to me.

"Who was that, and what did the napkin say?"

I handed John the note.

"Shit."

Siara joined us and read the note over John's shoulder.

"He's the one I started sketching on the napkin that got wet. He was keeping company with some radical faction members. Why would he tell you this?"

"I know him from my previous life. He was part of my last client's inner circle and developed an unnaturally possessive streak toward me."

Siara and John gave one another a look I'd seen before that meant they knew something I didn't but weren't ready to tell me.

"That he sent you the note means he knows who and what you are," Siara said.

The bar was empty, and the bodyguard and remaining staff were gone. John went back to the security office to check the outside cameras before we attempted to exit. Siara was hunched over the bar working on a new napkin sketch of Guerrera, and I paced the floor thinking about the numerous interactions I'd had with him.

A gnawing in the pit of my stomach told me I'd missed many signs about Guerrera, but the only way I could know for sure was to Skip, which John had forbidden me to do.

John emerged from the back and said he didn't see any suspicious activity outside but wanted to send Siara out first to bring the car around to the front, where the pedestrian traffic, even at 3:00 a.m., might dissuade an all-out assault. A tap of the horn would be her signal that it was safe for us to exit.

I heard the lock reengage after Siara slipped out the back door. Unable and unwilling to pry ourselves away from the video monitor, John and I watched her get into the driver's seat, strap in, and reverse out of the staff parking area. It should've taken less than two minutes for her to pull around front. We strained to hear a car horn but heard nothing.

John switched views to the entryway camera and saw the SUV parked at the front door precisely where we expected it. Someone was sitting in the driver's seat, but with the vehicle's tinted windows and the grainy footage, it was too dark to identify her. Or him. If it were Siara, why didn't she honk the horn? John's muscles flexed involuntarily, and my hands started to tingle.

"I have to make sure she's okay," he said. "Stay here and watch the monitors. If anything happens to me, don't wait. Go back."

"But how?" I asked, looking at the strappy sandals on my feet. "My hiking boots are at Siara's."

"The Kairometer is an alternate portal. Turn the bezel, tell it where and when to go, and it will get you there."

The Kairometer's face turned bright red as John, Desert Eagle drawn, slipped out the side door. He was visible on the monitor as he passed between the two, side-wall-mounted cameras but went out of view when he rounded the corner toward the front of the building. I switched feeds to the front camera where the SUV remained, but he wasn't there.

I understood his earlier instructions, but I'd be damned if I left them behind, fate unknown. My idea of crafting a rescue plan fizzled when I heard the sound of buckling metal coming from the back door. The video feed confirmed there were two male Pellicos, one of whom I recognized as Pietro, pummeling the door with their fists.

I locked the office door moments before they burst into the hallway, shouting at one another in Spanish. Knowing it would do little to slow them down but determined to do something other than becoming a victim, I positioned the desk and filing cabinet in front of the door and moved into the corner with my back to the wall. A voice floated underneath the door.

"*Ella es aqui.*" *She's here.*

"We don't want your friends. We need you to come with us," said the unfamiliar voice. "Please surrender and come out."

"Where are they?" I asked.

"Taking a *siesta* in the car," came the response.

I'd made up my mind that I wouldn't go willingly. The fight was on. I knew I had powers. I didn't know what they all were and how to use them but now was as good a time as any for some on-the-job training.

BAM, BAM, BAM. They were almost through the office door.

I planted my feet, anchored the first three fingers on each hand on my hip bones to prevent them from sliding down the shiny, sequined top, and waited.

With a final blow, they were through the door, Pietro in a disheveled suit, and his friend, whose face was new to me, in pressed dress slacks and a sport coat. Pietro cleared the desk and filing cabinet from their path, which was every physical barrier that had separated us.

I expected them to charge toward me, but they didn't. Seeing my stance, they both stopped, silently debating their next move while Pietro's accomplice brandished something that reminded me of a cattle prod. There was no way in hell that guy was going to use that thing on me. I closed my eyes, turned my palms toward them, and visualized them incapacitated on the floor.

Come what may, I said to myself.

My hands burned, and I heard a crackling sound similar to the one from the day I torched part of Siara's art studio, followed by two heavy thuds. When I opened my eyes, I saw the two men crumpled on the floor. I pulled off the borrowed heels and tossed them into the corner, leaped over the downed heaps, and ran through the front door to the SUV.

✝

My tab was growing. I now owed Siara a new art studio and a pair of slinky sandals. The doors to the vehicle were unlocked, and Siara and John, both groggy but stirring, were shackled in the back seat.

"Keys. Where are the keys to the cuffs?" I shouted in Siara's face.

She struggled to focus on my face and pointed to her cleavage.

I reached down the front of her sweater and felt the key wedged under her right breast. I liberated it from the snug spot, unlocked them both, and pleaded with Siara that we needed to move. She flopped into the front seat, started the car, and stomped on the gas.

I stayed in the back seat, delivered a hard and self-satisfying slap to John's face to rouse him, and encouraged the still groggy Siara to drive faster. The Pellico must've thought it was a two-person job because no one followed us back onto the highway. They'd be as embarrassed that they didn't capture me as John and Siara were about being captured by them.

We swapped stories on the drive back to the fortress. Siara said she'd made it to the SUV but was stunned as soon as she'd climbed in and closed the door. Pietro's friend, Allard, restrained her in the back seat and drove the car around front. He didn't honk the horn because he didn't know it was part of our plan.

John was jumped by Pietro on the side of the building, just out of camera range. During their struggle on the ground, Pietro had wrested the Desert Eagle out of John's hand and choked him out with a grappling move. The next thing John remembered was the slap in the face I delivered to him as we sped away from the bar. The grilling began once he was fully conscious.

"Why the hell did you risk coming after us? I told you to go back if there was trouble, and you defied my direct order. They could've destroyed you."

"Leaving you at their mercy was unthinkable. I made a judgment call. If I had a do-over, I'd make the same decision."

"Damned fool," he muttered, rubbing the side of his face that still bore my handprint.

"And what of Pietro and Alland?" Siara asked.

"I subdued them."

"With what?" John challenged.

"With these." The silver Xs were still visible on my palms when I held them up for John to see.

The tension in the car acted like a toxin, effectively paralyzing our vocal cords for the remainder of the drive. Back at Siara's, John resumed his tinkering with the drones, and Siara withdrew to her art studio to continue with her sketches, leaving me alone again with too many questions and not enough answers. Not knowing where else to go, I returned to the kitchen pantry and parked myself on the floor with my back to a shelf full of junk food.

What Guerrera knew about me before my death and whether his note at the club was a warning or part of a greater plan to draw me out were questions to which I needed answers. John wouldn't be happy if he found out, but I knew the only way to get answers was to Skip back to my encounters with Guerrera, starting with the night he showed up in my office with a bottle of gin.

With my left hand, I turned the dial of the Kairometer several ticks counter-clockwise and conjured the memory of my first personal contact with Guerrera. Time pulled me backward, and in a blink, I was standing behind Guerrera, who was about to pick the lock on my office door.

Thunder echoed through the empty office building, and the lightning flashes reflecting off of the outer windows created a strobe-like effect. The night unfolded much differently without the filters of depression and intoxication through which I'd experienced it in real-time.

I hadn't noticed that Guerrera had worn a tailored, dark-grey suit with a navy dress shirt open at the collar. His shoes were spotless, and even though I was nothing more than an eyewitness to the past, I swear I could smell his musky scent from where I stood.

He set the coffee mugs and bottle of gin on my assistant's desk and slicked back his hair as if he were working up some courage. Then he leaned into the door and asked if I was in my office. Without waiting for an answer, he pulled a small tool from his pocket and used it to pop the lock on the door. He collected the offerings and entered my office.

Seeing now through my own, preternatural eyes what he saw then, I wondered why he'd come and better yet, why he'd stayed. My past self was slumped in my office chair with my dress hiked mid-thigh to provide the maximum range of motion for my bare legs, which were crossed and resting on top of a stack of files on my desk. My hair was tousled and my eyes, pupils fully dilated from the pain pills, were ringed with smudged eyeliner and mascara. I could've easily passed for a heroin addict on an epic bender.

As the spectator, I followed him into the office and watched him strategically position himself between then-me and the only exit. I noticed how, when he offered me the cup of gin, he strained to lean forward far enough to be able to brush his hand against my exposed thigh.

That's when the game changed.

The instant his hand made contact with that personal real estate that was off-limits to anyone but Rynner, his form faded in and out so fast that it seemed as if the lights had momentarily dimmed. My mind had been so foggy at the time that I chalked up the phenomenon to the blinding flash of lightning that had struck at the same moment.

Even though I'd had both hands wrapped around the full mug of gin, the silver light from my palms peeked through the gaps between skin and ceramic. At the time it happened, I'd been so distracted by Guerrera's charm, the alcohol, and the storm that I hadn't noticed it.

But he did. His eyes widened as he realized, long before I would know, that he'd found an *X Triplici* in human form.

Just as I'd remembered, he did most of the talking, and I did most of the drinking. My past self flirted shamelessly with him until I was too drunk to form coherent sentences. Without the support of my office wall, I would've fallen over like a felled tree when I stood up to leave. That's when Guerrera moved in to guide me down to the parking garage.

I followed them in this 3-D movie as Guerrera walked straight to my car without the need to use the locator function on the key fob and saw him effortlessly lift my body into the passenger seat. Not knowing the full extent of my ability to Skip, I walked over to my car and climbed into the back seat to watch the remainder of the night unfold.

As we turned onto Elm Street and while soft jazz music played, Guerrera made the call. The person on the other end picked up the phone and waited for Guerrera's instructions.

"Get my lab ready," Guerrera said with a tinge of urgency, and then ended the call.

He drove straight to my house without the help of the navigation system and carried my inebriated former self into the bedroom. When Maverick appeared and growled at him, Guerrera threw one of my heels across the room, grazing Maverick's head and sending him running for cover. That's when Guerrera slammed the bedroom door and made a permanent enemy out of my cat.

I remembered feeling disgusted with myself the morning after this encounter, both for my imprudent behavior with the alcohol and for what I didn't know transpired in my bedroom. What I saw next validated those feelings and magnified my self-loathing.

Guerrera laid my limp human body on the bed, unfastened my arm sling, and threw it on the floor. Standing by the side of the bed, he reached a hand underneath my back and unzipped my dress with ease, peeling it off like a candy wrapper and leaving me exposed in nothing more than a bra and panties.

Leaning further over me, he grabbed my wrists, examined my palms, and positioned my arms above my head, which made my current self wince with the thought of how painful that would've been with my healing shoulder, had I been conscious.

Without releasing his grip, he moved his mouth to my neck, where he breathed in my perfume and ran his tongue down my carotid artery until he reached my collarbone. He rested his head on my chest and listened to my heartbeat.

He was confirming you were human, Lawyer Brain noted.

He used his thumb and index finger to unclasp my bra and tossed it into the pile of clothes on the floor. My stomach turned watching the intimacy with which he caressed my breasts, first with his hands, and then with his mouth, and then proceeded down to my hipbone, where he dug his teeth deep into my flesh.

The sour taste of bile burned my bystander's throat.

He licked the red stain from his lips, released his grip on me, and used both hands to remove the last of my lingerie. Visibly aroused, he stood up and began unbuckling his belt but stopped abruptly when my intoxicated self, without warning, uttered one word.

"Rynner?"

Guerrera's face contorted into a strange mixture of anger and frustration. He stood transfixed and stared at me for a few minutes before he refastened his belt. He reached into his jacket pocket and produced a leather case. He unzipped it and retrieved a small metal utensil and something else I couldn't see from my current position in the doorway. He straightened the instrument to reveal what looked like a retractable scalpel and turned my listless head for better access to the back of my neck.

He gathered my hair to the side, pulling it harder than necessary, and as adeptly as a surgeon, made a small nick at the base of my hairline and inserted something into it. He dug around in the case and pulled out a small needle and surgical thread which he used to close the incision, several syringes, and two glass vials that looked like the test tubes we used in high school chemistry.

He inspected the veins in my inner arms but rejected them in favor of the one protruding from the top of my left hand. As if it were second nature to him, he slid the needle into the vein and withdrew two vials of blood that he pocketed along with everything else he'd used on me. A small bruise started to form on the top of my human hand. Into my hip muscle, he injected the unknown contents of the remaining two syringes. He covered me with a blanket and engaged in what looked like a sweep of the house.

Starting in my bathroom, he rummaged through all of my make-up drawers, the medicine cabinet, and the linen closet before spending a few minutes in the master bedroom closet. He dug through the nightstand tables and clothes drawers and removed pictures from their hangers on the walls to inspect the backings.

Even if I'd known what to look for in my human form, I never would've found the pinhole cameras he installed that night, which provided him with unobstructed views of the bedroom and bathroom.

He went through the same motions in the other rooms. When he finished, he reviewed and downloaded all of the e-mails, files, and photos on my and Rynner's laptops. I stayed close to him throughout this part of the Skip but had no luck determining what it was he sought. When he completed his checklist, Guerrera walked through the kitchen, placed my keys on the counter, and left through the back door using the same tool he'd used at my office to defeat the door lock.

✝

Someone started yelling.

"Get your ass back here now."

It was John's voice. He must've realized I'd left Siara's garrison and was now summoning me back to answer for my transgression. With a turn of the Kairometer, I was back on the floor of the pantry, but before I could reposition myself, John yanked me upright by the arms and put me in a lock, with one of my arms pinned behind my back and the crook of his arm pressed against my throat.

"I told you to stay put, and I meant it," he said in a voice that betrayed the force he applied to my body.

He relaxed his grip but didn't release me when Siara rushed into the kitchen. He told her what I'd done and threatened to haul me down to the basement if I continued to defy his orders. With some coaxing from her, he let me go and stormed off to another part of the house. She leaned against the granite kitchen island and shook her head.

"John comes from a world where people followed his orders. His job is to protect you, and he can't do that when you go rogue."

"But we're not in that world, are we?" I regretted my snide comment as soon as it left my lips.

"How did he know I was gone?"

"From what I understand, he and those like him can sense it," she said, "although I don't think he's able to retrieve you himself."

"I think at least one Pellico member knows we're here, but I need you to confirm my suspicion."

I flipped my head over and exposed the back of my neck to her.

"Do you see a tiny scar on the edge of my hairline?"

She picked through my hair.

"I don't see anything but hang on. I'll be right back."

She returned with John, who was carrying an industrial flashlight and slapping it against his palm like a baseball bat. *Whap, whap, whap.*

"See if you can find it," she said to him.

I flipped my head down to provide him with a better view of the back of my neck. When he told me there were no discernible scars, I asked him to palpate the left side where Guerrera had made the incision to see if whatever Guerrera inserted there had made it to the Afterlife.

"There's something here," John said when he bored his fingertip into my skin.

He guided Siara's finger to the same spot and asked her if she felt a defining edge. When she concurred she felt something, he skipped over the paring knife in the knife block on the counter, opting instead for the butcher knife that could've sliced through bone.

"Whoever did this has a real gift with a needle and thread. There are no visible stitch marks," John remarked.

With the flashlight in one hand and the sword-sized utensil in the other, he approached me and told me to hold still. He was trying to scare me into submission, and it was working.

Point made, I said to myself.

Not wanting to disobey another one of his instructions so shortly after the last incident, I did as he commanded. Siara saw me wince and took my hand for support. Fortunately, I felt nothing as he cut a notch in my neck and popped out a small metallic disc.

"It's probably a tracking device. I won't know if it's active until I examine it more closely. How did you know it was there?"

"From paying attention to the details of the Skip."

Without getting into the perverse particulars, I told them the story of how Guerrera, a senior level employee of TSC and a confirmed member of the Pellico, figured out that I was an *X Triplici*. I described how he brought me home after I'd had one too many drinks, put me to bed, and performed the minor surgery. I also shared with them how Guerrera searched my house and computers for something he wanted but couldn't find. Not wanting to open up Pandora's Box, I omitted the more personal details.

"Did he alert anyone to your existence?" John asked.

"He made a call and mentioned something about a lab. Other than that, I don't know."

"It's strange he didn't capture you then when you were as naïve and vulnerable as you would ever be. Something held him back," Siara said.

"If that disc is active, he knows where you are now, apparently hasn't shared the information yet, and took a risk warning you about the others at the club," John added.

He wandered back to the control room to inspect the bug.

I rubbed my neck while Siara washed the knife and returned it to the safety of its wooden block. She stood with her back to me and let out a long sigh.

"I can feel the questions stacking up in your head. Here are the answers I'm willing to give you now. I can't read the minds or see the futures of those who are not of this world, but I can sense their feelings. I have no superhuman powers, but I age much slower than humans, have never been to the place you now call home, and have never formally met *The One*. Does that help?"

"Yes, but not much," I said mid-yawn.

The information was helpful, but I knew she was holding back. What she told me explained, at least in part, why our mission wasn't a simple search and rescue effort. We had a fair amount of intelligence gathered by Siara but were faced with the confounded unpredictability of the Pellico, both in their motives and their allegiances.

Siara left to check on John's progress with the disc, and I found a comfortable spot to rest my head in one of the guest bedrooms. The room was dark and quiet, and the silky, lavender-scented sheets eased me into a twilight sleep.

I strained to focus in the dim light. I knew I wasn't at Siara's because the caustic smell of industrial cleaner had replaced the sweet, floral scent of the guest bedroom. According to the ancient wall clock, it was 3:32 a.m.

I was in Rynner's room at Evergreen, sitting on the floor at Ray's feet with my head planted in his inner thigh. I couldn't see his face but sensed from the tension in his leg muscles that he was awake, trying hard not to move and disturb me.

The chocolate cake still wrapped neatly in foil lay untouched on the table. I twitched involuntarily.

"You dozed off there for a bit. Thanks for keeping me company when I know how busy you are. I paid the new nanny to stay the night with Jackson but really should get home."

I hugged him goodbye, and he departed with my mother's magic remedy and a promise from me that we'd share a relaxing meal once the trial was over. I kissed Rynner on the cheek and closed the circuit of my routine by driving home to get ready for work. I couldn't check e-mails on the way because my phone battery had died during the night. As a result, the ride gave me time to reflect on the sanative nature of Ray's companionship.

The house was quiet and as far as I could tell, remained unmolested during my absence. Maverick was on top of the refrigerator, waiting for breakfast, and I fed him and plugged in my phone to charge before showering. I noticed I had nine missed calls from an unlisted number and an e-mail from Wiley telling me he had an emergency and would be out of town for the next three days.

As usual, I arrived at work hours before my colleagues. Large envelopes buried my office chair, and before I could clear a place to sit, my phone chirped with a text message. It was from Gator.

"Got some stuff fo' yah," it read.

I texted him back with an invite to stop by the office and dumped the contents of the first package onto my desk. Neatly clipped together with cover sheets identifying the names and addresses of each potential jury member were the results of Gator's team's investigative work. What they collected crossed the line from compelling to frightening.

The first file was on Rowan Singleton, a thirty-two-year-old venture capitalist with a voracious appetite for online fetish pornography as evidenced by the dozens of pages of computer records that identified, with date and time stamps, Singleton's IP address and every kinky website he'd ever visited and paid to view. Copies of Singleton's credit card statements verified the transactions, as did the photographs, shot by people I hoped I'd never meet, of Singleton enjoying his purchases.

Buried deeper in the file were documents proving Singleton's complicated tax fraud schemes and disclosing his offshore bank accounts and other assets. Most interesting to me, however, were the records showing his ownership, through a straw man, of several real estate holdings in and around Radiant.

The next file was for Patricia Gillium, a fifty-year-old divorcee who used her teenage son's attention deficit disorder medication as an upper and employed undocumented house staff whom she paid well below minimum wage. Gillium's former mother-in-law was buried in Radiant.

I reviewed file after file replete with people's dirty laundry, from drugs and prostitutes to extramarital affairs and hits for hire, corroborated by pictures and records that had to have been excavated to be found. Gator and I both knew that although his team had obtained the stuff on my desk through shadowy legal channels, I would never ask him to disclose his sources, and he would never offer to tell me about them. I'd filled two notepads with useful tidbits by the time my assistant sent me an e-mail telling me she was leaving for the night.

A few hours later, I did several laps around the office to stretch my legs and ended up in the break room, where I finished off the last of my brother's lasagna, cold as I preferred it. I must've eaten it too fast because it didn't stay down long. After the unexpected trip to the bathroom, I texted Ray, who was visiting Katherine, and told him I wouldn't be stopping by Evergreen tonight because I needed to get some sleep before tomorrow's hearing. He texted me back, said he'd tell Rynner where I was, and wished me good luck.

With my briefcase stuffed with everything I needed for the pretrial hearing, I went home, managed four hours of fitful shut-eye, and woke up at the usual time ready for the beating I knew I'd take in court. I blew off some steam with a run through the neighborhood and was dressed and ready to go with a few hours to spare.

The courthouse officially opened at seven, and Judge Cordan's deputy unlocked her courtroom doors around eight. At ten minutes after seven, I parked myself, with a can of warm diet soda and a package of stale cheese crackers, in the Courthouse Café located in the basement of the building.

Lawyers holding last-minute meetings with their clients filled the tables around me, and court personnel passed through for coffee and donuts. I didn't see anyone I knew, which was fine because I didn't feel like socializing. At five minutes to eight, I boarded the elevator with four other attorneys on my way to the fifth floor.

After passing through the second security checkpoint, I entered the courtroom and had to weave through the reporters and onlookers to reach the bar, the swinging doors that separate the gallery where the public sits from the area where the judge, jury, and counsel play their respective roles. As custom dictated, and as the lawyer for the defendant, I checked in with the bailiff, who was seated just below the judge's bench, and found my place at the counsel table furthest from the jury.

Butterflies danced in my stomach as they always did when I passed through the swinging doors. I was used to having an audience when I attended hearings because the judges often scheduled them back-to-back, and most attorneys appeared early for their hearings and waited in the gallery until the bailiff called their cases. Today was different because members from the local and national press were present. If I made a fool out of myself, a large swath of the country would know about it.

Frantsen's team arrived while I was unpacking my briefcase. Frantsen, as usual, carried nothing, not even a pen, as the sea of spectators parted to allow him and his posse, toting boxes and trial bags, to proceed to the counsel table closest to the jury box. They stood close to me facing their first and probably only dilemma of the day because their table, like mine, had only three chairs for the ten occupants. Two of the junior attorneys I recognized from the disgraced expert's deposition must've drawn the short straws and had to sit with Frantsen.

It took four people to unpack the dolly full of boxes and arrange the pleadings and miscellaneous papers on the table in front of Frantsen, and a fifth to sign in with the bailiff.

The sixth person produced a small wooden box filled with fountain pens and presented it to Frantsen as if he were an emperor receiving a scepter. Once his helpers had arranged his courtroom camp to his liking, Frantsen banished the extra bodies to the gallery, which was now standing room only.

No one at Frantsen's table acknowledged my presence. I watched the minutes tick by on my watch because the clock in the courtroom was set high in the wall at the back of the gallery behind the lawyers. Twenty minutes later, the court reporter took her seat below the witness box. Thirty minutes after our hearing was scheduled to start, a loud knock on a door behind the bench signaled the judge's arrival.

"All rise," called the bailiff.

And all did. Judge Cordan stepped up onto her bench, opened her docket notebook, and appraised the crowd.

"You may be seated," she said, clearly enjoying the attention.

Two additional deputies appeared at the back of the courtroom to quell any disorder. We waited a few more minutes while Judge Cordan studied her file. When she was ready, she read the case number and the list of motions in the order in which she wanted to hear them.

As the first order of business for the day, Judge Cordan had chosen Frantsen's motion for a continuance of the trial date, which he wanted so he could have more time to find and designate a new expert. The Judge's choice made sense because if she granted his request, the other motions in the queue would be moot.

"Mr. Frantsen, it's your motion, please proceed," she said, without looking up from her computer.

With some difficulty due to his size and the fact he'd chosen the middle seat at the counsel table, Frantsen stood to address the court. With full command of the room, he spoke for nearly an hour about the complexity of the case and the importance of sufficient time for the parties to prepare their respective sides. Not once did he mention his expert problem, even though it was the real reason he wanted more time. He ended his speech with a request to move back the trial date another four months.

"Thank you, Mr. Frantsen. Response?" The judge's tone didn't indicate which way she was leaning at that moment.

Tessa's instructions were crystal clear. No continuances. I stood up, and with nothing more than a piece of paper full of scribbled notes, countered every one of Frantsen's arguments in a fraction of the time it took him to make them. After my counter-arguments, the judge thanked me and leaned forward toward the microphone mounted on the bench.

Before she said anything, Frantsen stood up again and asked if he could have a few minutes for a short reply to my arguments.

"Mr. Frantsen, I believe I've heard enough argument from the parties. I'm going to deny your motion to continue the case and keep it on the docket with its priority trial setting."

Nothing in Frantsen's demeanor betrayed the stalwart façade to reveal whether he was surprised by the ruling. Next on the list of motions was my motion to strike Frantsen's expert. I stood up again to start my argument but was cut off mid-sentence by Frantsen.

"Your honor, I'd like to advise the court that plaintiffs will voluntarily withdraw the expert designation of Dr. Richard Perryman."

"Any objections from the defendant?" the judge asked me.

"None your honor."

"Motion granted," she noted for the record.

Frantsen's decision to withdraw his expert was a gamble. Without an expert, the plaintiffs had no scientific evidence to link the explosion to TSC. If Frantsen allowed Dr. Perryman to testify, I could thoroughly discredit him on cross-examination, which could cost the plaintiffs their case.

The eleventh-hour expert withdrawal was the last bit of good news I'd have during the remainder of the hearing. It came as no surprise to me when the judge sided with Frantsen on the rest of the evidentiary issues we argued. The result was that TSC would be far more restricted in what it could say about the plaintiffs during the trial than what the plaintiffs could say about TSC.

Before concluding the hearing, the judge asked if there were any other matters to discuss, and when neither side raised any, she dismissed the parties and retreated to her chambers. Frantsen left the courtroom in the same manner in which he'd entered, with his underlings scrambling in his enormous wake to pack his papers, books, and pens.

I waited several minutes to allow Frantsen and the press to clear the building before I started stuffing my documents back into my briefcase. As was his custom, Frantsen liked to hold impromptu press conferences just outside the courtroom doors. Based on the commotion in the hall, I knew he was holding one now. The bailiff straightened the chairs and turned off the microphones.

"It's gonna be some show," he remarked.

We were now the only ones remaining in the courtroom.

"I heard the Judge talking about sequestering your jury," he added.

He shouldn't have revealed this information to me, but Steve Cozen had been the bailiff assigned to this courtroom since I began practicing law and was the older brother of a friend from law school.

"What do you think about the case?" I asked.

Steve had been present for every hearing we'd had, knew Frantsen's trial skills, and was privy to the water cooler talk from the judges and both sides of the bar.

"Frantsen's got a silver tongue and a sympathetic case, but if you can get a smart jury in that box, his lack of an expert will bite him in the ass. And even if it didn't, he has to know there's a strong chance the court of appeals would reverse a jury verdict in his favor because he won't be able to prove that anything your client did caused the explosion."

For someone who'd never been to law school, Steve had a grasp of jury trials that most lawyers would never develop. Without my having to ask, he peeked out the courtroom door and told me the hall was clear. I told him to say "hello" to his sister and left.

†

Only a few more days separated me from the trial date. Once I returned to the office, I called Wiley and left a message asking him to call me for an update. The partners summoned me to Main for an early afternoon briefing on the hearing and offered unsolicited advice on everything from my trial wardrobe to my opening and closing arguments. With their curiosity sated, they left me to my work and went wherever people with time and money go to relax.

Gator was raising and lowering himself in my office chair when I returned from the meeting with the partners.

"*Ca viens?*" he asked. *How's it coming?*

"*Laissez les bon temps rouler,*" I replied. *Let the good times roll.* It was one of the few Cajun phrases I'd learned from a college trip to New Orleans to celebrate Mardi Gras.

"Yah Cajun's gettin' bettah." I saw what could've been a wink from his twitchy left eye. He leaned across the desk and produced a large package from underneath my desk.

"Mowah ta read."

I took the package from him and asked if there was anything else we needed to discuss. He reached into his back pocket and pulled out a giant claw.

"Issa *Gris-Gris,*" he said as he handed it to me. *A voodoo good luck charm.*

He left me with the mysterious package and the sharp claw I determined came from an alligator, probably the same one that gave its life for his beloved pair of boots.

By the time I left the office to visit Rynner, the mounting headache was in fierce competition for attention with my churning stomach. I worried that regardless of his condition, he'd somehow sense my absence, and even if he didn't, I would feel the emptiness. And the guilt. I'd had enough for the day, locked the creepy

157

Gris-Gris and the unopened package in my desk drawer, and called it a night.

The Evergreen parking lot was sparsely populated, and the one car I'd hoped to see wasn't there. The staff was focused on their shift change duties and didn't notice me as I wandered down the corridor toward the stairs. I stopped just inside the door to the third floor to silence the ringer on my cell phone.

The hallway was empty except for the man in scrubs with a medical cart, who was waiting for the elevator at the far end by Rynner's room. He had his back to me, and an alarm sounded at the moment the elevator doors closed behind him. Strobe lights flashed from the ceiling, and a bodiless voice echoed off the walls.

"Code Blue, Room 302. Code Blue, Room 302."

When the elevator doors reopened seconds later, a code team with a crash cart rushed into Room 302.

Rynner's room.

I bolted down the hall and stopped just inside the doorway to avoid entangling myself in the trauma team's work on Rynner, but Rynner wasn't the object of their attention. Across the room, Katherine was surrounded by medical personnel who were attempting to shock her heart back to life.

Remembering a comment by Ray that their aunt had raised them as Catholics, I flagged down a passing nurse and begged her to summon the resident Priest. She made the call and told me he was on the way up. I stepped back into the room and stood frozen on the perimeter of the circle of chaos.

"Clear," the lead doctor shouted.

I heard the sound of the electrical charge connect with Katherine's body. For the first time since I'd met her, I saw her move as the current surging through her caused her limbs to contort involuntarily. Katherine's eyes were wide open, but she wasn't breathing.

The Priest arrived, and the team shifted in a religiously deferential choreography to allow him the access he needed to administer the Last Rites.

A second doctor started chest compressions while the Priest prayed calmly. Over and over the second doctor counted rapidly from one to thirty as her interlaced hands tried to coax Katherine's heart to restart.

The heart monitor continued to broadcast the familiar flatline tune, and after another ten minutes of compressions, the first doctor pronounced Katherine dead.

With tears welling up in my eyes, I stepped out into the hall to call Ray. I choked out that Katherine had just passed and that he needed to get here. In a voice much calmer than mine, he said he'd collect Jackson and be there as fast as he could.

The crash team reloaded their cart and left the room with the Priest in tow, leaving Katherine's frail and lifeless body covered by a thin bedsheet. The oil the Priest had placed on her forehead had seeped through the flimsy material, causing an unsightly blot on the white cloth.

I walked over to her, folded back a corner of the sheet covering her head, and used it to dab the excess oil off of her forehead. I pulled my hairbrush out of my purse and smoothed the knots from her tangled hair. With her cool hand in mine, I sat and waited for Ray to arrive.

Within an hour, Ray crept into the room, placed his sleeping nephew in the guest chair, and stepped around to the other side of Katherine's bed. Just as I'd done, he wrapped his hands around his sister's limp hand and sat quietly for several minutes. When he was ready, he kissed her cheek and called to Jackson.

"J-Man? Wake up, buddy. It's time to say goodbye to your mom."

Jackson wiggled his way off of the chair and into Ray's waiting arms.

"Is she going away?"

"Yes. Do you remember what Father Castraverde told you?" Ray said, hugging Jackson tightly.

"That people who die go to Heaven?"

"That's right. The Angels came and told her it was time to go."

Jackson's face registered confusion as he looked at his mother and tried to reconcile how she could be in two places, Heaven and here, at the same time. He climbed up onto the bed and did his best to wrap his little sausage arms around Katherine.

"I love you, Mommy. Be good and don't forget us." He climbed back into Ray's lap and was asleep in minutes.

Hollow was the only word I could find to describe how I felt at that moment. I'd lost Rynner, but Katherine was *gone*. Not knowing what else to say, I hugged Ray and asked if there was anything I could do to help.

"I've got this. Besides, you've got trial around the corner."

I hugged him tighter.

"I can make the funeral arrangements, and the custody papers for Jackson can be fast-tracked. It would mean a lot to both of us if you could attend the funeral service."

I promised him I'd move mountains to be there for them. He hoisted Jackson over his shoulder and turned toward me.

"Thank you for being here for her, for calling the Priest, for calling me. On some level, I know she knew you were with her."

Orderlies were waiting outside the room with a gurney and came in to retrieve Katherine's body as soon as Ray was off the floor. I pulled my chair over to Rynner's bedside, intending to spend some quiet time with him, but the thoughts confined in my head broke free.

The result was an extended confession of sorts, where I shared with Rynner how adrift I felt. I talked and talked, but as much as I wanted to, I couldn't convince myself to tell him what was really bothering me. How could I admit to him that I was intellectually attracted to a man who just lost his sister and carnally attracted to a man who, when I was sober, scared the hell out of me?

When I ran out of words that weren't on the self-imposed quarantine list, I pressed my forehead against Rynner's and told him that with the trial around the corner, my visits would be more sporadic. I stopped by the nurse's station on the way out to give them instructions to text me over the next few days if there were any changes in Rynner's condition. The Charge Nurse said I looked peaked and suggested I get some rest.

Wash. Rinse. Repeat.

Work. Evergreen. Home. This was the orbit around which my personal planet rotated.

I caught a few hours of sleep and schlepped back to the office at 4:30 a.m. The first item on my to-do list was to inspect Gator's most recent gifts hidden away in my locked desk drawer. I removed the package and tore it open to find supplemental dossiers on the plaintiffs. As I'd come to expect, the information about each person fell into one or more of the categories of kinky, illicit, or profane. I added some notes to my working witness outlines and sealed the information back in the envelope.

The alligator claw talisman wasn't that large but gave me a good case of the willies when I touched it. I tore a page from my yellow legal pad, wrapped the claw in it, and shoved it into the bottom of my purse in case there was something to Gator's bayou voodoo.

The next time I dug into my purse was when I needed a mirror to help me find an errant eyelash lodged somewhere underneath my eyelid. I unzipped the little pouch where I kept my cosmetics and saw something poking out from my powder compact. Stuck to the inside of the mirror was a scrap of paper with a message in handwriting I knew.

"*I told you not to make me jealous,*" it read.

Acid churned in my stomach. What had I done to make Guerrera jealous? What had he done in response? I called Evergreen and confirmed that Rynner's condition hadn't changed in the few hours since I'd left him. Next, I texted my brother, who predictably slept later than most but close to his phone, and asked if everything was okay at home.

"Fine. R U OK?" he texted back.

"Yes, all good."

Without warning, my stomach contracted. The second time it happened, I embraced my office trashcan and threw up until my abdominal muscles cramped so tightly that I had to curl into the fetal position on the floor for relief. The question beat against my skull like an angry prisoner banging against cell bars.

Was Guerrera involved in Katherine's sudden death?

If he were, what point would it serve? I thought about the figure who'd stepped into the elevator just before Katherine's alert monitors sounded. Maybe it was paranoia. After all, I couldn't see his face, and he wore Evergreen staff garb.

A chime from my phone indicated I had a new e-mail message. It was from Ray and included the details for Katherine's funeral, which he'd managed to coordinate for the next day. The next two people I contacted were my favorite florist and my mother. I ordered a large bouquet of white lilies to be delivered to the church and sent Mom an e-mail alerting her that I'd need to borrow her and her kitchen later in the day to make meals to last Ray and Jackson through the remainder of the week.

Mom responded and told me she'd make a grocery run and enlist the rest of the family to help with the planning and cooking for Ray's dwindling family. For the next few hours, I tinkered with my *voir dire* questions and met with my paralegal to ensure the trial exhibits were ready. Just before 5:00 p.m., I locked my office door and changed out of my suit and into a pair of jeans. I instructed Kathy that unless there was a life-threatening emergency tomorrow, I'd be unavailable and didn't wish to be disturbed.

Preparations were well underway when I walked into the house. Bags of groceries cluttered the kitchen countertops leaving no extra space for me to unload my purse and briefcase. I tossed them onto the living room couch and joined the work detail.

Chris was mixing a bowl of chocolate chip cookie batter, and Mom was smashing a bag of crackers to use for the Southern-style fried chicken coating. Neither was aware that both stirred and pounded in sync to the beat of the music playing in the background. Watching them, I didn't doubt that Chris was his mother's son. His eyes were the same shape and hazel color as hers, and their noses matched in size and slope. Like our father, he was tall with big hands and a bigger smile. All three of them shared a naturally healthy complexion.

I caught my distorted reflection in the oven door and wondered, as I had in my younger years, about the deep end of the family gene pool. When I'd asked my parents why I looked so different from them and my brother, they explained that I bore a striking resemblance to Evalina, my maternal, great, great grandmother, who was instantly recognizable by her height and her dark red locks. No photographs of her had survived the Great War, but my grandmother told tall tales about Evalina's beauty and notoriety. According to one such story, Evalina, who'd wanted to go to law school long before women would be admitted, settled for a job as a secretary to a local judge.

When the judge developed dementia, Evalina, aware of his failing health, began ghost-writing his legal opinions for him. They were so well-written that the judge was offered an appointment to a position on the court of appeals, which his wife convinced him to decline. Evalina never divulged the judge's declining health to members of the bar and disposed of all drafts of the opinions she wrote on the judge's behalf. The judge's wife caught on quickly and in gratitude, introduced Evalina to a bachelor friend who won Evalina's heart and became my great, great grandfather.

Mom and the smell of fresh pound cake interrupted my thoughts.

"Hi Honey. Wash your hands and come join us."

"I didn't think you'd start without me although it looks like you've made good progress. What's on the menu?"

"I researched the favorite foods of five-year-old boys and came up with a list of suggestions. We're making fried chicken for Ray and chicken fingers for Jackson, homemade macaroni and cheese, cheese enchiladas, green salad, and chili. Your brother's working on the cookies and the pound cake's already in the oven."

"Where's Dad?" I donned an apron and started grating the five-pound brick of cheddar for the macaroni and cheese sauce.

"He stopped on the way home to pick up Chinese food. He'll be here shortly."

Without realizing it, I too began shredding cheese to the rhythm of the music while keeping an eye on the rapidly depleting bowl of cookie dough. When the last spoonful of batter hit the cookie sheet, it would be a race to see who would have the honor of licking the mixing bowl clean. My mother's contrived indifference didn't fool me. She knew the stakes of the game, and I knew how fast that woman could move across the kitchen to grab the bowl.

We were poised to pounce when Dad appeared in the doorway from the garage to the kitchen with a bag full of take-out. Mom took advantage of my momentary distraction and lunged, spoon in hand, for the batter bowl.

I conceded the victory to her and took the steaming bag to the dining room to distribute. The gathering reminded me of the dinners of my childhood days when my parents insisted that we sit together as a family around a properly set table to eat and swap news, stories, and gossip. The conversations had matured with time, and despite our age difference, Chris and I never outgrew our sibling rivalry over which one of us would get the last piece of whatever was left on the table.

In this case, it was the eggroll orphaned when Dad devoured its mate. A duel with chopsticks decided the battle for the cold, soggy, wonton-wrapped goodness. I lost to Chris but earned the honor of passing out the fortune cookies, a task that required the skill of divining the cookie with the fortune explicitly meant for each recipient.

"*Your future will change abruptly,*" my fortune read.

I tossed the slip of paper into the empty wonton container.

It already has, I thought.

We cleared the table and returned to the kitchen to finish the cooking. Worried as most mothers would be that Ray, a single man, would starve to death in the aftermath of the funeral, Mom threw together a double batch of meatloaf and whipped up a bowl of mashed potatoes to add to the smorgasbord.

Dad and Chris carried the two coolers, crammed with ice and enough food to last Ray and Jackson through a famine, to my car. Before she allowed me to leave the kitchen, Mom gave me a primer on what to expect at a Catholic funeral Mass.

My purse felt like it had picked up some weight, and it had because Dad had dropped several boxes of ammunition into it. This small act was one of the many unconventional ways he expressed his love for his only daughter. Chris opened the car door for me and put his hand on my shoulder.

"Are you sure everything's alright? You've got us all worried about the stress you're under with Rynner, the trial, and now Katherine's death. Promise me you'll take some time off when the case is over so you can level-set."

He closed the car door, rapped on it twice, and went back into the house. With the windows down to take in the fresh air, I took a circuitous route home. Too wound up to sleep, I counted down the hours to sunrise and busied myself with mundane tasks like cleaning the bathroom.

✝

I arrived early for the service at St. Rita's, took a program, and stood at the font in the vestibule wondering if I should bless myself with the holy water as other mourners were doing. Deciding that even though I wasn't Catholic, it shouldn't offend *My God* if I did, I dipped my fingers into the pool and made the sign of the cross.

I'd never been in a Catholic church before and picked a pew toward the middle of the nave to study my surroundings. The inside wasn't as ornate as I'd expected it to be. The north and south walls featured biblical scenes in stained glass and candles in gilded candelabras on the chancel waited patiently for an Altar Boy to set them ablaze. Statues of the Virgin Mary gazed down from their alcoves at the growing number of flower arrangements the volunteers placed on the stairs leading to the altar.

Many of the songs in the hymnal tucked into the wooden pocket in front of me were foreign, and when I leaned over to pick up the program that had slipped off of my lap, I couldn't resist unfolding the kneeler to see how hard it was to move and how much noise it made. It must've been loose because once I returned it to its upright position, it fell back down with a reverberating *clunk*.

"Don't worry, just do what everyone else does," someone whispered to me.

Embarrassed to be caught playing in church, no less at a funeral service, I returned the kneeler and myself to the upright position. I was relieved to see Ray, dressed in a dark black suit with a charcoal tie, standing in the aisle. Next to him was a middle-aged woman in a plain brown dress. The only jewelry she wore was the gold cross around her neck. Ray introduced her as "Julie," his new nanny who also taught Sunday School at St. Rita's.

Jackson, dressed similarly to his uncle in a dark suit with a gray tie, clutched Julie's skirt and rocked from side to side. I never would've said it to Ray, but I thought Jackson, at age five, was too young to attend this type of service. Julie carried a large tote bag on her shoulder that I hoped was filled with distractions to get Jackson through the service. I moved out of the pew and positioned myself on bended knees in front of Jackson.

"Don't you look grown-up? I know your Mommy is watching you from Heaven and hoping you'll be a good boy and take care of Uncle Ray."

Jackson nodded and tilted his little head to the ceiling.

"I don't see her up there."

"You can't see her, but she can see you," I assured him.

I was glad Ray wouldn't put him through the trauma of attending an open casket service like the one I attended when I was a young kid. By that age, I understood the concept of death, but that didn't stop me from staring at the dead man's exposed face and expecting him to blink or flinch. The images of his pasty skin and unnaturally made-up face gave me nightmares for months. Jackson was already confused about his mother's whereabouts and seeing her dead body again could've caused deep emotional scars.

The trio found their front-row pew, and Julie pulled a pad of paper and a handful of crayons from her bag. Oblivious to the fact the service had started, Jackson, whose outstretched legs barely reached the edge of the wooden bench, slid off the pew, turned around, and used the hard surface as a drawing table.

Ray was right about following the lead of the other parishioners. I stood when they stood, sang when they sang, and recited the Lord's Prayer when they did, although I was the only one who added the additional words at the end that Lutherans used in their version. Ray read several passages from the Bible, the Priest offered Communion, and the service closed with a final hymn.

Escorted by police officers, the funeral procession, consisting of me, the Priest, Ray's little family, the hearse, and Katherine and

Ray's friends, wound its way across town to the Catholic cemetery for the Rite of Committal. In a show of respect, cars pulled over to the side of the road, and a few drivers made the sign of the cross as our cavalcade passed.

Clouds had rolled in during the service, and the smell of rain was heavy in the air when we arrived at the cemetery. Few visitors were visible among the tombstones in the graveyard that dated back to the 1800s. Feeling the need for some personal reflection time, I parked a fair distance from the hearse and made my way to the gravesite across the manicured green grass, which seemed brighter against the darkening sky.

The grave markers I passed varied in shapes, sizes, and materials, from weathered blocks of sandstone to marble obelisks. The choices of material and construction made by the family members had hidden meanings, but the universal message conveyed by all of them was, *here is someone who lived and was loved.* The inscriptions on several of them confirmed my theory. "*Blessed wife, peaceful be thy silent slumber,*" read the inscription on a pink granite headstone belonging to Betty Ashlock, who'd died in 1919 when she was just two years older than I was as I stood there.

"*Someday we shall meet again,*" read the cursive inscription on Thomas Covington's smaller black slab. *Was this a message from the dead to the living, or from the living to the dead?* I thought.

I was so immersed in my thoughts that I tripped over something in my path. I hadn't seen it because it was in a horizontal position, partially covered with a thin layer of dandelion-inhabited dirt. After serving a sentence of more than one hundred fifty years, one edge of the stone, the entirety of which was no larger than a sheet of notebook paper, had managed to free itself from the prison of the surrounding soil where it had fallen. I brushed away the dirt and weeds and saw that carefully chiseled into the little block were the words, "*Rose Thomas. b. 1846. d. 1846. The Angels Called.*"

While I didn't consider myself to harbor any irrational super-stitions, I felt that something otherworldly had drawn me to this spot. Maybe Rose, who ironically was one of the oldest residents in the cemetery, wanted to remind me specifically, or the world generally, that she'd lived briefly but mattered greatly.

I was probably her first visitor in a century and couldn't bear the thought that the earth was swallowing her tiny tombstone. With my bare hands, I dug a small trench that was deep enough to keep the marker upright and reinforced the base with extra soil. By the time I was finished, I'd filled my fingernails with dirt and my knees with grass stains, but I felt relieved that Rose could again be acknowledged through the ages.

The graveside party was already assembled when I reached the burial plot. The Priest recited a prayer in Latin and held a bowl of dust from which each person took a pinch to sprinkle on top of the casket. Undeterred by my dirty hands, I too engaged in this ritual, although the wind from the approaching storm carried the dust away from the coffin and into the universe.

Before the cemetery workers lowered the casket into the ground, Ray and Jackson placed their hands on the polished wood and said their final farewells. I said a parting prayer for Katherine and hurried off to Ray's house to deliver the food and make the final preparations for the post-service gathering.

✝

Ray lived northeast of downtown Dallas in the City of Richardson. The houses in his neighborhood were older by Dallas standards but coveted for the mature trees and large lots, some covering more than an acre, that went with them. I pulled up to the curb in front of his house and saw the *Sale Pending* sign in Katherine's yard next door. Ray told me he planned to sell the house he'd bought for her and integrate Jackson into his home.

I let myself into Ray's home with the key Julie had given me at the church and propped open the front door to get the coolers inside. I found the kitchen, unloaded the food, and popped the cheese enchiladas into the oven. I arranged some cookies on one of the plates Ray had left on the counter and filled the ice bucket next to the bottles of soda. Certain it would be another half hour before Ray and the other mourners arrived, I gave myself a tour of the house.

In the living room, a black leather sofa and matching chairs complemented a metal and glass coffee table covered with architectural magazines. The speakers mounted in the ceiling indicated he had a high-end sound system controlled by one of several remotes on the table. Breathtaking black-and-white photographs featuring people, places, and things graced the walls. I looked around the borders of each picture but didn't see a lithograph number or mark of any kind identifying the photographer.

Jackson's room was down the hall and easily identifiable by the superheroes painted on the walls. His bookshelf was crammed not with video games, but with story, comic, and coloring books. Stuffed animals, including dragons, dogs, and bears, covered his bed. Ray's room, decorated in shades of navy, cream, and crimson, was next to Jackson's. There were only two framed photographs in the room. One was of Ray, Katherine, and Jackson, and the other was of Ray and Katherine with a woman I presumed was the aunt who raised them. The guest room, Ray's office, and several bathrooms occupied the rest of the square footage.

A door off of the living room led to the large backyard, a portion of which was protected by a pergola covered with bougainvilleas. The covered deck had an outdoor kitchen with a grill, smoker, and wine and beer refrigerator, along with seating for six. The rubber balls, plastic bats, toy cars, and action figures scattered amongst the Bermuda grass marked the remainder of the area as belonging to Jackson.

I was startled when a dark blur streaked past me and landed, face-up, in the middle of the yard. It was Jackson, still in his suit and giggling hysterically. Ray, who'd pierced his canine teeth with two pieces of celery so they stuck out like vampire fangs, was growling like a monster in hot pursuit. Jackson's laughter was infectious. Ray made it halfway into the yard before his laughter dislodged the vegetable fangs and sent them flying into the grass.

"Hey, kiddo. Let's get you out of that suit before you start playing," Ray said, picking up the bundle of energy.

Large drops of rain chased us back inside where Julie was waiting to get Jackson changed into play clothes. At least a dozen of Katherine's nursing school classmates and her two favorite professors stopped by and mingled with her childhood friends. The single mothers from Jackson's class swarmed around Ray and his male colleagues. Ray and Katherine's neighbors kept to themselves in small cliques.

I came out of the kitchen with a plate of cookies and collided with the Priest, who introduced himself as Father Pablo Castraverde, on loan to St. Rita's from Linares, Spain. I shook his hand and complimented him on the service, which I professed was my first Catholic Mass. He mumbled something, abruptly excused himself, and disappeared into the kitchen. After I'd made the rounds, I found Jackson in his room working thoughtfully, for a five-year-old, on a new drawing. I sat down on the floor next to him.

"Tell me about your picture."

He'd drawn a piece of abstract art that resembled a large box around a cross, with a small, jagged star in the middle of it.

"I keep seeing this, so I drew it."

"What's it supposed to be?"

"I don't know, I just see it. Will you read to me?"

"Of course, I will."

Jackson set the drawing aside and pulled several stuffed animals from his bed to join us. He leaned against my shoulder to get a closer look at the picture of the sloth I'd found in a nature book and listened as I described how the animal spent its days. He was asleep in minutes. Julie, vigilant but not overbearing, helped me put him to bed.

The last of the visitors left around dusk. The rain had tapered off, but the sky remained dark. Ray sent Julie home for the night and offered me an adult beverage. He loosened his tie, took off his jacket, and rolled up his sleeves to mix two cocktails. He handed me one and took a seat on the couch across from me.

"This won't sound the way I mean it, but I'm glad it's over. Death is final and brings with it the peace of knowing that Katherine is in a better place. I can now move forward through the grief so I can figure out how to raise a child as a single parent."

"Judging by the number of women who stopped by, I doubt you'll remain single for long if you don't want to."

I begrudgingly meant what I said.

"They mean well, but they've been hovering like vultures. I need to focus my energy on maintaining Jackson's routine, and dating would be nothing more than a needless distraction."

I sipped my drink and admired the framed photograph on the wall in front of me. In the foreground, and surrounded by nothing but sagebrush, was a one-room chapel topped with a simple cross.

In the background, and perfectly centered behind the church, was the snowy, shark-finned shape of the majestic Grand Teton, the highest peak in the Teton Range.

"Lovely artwork. Who's the photographer?"

"I took all of the photos you see on the walls."

Ray pulled a point-and-shoot camera out of a drawer in the coffee table and snapped a photo of me.

"I photograph what inspires me."

My face felt warmer. It had been a long time since I'd received a personal compliment.

"How do I inspire you?"

"It's simple. You persevere."

"Perseverance is an interesting trait to compliment, but I'll take it."

I finished my drink and set the empty glass on the table.

"I meant to ask you if you know how Father Castraverde burned his right hand. I found him standing over the sink in the kitchen running cold water over some nasty-looking blisters," Ray said.

"His hand was fine when I met him and shook it, and I didn't see anyone else handling hot food, although he could've burned himself while trying to help in the kitchen when I wasn't there."

Ray grabbed a bag of chips that we passed back and forth until only crumbs remained. We ran out of grapefruit juice before we ran out of vodka, but that didn't stop us from finishing the small bottle of the latter. I was tipsy and relaxed, and Ray's eyelids were fluttering from exhaustion.

"Why don't you stay here tonight?"

I did my best to give him a look of shock at such an indecent proposal. The thought of his body pressed against mine made my warm face burn.

"In the guest bedroom," he added, realizing how the original offer must've sounded.

I knew I could get a ride home and make arrangements to retrieve my car later. What I wanted right now was to feel safe in Ray's company, even if it meant that I slept in another room and not in his arms. He walked me down the hall and stopped in Jackson's bedroom. Ray pulled a blanket over the sleeping child and returned a picture book to its place on the bookshelf.

After a quick orientation on where to find towels and toiletries and the gift of an extra-large, college t-shirt to sleep in, Ray, ever the gentleman, hugged me goodnight and closed his bedroom door behind him. I acclimated myself to the acoustics of the house as I got ready for bed.

The air conditioning unit hummed outside, and the internal air pressure caused several door hinges in the hallway to creak. I closed the door to my room, undressed, and pulled on the t-shirt that meant enough to Ray for him to keep it in pristine condition for all these years. I slipped under the unfamiliar covers and eventually sank into my body's version of sleep.

In my dream, I was sitting alone in the single-room church in Ray's photograph trying to locate a song in the hymnal, but all of the pages in the songbook were blank. I checked the other five books, and their pages were also empty. I wanted to leave, but the only door at the back of the church was locked. I repeatedly flung my body against it, but it wouldn't open.

†

I woke up feeling the residual panic from the dream and something warm curled up by my feet. The shape, which was more significant than Maverick, required further investigation. I turned on the bedside lamp, saw that it was 3:32 a.m., and identified the warm ball at my feet as Jackson, who'd sneaked in sometime after I'd fallen asleep.

Neither the light nor my movements affected his slumber, and while I could've easily carried him back to his room, I was touched that he chose to bunk with me instead of Ray. I moved him to the center of the bed and changed back into the clothes I'd worn to the funeral. The piece of abstract art Jackson had shown me earlier was on the nightstand so I wouldn't miss it.

I left a note on the kitchen counter for Ray and told him I'd check in with him tomorrow evening, which was the last Friday before I started jury selection. Remembering I'd silenced my phone for the funeral service, I dug it out of my purse and switched it back on. E-mail and voicemail messages flooded the inboxes but would have to wait for attention until I reached home.

I knew something was off when I pulled into my driveway, and the motion-sensing lights that led to the front door didn't trigger. Using my phone as a flashlight, I hustled into the house, locking the door behind me.

I flipped the light switch in the kitchen, but nothing happened. Every wall switch I tried was dead, as was every lamp. Porch lights blazed from my neighbors' houses which told me the power outage was confined to my house. Maverick didn't come when I called him, even though his food bowl was empty. I quelled my jittery nerves by reminding myself that the house was old, and wayward squirrels had already caused more than one blown transformer.

Not having fully convinced myself of the lack of foul play, I extracted my .380 from underneath Rynner's pillow in the bedroom, checked to see that the safety was still on, and went into the guest bedroom to find the circuit breaker box on the wall in the back of the closet. The latch on the breaker box was closed, but all of the switches inside it were tripped to the off position. Pleased that I knew enough about domestic maintenance to troubleshoot the problem, I moved each switch back into the correct place.

A test of the lights in the room confirmed I'd restored the power. The next task was the room-to-room search for Maverick, who must've found another new hiding place because I couldn't find him in any of the usual spots. As anyone with cats knows, you won't find them when they don't want to be found.

I put the gun on the bathroom vanity, stripped out of my day-old clothes, and turned on the shower. The small space filled with the smells of lavender, sage, and lemongrass.

I took a deep breath and let the scalding water pour over me until my skin glowed bright red.

The sudden blast of icy cold water made me squeal, reminding me that it didn't take long to consume every drop of hot water in the aging water heater. Not wanting to spend another second in the cold deluge, I turned off the shower and grabbed the towel hanging over the door. Out of habit, I flipped my head over and wrapped my hair in a towel turban before drying myself.

I grabbed a bath sheet from the towel rack but dropped it on the floor when it registered.

The gun was gone.

I wasn't alone.

I hastily converted the towel on my head into a body wrap. Assuming the intruder was Guerrera, I had no choice now but to confront him.

I walked into the bedroom and found Guerrera, shoes off, lounging on Rynner's side of the bed. His shirt was unbuttoned past his navel, exposing a thick scar that snaked down his otherwise perfect chest and disappeared at his waistline. His hands were clasped casually behind his head. One of them was wrapped around the grip of my .380.

The bedroom door was closed. The safety was off.

"You spent the night with him," he seethed, his accent thicker than usual.

He didn't give me time to respond.

"I've protected and indulged you long enough. My patience has worn thin. You don't understand what's at stake, and I can't wait any longer."

His words made no sense to me. I didn't think he'd shoot me but believed he was capable of inflicting pain in more ways than I could imagine.

The only way out of the bedroom was through the closed door, and those eighteen or so feet to reach it might well have been eighteen miles because to make it, I'd have to get past Cerberus in the flesh.

Guerrera wasn't the kind of man who could be talked off a ledge or swayed by tearful pleas. Any words I used would be wasted on him. To communicate, I'd need to use the language he preferred and understood best, the language of the physical. He'd chosen the venue for this Gordian knot that would strangle me if I couldn't break free.

It was my move. I looked into his eyes and dropped the towel.

My lack of inhibition surprised him. And me.

His face softened.

"*Te deseo*," he sighed. *I desire you.*

Mindful of the location of the gun, I kept my gaze locked on his while I climbed on top of him, moving slowly to distract him and hopefully dissipate his anger.

By the time I parted his lips with my tongue, I'd unfastened his belt and undone the zipper on his slacks.

He wore no underwear, and my actions immediately freed the sizable package from its wrapping.

His eyelids dipped.

"*Te necesito,*" he whispered, his voice tinged with urgency. *I need you.*

He grunted approvingly as I slid his pants down his legs and hovered above him on all fours with my damp hair tickling his face.

I never broke eye contact as I unfastened the remaining shirt buttons, revealing a wash rack of abdominal muscles and the lower part of the scar that ended just below his right hip bone.

At this moment, what terrified me most wasn't the gun or the tempestuous man between my thighs who brandished it. It was a new inner voice, the latent Sexual Deviant, who found this sex and danger combination to be an irresistible, erotic elixir.

You want it as much as he does, Sexual Deviant taunted. The realization was the horrifying truth. *You could wrap your legs around him, rake your nails down his chest, and finish what you started. Did I mention all the things he could do to you?* Sexual Deviant was persuasive.

Lawyer Brain, who could've countered with something intelligent, was AWOL.

I quivered at the thought of the impending physical connection.

Just when I was about to give in for the second time, what little of my conscience that remained hijacked my attention and forced me to read the list of reasons it hastily constructed to explain why I shouldn't.

Each word stacked on top of the next:

Rynner.
Ray.
Morals.
Ethics.
Risk.

Exposure.
Uncertainty.
Danger.

Every part of Guerrera was now rigid with anticipation. A smoky shadow settled across his face, and I could see he was done with his version of foreplay and eager to move to the next level.

He absentmindedly set the gun on the bedside table, seized my hips with his now free hands, and guided them forcefully down toward him.

His eyes closed in anticipation of our joinder.

Time was up.

My decision made, I clenched every muscle in my body, arched my back, and grabbed the headboard with my left hand.

My right arm shot out to my side and snatched the .380 off the nightstand, gripping it by the barrel.

With as much force as I could muster, I slammed the butt of the gun into his left temple, cold-cocking him.

He didn't make a sound in response to the metal on bone contact. His eyes rolled back into his head, and his body went limp.

I clicked the safety on and jumped out of bed, frantic to grab some clothes and get out before he stirred. With my pulse thumping in my ear, I plunged myself into the closet, snagged the closest dress from a hanger, and slipped it over my head.

No sounds came from the bedroom.

I stepped further into the closet and clawed through a pile of shoes but stopped when I heard a soft, brushing sound overhead. Peeking out of the boot box on the shelf above me was Maverick's tail banging softly against the box top. He was a smart cat and would be safe as long as he stayed put.

The slingbacks I wanted weren't in the shoe pile, which meant they were either stuffed under the bed or in my gym bag. I reached for another pair of shoes and felt a sharp pinch on my neck.

✝

Father Davila sewed out of piety. Herr Bauer stitched out of savagery. I sewed because I was good at it, and it served me well. And because a surprising number of things in my life required stitches.

My emergency medicine practice began in the ER at the San Cristóbal General Hospital, where in those days, we were perpetually understaffed and plagued by supply shortages of all kinds. One week we'd run out of bandages. Another week, antibiotics. I never knew what we didn't have until I desperately needed it. I'd witnessed squalor, poverty, corruption, and licentiousness over the years, but these things paled in comparison to the level of violence that kept a steady flow of patients streaming through the ER doors.

The hospital wasn't the kind of place that treated heart attacks or routine domestic mishaps. I'd been working there for five months before I saw my first cardiac arrest patient. The disappearance of the blood samples, along with the lab technician who ran the drug screen tests before the results made it into the medical chart, indicated that the patient's condition was anything but naturally occurring.

Daniela dutifully stayed on as my housekeeper after Herr Bauer's death. She kept the house spotless and the pantry stocked, which I would've appreciated if I'd ever been home.

I worked twenty-hour days, sometimes more, and snatched minutes of valuable sleep wherever and whenever I could. My favorite spot to catch a quick nap was in the toilet stall in the male physicians' bathroom, where I'd lock the door, put the lid down, cover it with a sterile drape, and all but pass out with my head against the cold tile wall.

One of the newer surgeons discovered my hideaway when he couldn't unlock the stall to use it for its intended purpose. In exchange for my agreement not to expropriate the men's toilet,

he supplied me with bottles of pills usually prescribed to narco-
leptics to help keep them awake.

Late one summer evening, after spending hours digging pieces
of glass, asphalt and other debris out of the body of a motorcycle
rider who'd been run off the road and into a storefront window, I
was scrubbing down intending to sleep in my own bed. I disposed
of the bloody surgical gown and the sweat-soaked t-shirt I wore
underneath it and threw on one of the extra shirts I kept in my
locker.

I needed fresh air, and although I rarely did, I walked out the
ER through the front doors, which were propped open for better
air circulation in the lobby, so I wouldn't have to walk around the
building before heading home

I didn't get very far. Before I could cross the circular drive
to reach the parking lot, a line of black Range Rovers charged
up onto the sidewalk in front of the ER doors. Five men in the
lead vehicle joined the six men in the tail car to form a protective wall around the doors to the middle vehicle. A middle-aged
man in a tuxedo emerged with a blood-soaked child in his arms.
Immediately behind him was an attractive woman in her 20s wearing a body-hugging, white dress splattered with blood.

Within seconds, my pager went off, and I swallowed two of
the stay-awake pills on my way back to the ER. I ripped off my
clean shirt and tossed it at the intake nurse, who threw me a new
set of scrubs that I pulled on before I reached the door of the
triage room. Men with guns in their hands physically restrained
me, inspected my hospital identification badge, and questioned
me before I could tend to my new patient. Inside the room were
more men with guns and the hysterical mother whose speech was
incoherent.

The father sat on the bed with the little girl in his arms. She
was three or four years old, and her face and the remains of her

lacy dress were saturated with so much slick, red blood that I was unsure of the nature and location of her injuries.

"What happened to her?" I shouted above the clamor.

When the parents didn't respond, one of the armed men told me a guard dog had attacked the girl at a party. I ordered everyone out, wrested the girl out of her father's arms, and called for my trauma team to prep the operating room. While staff transported her to surgery, I splashed cold water on my face to sharpen up and scrubbed in. My lead surgical nurse had just cut off the remains of the frilly clothes when I entered the surgical suite.

Something had attacked the child, but no dog I knew had that wide of a bite radius and that kind of a scratch pattern. Every one of us in that room knew it was some kind of carnivore, much larger than a canine, but we had no time to dote on the details. She'd already lost a lot of blood, and her pulse was dangerously low.

The resident in the ER rotation worked on cleaning up her face as I performed several bypasses to repair the extensive vascular damage. Satisfied that I'd stopped the bleeding, I turned my attention to her head. Razor-sharp claws had dug trenches into her face that ran from her forehead to the bottom of her chin. The nurse paged the plastic surgeon on call, but he didn't respond.

"We can't wait. Get me his tray."

I studied the depth and angles of the gashes until someone placed a tray of fresh instruments in front of me. She'd need subcuticular sutures to close the wounds and minimize the scarring. I'd learned the technique in medical school and perfected it on the cadaver heads the cosmetic surgeons used to practice their facelift, blepharoplasty, and rhinoplasty skills, but it was technically out of my specialty area of emergency medicine.

Failing to finish the repairs I'd started wasn't an option. Needle in hand, I began my work. The harder I concentrated, the more obscure her delicate features became. In my eyes, her skin and bone morphed into a priceless, damaged canvas I alone had the skill to restore. With the swelling and bruising it didn't look like much now, but I knew that if her parents followed the recovery protocol, there was a good chance the girl would have minimal disfigurement.

God couldn't save that child from death, but I could, and I did. The last thing I ordered before exiting the operating room was a series of rabies and tetanus shots to cover the bases.

More than eight hours later, I found the parents and their henchmen waiting in the Chief Administrator's office. I announced my arrival with a knock on the door and entered to find more people crammed into the space than the fire code would've allowed.

The husband had shed his tuxedo jacket, bow tie, and cummerbund and had his shirtsleeves rolled up to his elbows. He paced the floor with his cell phone glued to his ear. His wife had draped herself across the couch with her bare feet hanging over the armrest. The silk handkerchief she held across her eyes lowered when I started to speak.

I reported that the child had made it through surgery and was in the recovery room and told them in broad strokes about the repairs I'd made. When the mother asked me about the girl's face, I assured her I'd done everything I could and recommended hyperbaric oxygen therapy, if they could find it, to speed the healing process. The husband shook my hand and told me he wouldn't forget me before the large group made its way to the recovery room.

With her office cleared, the Administrator, who was also my boss, took a seat at her desk and sighed.

"You don't recognize them, do you?"

"Other than parents who allowed their child to be mauled by a wild animal, no."

She chuckled.

"His name is Gilberto Miguel Santacruz, the new President of the largest gemstone and gold mining conglomerate in Colombia. The woman wasn't his wife. It was one of his mistresses, whose uncle is a Commander in the Colombian military."

"Who gives a shit if he's the King of France? My shift is over, and I'm too tired to go home. Your couch is mine tonight."

The utilitarian couch was more comfortable than it looked. I stuffed a few throw pillows behind my head to mask the faint, metallic smell of dried blood and closed my eyes.

"Dr. Sánchez gave a shit. He didn't answer your page because he knew, courtesy of one of the nurses he's been screwing, that Santacruz was here and would've killed him if he tried to stitch up that girl's face while high on coke."

I fell asleep before I could respond.

☦

A few days later, I learned that the child was transported to a Swiss facility for oxygen treatments and rehabilitation. I had a few consultations with her new medical team, reviewed her progress notes, and moved on to treat my self-populating ER. To avoid losing his job, Dr. Sánchez was forced to be the heavy and arrange for coverage for my on-call shifts for a month, which meant I could become reacquainted with my bed.

The fault line beneath my feet shifted again the night I got home and found an elegantly wrapped gift on my dining room table. The card that went with it contained an invitation to spend a weekend at the Santacruz's *Hacienda* in Quindio, Colombia. All I had to do was call a phone number to set the date and arrange for transportation. The gift was a Moinet watch with a gold bezel, black face, and black leather strap. I retired Herr Bauer's old Tagheuer, which I'd worn since his death, and replaced it with the lavish new timepiece. Not wanting to seem too eager, I waited two weeks before setting up the weekend trip.

On a Friday afternoon, and after completing a twelve-hour shift in the ER, I met the Santacruz's pilot, a flight attendant, and a security escort at a private airstrip. This was my first trip in an airplane, and with no point of reference, I had no idea how richly the Gulfstream was outfitted.

We landed at another private airstrip hidden in a deep, green valley where additional security officers met me and drove to the *Hacienda*. At the center of the sprawling compound was a multi-level main house surrounded on three sides by several smaller, private guesthouses. The grounds included an outdoor pavilion with a swimming pool, stables, and a golf course among the lush, verdant landscape.

My assigned guesthouse was nearly as big as Herr Bauer's entire home. When I was dropped off, the driver told me I had an hour to freshen up before dinner. What I needed was a full night of uninterrupted sleep, but I settled for a handful of stay-awake pills I pulled from my medical travel bag and a glass of red wine from the bottle on the dresser.

An attendant driving a golf cart pulled up to my front door at 7:00 p.m. sharp to ferry me to the main house for dinner. I was escorted into the formal dining room and surprised when I was met not by Señora Santacruz, but by Gilberto and the girlfriend, who introduced herself as Ambar. They greeted me as if I were an old friend and told me they had a surprise for me.

On cue, the little girl I'd treated walked into the room, curtsied, and presented me with a bouquet of flowers. She was a beautiful child who looked nothing like the bloody mess I'd treated back home.

"*Qué bonita estás hoy.*" *How pretty you are today.*

She beamed at my compliment and waited patiently for me to inspect my handiwork. The outcome was far better than I'd anticipated, and even when her face was just inches from mine, I had trouble finding the scars. Dayana, who had her daddy wrapped around her finger, kissed my cheek and hugged her parents before being escorted away by a nanny.

Gilberto and Ambar praised my skills and treated me to an eight-course meal suited for royalty. Setting aside the fact that Ambar could've been Gilberto's daughter, she was as intelligent as she was charming. She made Gilberto blush when she recounted how they'd met on the beach after he'd lost his swim trunks in the surf.

When the servants cleared the last plates, Ambar excused herself, and Gilberto asked me to join him on the veranda for tequila and cigars. Out here, we were far from the city with its ambient light pollution. I marveled at the dark sky and how it looked like someone had thrown a dark cloth over the earth, poked millions of tiny holes in it, and backlit it with a spotlight.

We talked about how well Dayana was doing, how much the family enjoyed their time at the *Hacienda*, and the challenges of running the largest gold and emerald mines in the country. Gilberto asked me questions about my practice and whether there was anyone or anything that tied me permanently to San Cristóbal, although I sensed he already knew the answers to the questions he asked.

When I admitted I had no permanent ties there other than my job and Herr Bauer's house, Gilberto said he had a business proposal for me, but he wouldn't discuss it until I'd had a chance to enjoy the *fiesta* planned in my honor. He told me that if I needed anything, all I had to do was ask.

Around 2:00 a.m., an attendant drove me back to my villa, where someone had opened all of the windows to allow a comfortable cross breeze. That person had also pressed my clothes and put them in the closet, turned down my bed, and placed additional garments across a chair.

A bottle of brandy waited on the nightstand. I took a long drink, shed my clothes, and sank into the bed. I'd come a long way from sleeping on plywood and bricks. If this was how the other half lived, I liked it and wanted to join the club.

I slept like the dead. Rays of sun were barely visible from the Plantation shutters that had been surreptitiously closed in the pre-dawn hours to prevent the light from disturbing my sleep. I detected movement on the private patio. Upon investigation, I found that my stealthy weekend assistant had just delivered a full breakfast to the table on the balcony. Wrapped in a plush robe, I meandered outside, lured by the nutty scent of rich, dark coffee. Across the grounds, I watched trainers outfitting a dozen *Criollo* horses with saddles and supplies for a riding party.

Atop my napkin was a calligraphy-graced schedule featuring the day's activities. The list included a group trail ride followed by individual massages and ending in *tapas* and entertainment at the main house. According to the instructions, I was supposed to don the riding clothes delivered to my room the night before and meet the party at the stables. The riding outfit and boots fit well, and I joined eleven additional men, including Gilberto, who were similarly clad and ready to ride.

Gilberto introduced four members of his executive team and six business associates who were saddling up and becoming acquainted with their horses. Having grown up in the slums, I'd never ridden a horse, so to avoid embarrassing myself, I watched and mimicked the actions of the other men.

Throughout the trek, we alternated our positions in the procession so that everyone had personal time with our host. The ride took us up and across a rocky spine that was part of the surrounding mountain range, which gave us a spectacular view of the neighboring valley that was home to thousands of grazing cattle. Attendants met us at the halfway point of the ride with cold *cervezas* and gourmet sandwiches. When I asked about the entertainment for the evening, I was assured I wouldn't be disappointed.

We had little trouble encouraging the horses to compete in a race down the hill to the stables. Mine came in second and sulked in disappointment at his loss. Horses and riders alike were taxed by the friendly competition and gladly submitted to the pampering that followed. We had time for customized massages and a *siesta* before the party began. Several hours later, we regrouped by the pool.

The first thing I noticed was that the staff had changed from male attendants to beautiful and barely clad young women. The second thing I noticed was the absence of Ambar, Dayana, or any other female member of the extended Santacruz family. When I asked Gilberto if they'd be joining us later, he laughed and said he's sent them to the city for a weekend shopping trip.

At sunset, a woman in a thong bikini stepped into the DJ booth at the edge of the pool and began spinning Latin dance music. Two dozen more women, who must've arrived after Gilberto's girlfriend and daughter were in the air, emerged from the main house to join us, and the party kicked into high gear.

Female bartenders poured shots directly into the mouths of the daring, and several of the escorts volunteered their breasts as holding stations for the tequila-chasing lemons. Ladies toting silver trays filled with cups of pills in a rainbow of colors, bags of white and brown powders, cigarettes, needles, and pipes circulated through the crowd, passing out their goodies like Halloween candy.

One of two buxom twins placed a highball in my hand. The other leaned over me and stuck her tongue in my ear. A few sips into the drink, I felt a strange sensation, as if I were having an out of body experience. I vaguely remember commandeering a golf cart and relocating the twins and some of their friends back to my villa.

"*Señor? Señor?*"

I opened my eyes and found one of Gilberto's male attendants standing over me looking nervously and impatiently toward the door. He diverted his eyes because I was stark naked on top of the covers in my bed, sandwiched between the very nude twins. The gentleman told me I was needed immediately in the main house. He grabbed my small medical bag and waited for me to throw on a pair of pants and a shirt.

I found an unconscious man and a terrified woman wrapped in a bedsheet in a third-floor bedroom at the back of the *Hacienda*. At the sight of my medical bag, the woman stammered through the list of drugs her partner had ingested before he collapsed. The idiot I recognized from the trail ride had overdosed and earned himself several doses of Naloxone.

Gilberto was waiting for me downstairs in his private dining area. Between sips of dark, steaming coffee, he inhaled pure oxygen from a personal oxygen bottle and offered me one to speed my recovery from the previous night's festivities. After I'd taken a few hits, he shared his business proposal.

In exchange for my agreement to become the mining company's physician, reporting directly to him, I would enter the elite stratum of society as one of his trusted counselors.

He offered me an outrageous salary and a private residence, as long as it was close to his, gold and gemstones if I wanted them, and access to all of the executive perks, including the jet, the yachts, and other playthings, which I understood to mean drugs and women. I would be expected to treat anything and anyone at his request, no questions asked, and maintain complete discretion and confidentiality.

I accepted on the spot, and we agreed I'd have two weeks to get my affairs in order before undertaking my new responsibilities. Gilberto was delighted and told me the twins were at my disposal until my departure that evening.

The twins entertained me for another hour and disappeared while I was in the shower. With time to kill before my trip home, I wandered across the golf course to investigate a large complex of concrete buildings protected by a double layer of fencing. A man who looked like a groundskeeper met me at the outer gates of the complex and asked if I'd like to view the collection. He brought me through several additional sets of gates and into a room with a view looking down into a concrete enclosure.

The area was partitioned into two sections, one indoor and one outdoor. Inside, boulders surrounded a wading pool, and tires and logs covered the floor. Outside was a sizable area filled with trees, a treehouse, and a larger pool. At the far end of the inside compound, a pulley squeaked to life, opening a square door in the wall.

A full-grown Bengal tiger followed by two cubs sauntered in and made herself comfortable on top of a pile of tires. The cubs tussled with each other and practiced their growling while their mother took a nap. The keeper pointed to the two cubs and said that Señor Santacruz had given them to Dayana for her birthday. While I was confident that one of the cats below was responsible for the child's near-death experience, I held my tongue.

We toured the rest of the facility, home to a lion, a black panther, and a cheetah, all of which were cared for by a veterinary staff and animal keepers. The cheetah keeper told me Gilberto admired the ruthlessness of his carnivores and kept them fed with livestock from the neighboring ranches. I had enough time to return to the guesthouse and pack my bag before a driver and the crew brought me back to San Cristóbal, where I promptly handed in my resignation notice at the hospital and began planning for my future.

Daniela helped me pack up my medical books and supplies, sewing needles, clothing, and the photographs depicting the life Herr Bauer had given me. The last item I packed was an ancient *Adventskalendar*, long relieved of the chocolate surprises behind the doors, which I'd kept all those years. It evoked happy memories I hoped I'd never forget. Daniela agreed to watch the house, and just as Herr Bauer had done for me, I set up a bank account for her to keep her comfortable in her retirement.

✝

Gilberto moved me into a downtown apartment near his head-quarters in Bogota. My new home occupied the entire forty-ninth floor of the fifty-story building. His semi-permanent residence was one floor above me in the penthouse suite. He gave me a private cell phone preprogrammed with his, his family's, and his girlfriends' contact information, and asked that I keep it on me at all times.

Ambar had hired a famous Italian decorator who'd bathed my eight-thousand square foot residence in luxurious leathers, silks, and hardwoods. Antiquities of all sorts, including roman busts and frescoes, filled in the spaces on the walls and shelves, and while I didn't know much about fine art, I knew these pieces were expensive.

The fourteenth floor of the building had been converted from office space into my surgical suite, which included multiple recovery rooms. I interviewed and hired a medical staff of six, including an anesthesiologist, a general surgeon, and four Registered Nurses. They lived in much smaller apartments on the ground floor.

It didn't take long before the patients started arriving. The inaugural one was a man in a three-piece suit with orbital and zygomatic arch fractures, a nose that had been flattened to his face, and a row of missing front teeth. When I asked what happened to him, he told me, as would every subsequent patient, that the injuries occurred in a mining accident.

To honor my deal with Gilberto, I asked no questions that would reveal the real cause of the injuries and instead learned how to gather the medical information I needed more unobtrusively. Instead of asking if a knife had cut someone in a fight, I'd tell the patient that contact with metal would require a tetanus shot and asked if one would be required.

From botched abortions to complications from venereal diseases, I treated men and women who were important enough to the Santacruz family to benefit from my private services. Although infrequent, I made house calls to the Santacruz penthouse, the first of which was inconveniently required on a Friday night during one of the countless one-night stands masquerading as my social life.

I disentangled myself from the blonde beauty when the special phone rang and was surprised to see Señora Santacruz's name appear on the caller I.D. She said that shortly after he'd returned from a trip abroad with friends, her teenage son had developed a high fever and had refused to eat or drink anything for several days.

She met me on her end of the private elevator connecting our floors and ushered me to the kid's room, where I found him delirious with fever. She said that before he stopped talking, he complained of stiffness and headaches. One of my nurses came up to draw blood for testing and start fluids.

The results indicated a massive infection, and I suspected bacterial meningitis. I told Señora Santacruz that to confirm the diagnosis, I'd need to perform a spinal tap, which she reluctantly authorized. I started Julien on antibiotic therapy before the test results came back because I knew what they'd say.

I stayed by his bedside for a week leaving only to shower and change clothes. Gilberto was away on business the entire time, although I checked in with him periodically to assuage his concerns about the health of his oldest son. Señora Santacruz sat with me for hours and poured her heart out about how difficult it was to be married to a man like Gilberto. She was probably fifteen years older than Ambar but just as beautiful and far less naïve.

She knew about her husband's girlfriends, prostitutes, parties, and drugs, and had recently learned that in addition to Dayana, Gilberto had three other children with other women he supported on the side. As Gilberto's wife and the mother of his first son, Señora Santacruz knew she had dibs on the money, jewels, and material aspects of the marriage, but knew she no longer had first dibs on his affections.

Divorce wasn't an option, so she had to find other creative outlets for her needs and desires. I wasn't sure whether she was sharing this intimate information because she was lonely or because she was testing the waters with me. No matter what she thought, as the boss's wife, she was strictly off-limits.

Julien made a full recovery, and when I wasn't sewing up, medicating or otherwise fixing my patients, I was enjoying my new-found wealth.

But as I was to learn, wealth didn't equate to status, and money didn't equate to happiness.

Gilberto's niece, Carolina, was a budding star on a popular *telenovela* and visited Gilberto's family while shooting on location in the city. She showed up on an evening when Gilberto and I were having drinks on his terrace and discussing his latest business ventures. Carolina was a beautiful woman, tall and tan with a mane of luxurious, chestnut hair that caressed a face framed by large eyes and thick, dark lashes. It didn't matter that her glamour camouflaged her shallow and materialistic personality because it never occurred to me to spend time with women for intellectual stimulation.

When Gilberto suggested that I act as her escort during her breaks in filming, I happily accepted. Once away from her uncle, she flirted provocatively with me and quipped that as long as I worked for Gilberto, she, like he, would own me. Her make-up artist welcomed my presence on the set, but her wardrobe assistant, an older busybody, tracked my every move from behind her small, dark spectacles and refused to acknowledge me.

No woman had ever rejected me. Carolina's constant teasing, especially when she couldn't keep her hands off of her male co-star in my presence, got under my skin and made my temper flare.

I'd seen her use cocaine on breaks, but at a shooting wrap party, I learned she was more than a recreational user. Coke wasn't my thing, but I did enjoy other recreational drugs and knocked back a handful of pills courtesy of a cast member. Carolina ignored her love-struck co-star and me throughout the party in favor of a cocky rich boy who'd arrived with his entourage. Someone told me this newest object of her affection was the son of a movie producer who financed blockbuster films around the globe.

When she left his side and tottered toward the bar for another drink, I moved in to divert her to a place where we could be alone. Halfway to my destination, I was grabbed by a hand with sharp fingernails that dug into my arm. The wardrobe assistant forced her nails deep into my flesh until small dots of blood-soaked through my shirt.

"You fool. Carolina will never be yours. Leave now or lose it all."

Whatever I'd ingested emboldened me and made me feel invincible. I forcefully removed the wardrobe assistant's arm from mine and whisked Carolina through a set of doors into a stairwell. Carolina's pupils were huge, and her head wobbled as she spoke.

"What are you doing? I don't need you to babysit me."

"Ditch the asshole and let's go."

I tried to kiss her, but she spat in my face.

"You're a nobody. You have no family name. Without my uncle's money, you'd still be a poor doctor in a shitty slum."

I only meant to slap her face when I raised my right hand and pulled it back. I didn't realize I'd clenched my fist when it connected with her jaw and drove her tumbling backward down the stairs. I saw her neck flop awkwardly to the side and knew she'd broken it before she reached the next landing.

Dumbfounded, I stared down at her. Whether it was my own sense of disconnection or the effect of the drugs, I felt nothing, and I didn't care. Like those before her, she was replaceable.

The wardrobe assistant was the first person through the stairway door. As if she already knew what had happened, she leaned over the railing and saw Carolina's twisted body on the concrete below. For the first time since I'd met her, the older woman repositioned her dark glasses to rest on top of her head, unveiling red eyes that glowed like a demon's.

"You'll never have the one you'll truly love, and your desire will kill her."

I didn't comprehend the severity of the situation until I saw the two men charging up the stairwell, guns drawn on me. One of them stopped and snapped photos of Carolina with a cell phone while the other grabbed me, zip-tied my hands behind me, and threw a cloth bag over my head. I blacked out after a barrage of kidney punches, and the last thing that went through my head was how unpleasant it was going to be to piss blood for days.

✝

I came to, but my vision remained obscured by the bag on my head. Based on what it felt like when I tried to move them, my arms and legs were bound to a chair with something that felt like razor wire. Struggling to free myself was out of the question because the slightest movement caused the metal to slice further into the already bleeding skin on my exposed wrists and ankles.

Stale sweat glued my shirt to my body, and the warm air made breathing difficult through the thick cloth. I wasn't claustrophobic, but I found myself on the verge of hyperventilating from a lack of oxygen. And fear.

If this was a scare tactic meant to punish me for my misstep with Carolina, it was effective. I'd spent years using drugs and alcohol to suppress the memories of Father Davila, and now that I had neither and was sober, the feeling of helplessness crept over and through me and made me feel like the child victim I once was. I knew it wouldn't be long before Gilberto appeared and gave me a stern warning before letting me go.

I thought the sound of an opening door and footsteps moving toward me were my salvation.

A man I didn't know, but whose features seemed vaguely familiar, yanked the bag from my head and threw it on the floor beside me.

"Do you know who I am?" he asked, leaning in to look me in the eyes.

I shook my head from side to side.

"I'm Gabriel, Gilberto's older brother."

He was Carolina's father.

"Let me speak to Gilberto. I'm sure we can straighten this out," I said, trying to remain calm.

"My little brother favored you, but he understands that to pre-serve our family's honor, you must pay for killing my daughter. *Dios ten piedad.*" *God have mercy.*

He left without another word.

At that moment, I knew I had two choices. Flee or die.

Anxiety displaced my feeling of helplessness. Praying the chair would break, I pushed hard against the back of it, lifted my feet, and rocked to the right, causing it to tip over onto its side. It must've been built to withstand this type of abuse because it did nothing more than hit the floor with a *crack*.

I thrashed around thinking that the friction might loosen the wire, but that didn't work either. Instead, fresh streams of red emerged from the thinly coagulated wounds.

I heard the door open again but couldn't see if anyone entered because I was facing the opposite direction. I ratcheted my neck around and saw a small man walking toward me carrying an atta-ché case.

"*Tsk, tsk, tsk,*" he whistled when he reached me.

He looked at me impassively, repositioned the chair so I sat facing him, and opened his case.

He slipped on a pair of industrial rubber gloves, donned an apron, and pulled out a skinning knife. My pulse echoed in my ears, and I redoubled my efforts to free my hands from behind me. Using the tip of the blade, the man sliced through my shirt to expose my damp chest.

He plunged the blade deep into my left sternum and sliced diagonally down my chest ending with a flourish at my right hip bone.

The initial pain was indescribable but short-lived due to the massive amount of blood seeping out of me. Despite my extensive surgical training, I couldn't look at the carnage and clenched my eyes shut. I could've prayed to God, but all the praying I'd done as a child had gotten me nowhere. As far as I was concerned, there was no God.

I couldn't breathe. I heard nothing but white noise and watched the red starbursts float around inside my eyelids.

Factum est. It is done.

Life closed at the age of thirty-four.

☦

The sound of a stopper being pulled from a bottle of *Gran Orendain* tequila makes a sound unlike any other. Liquid splashed into a glass, and then into another.

I tasted agave on the tip of my tongue. I was in a reclined position where my hands were no longer bound, and my feet moved freely. Alarmed that this was a prelude to a new form of torture, I ran my fingers across my chest and was relieved to feel nothing more than the crispness of a fresh, linen shirt.

A gentle warmth penetrated through the skin on my face and made my eyes burn and water. It took several dabs of my sleeve to dry them enough to behold the brilliance.

What met me was not what I expected. I was in a Barcalounger with my feet stretched out in front of me. A generous pour of tequila was in the chair's cup holder, and the bottle I could identify by sound was an arm's length away on a small table.

Across from me on a couch sat a Native American man dressed as a Westerner, except for the silver necklace adorned with thick strands of shells, beads, and stones around his neck and the glossy black ponytail, tied with a red strip of cloth, that hung down to his waist. He held his glass of the golden liquid up to the light, examined it, and drained it with one gulp.

"I'm glad you had good taste in tequila. Many moons ago, I made my own, but it was never this smooth. Now I drink it only for business, not pleasure."

I took a sip from my glass and relished the sensation of heat down my throat.

"Am I hallucinating?"

"Does it taste like you are?"

"This looks and feels real, but it can't be. I know I bled to death."

I sucked down another round as if it were the last liquid I'd ever consume.

"It's surprising you remember it. Most people I meet have no memory of how they passed."

"Why are you here?"

"I'm a Soul Decision Maker assigned by the Almighty to determine your fate. After much thought, I've done so, and it's time to discuss your verdict."

I poured the remainder of the bottle down my throat, not because I was thirsty but because the sting of it made me feel alive.

"I don't believe in God. Even if there is one, he's certainly not mine and has no right to pass judgment on me."

I stood up to leave but had nowhere to go. I was a hostage in this space with nothing more than an empty bottle of booze and an Indian, who claimed he was a proxy for God, who was quickly grating on my nerves. From nothing, he produced a second, identical bottle and handed it to me.

"That you choose not to believe doesn't change the fact that a higher power exists," the man replied.

I told him to go to hell.

A look of sadness crossed his face.

"I prayed I'd see the other side of you, but if you prefer to get down to business, we can certainly proceed."

He then pronounced judgment. That I took Carolina's life with no remorse, when considered along with my other behavior, prevented my ascension. My descension was mitigated by the childhood abuse I'd endured at the hands of Father Davila as well as the hundreds of lives I'd saved as a physician.

The elimination of those two choices left just one.

"You are sentenced to Purgatory on earth, where you will continue, possibly for eternity, to grapple with the everyday frustrations of the human existence. There, you will retain whatever skills you've developed during your life, and in accordance with the *Rules*, every thirty-four years, at the exact hour and minute of your actual death, you will relive every detail of the agony and pain followed by a meeting like this one where you will once again be judged on how you've spent your time."

Good behavior could save me. Bad behavior or no positive changes could result in the status quo. Evil behavior would earn me a one-way ticket Below courtesy of a personal escort.

If this is the middle ground, how bad could it be below my feet? I thought.

"*Cave. Deus videt,*" he said. *Beware. God sees.*

"Is that all you have to say to me?" I asked.

"It is, and remember that hope is not broken."

Pissed off that I was forced against my will to participate in this Grand Scheme, I made myself a promise. I would spend every life cycle foraging the planet for kindred spirits to help me plan and stage a revolution against this *higher order.* Casualties would be inevitable. I'd make sure that the Indian would be part of the collateral damage.

Before I could ask him any practical questions about the other *Rules* and how I'd navigate through a known world in a new form, he placed his hands on his necklace, rolled the beads, shells, and stones between his fingers, and disappeared, leaving me in the blackness of oblivion.

✝

My first day of existence in *Limbo Land* began with the annoying chirp of a text message notification from a cell phone near my head. I was lying on my back in bed, and one look at the ceiling confirmed I wasn't at home. A tight, tugging sensation that ran the length of my chest restricted my ability to roll over and grab the phone, so I slid myself sideways until I could reach it.

"Your shift starts at 9:00 a.m.," read the message on the screen. I noticed I was already dressed in green surgical scrubs. The hospital name badge clipped to the shirt pocket read, "*Dr. Guerrera, OB/GYN.*"

Maybe this really is Hell.

I knew how to deliver babies but was sure it was never my calling as a physician. My skills were better suited for the ER, and for a man who enjoyed the physical act of sex as much as I did, the thought of spending my days on the business end of women delivering babies was real punishment.

The tugging sensation I felt when I stood up reminded me of how my former patients described the feeling of stitches pulling apart, so I wasn't surprised when I looked down the opening of my scrub top and saw the hundreds of sutures holding my chest together. Second-rate grandmothers could stitch better than this. The wound would heal slower than it should due to the sloppy suture placement, and the inevitable, prominent scar would ruin what had once been a perfect chest.

None of this was lost on me. The choice of my new profession and the amateur work on my body were intentional and meant to teach me lessons about humility and sacrifice.

They had the opposite effect.

Time was the great equalizer, and I had plenty of it to learn the *Rules* and figure out how to break every one of them.

†

I opened my eyes and found Siara sitting on the edge of the bed with her fingers resting lightly across my face.

"I could sense your feelings of distress from across the house. They were so strong that any Seer within a hundred miles could've felt them. What kind of memory could make you feel that way?"

With the remainder of the memory involving my struggle to flee from Guerrera lost, for now, I told her it was just a bad dream. I could tell from her expression she wasn't buying it.

"I have some good news. John's had time to examine the disc from your neck and wants to brief us on his findings. Let's not keep him waiting."

She pulled me out of bed and followed me downstairs to the control room where John was banging out new computer code. John stopped typing when he heard us.

"As I suspected, it's a tracking device, and it's still active. The technology is more sophisticated than I expected, which explains how it survived your transition, but I've hacked into it, run a trace, and narrowed the source of the signal to a four-square-mile radius in the southern sector of the city."

We spent hours debating our next move. Siara wanted to wait for Guerrera, who most likely knew where we were, to come to us. John vetoed that idea because he thought Siara's fortress was too imposing to penetrate.

Not known for my patience and with no intention of remaining caged up at Siara's, I proposed a bolder plan. The Pellico didn't know we'd found the tracking device, which meant that leaving the disc at the fortress would give the impression that I remained safely ensconced within its walls. John and I would head out, locate the lair, grab the first Pellico member we found, and return to base.

"Not a bad plan but you realize neither of you can go anywhere without me, right?"

"I have destructive capabilities, can move backward through time, and travel between earth and the Above, but can't drive a car while I'm here?"

"You forget you're no longer of this world. I didn't make the *Rules*. If you don't like them you can take your complaints up the chain," Siara responded, clearly amused by this contradictory limitation.

"What about using our portals to travel?" I suggested.

"Out of the question. We could arrive in the middle of a pack of Pellico members, and even if we didn't and could capture one of them, neither one of us could use our portals to transport him back here."

Our circumstances dictated the outcome. Siara would join us on what was either a successful *smash and grab* or a suicide mission. John handed Siara a scribbled list of equipment and supplies and tasked us with procurement.

It was more like a shopping list for a hitman and included two helicopter drones with remote controls and extra battery packs, three sets of high-powered binoculars, four sets of double cuff disposable handcuffs, two bandanas, a box of black trash bags, fifty boxes of ammunition, four assault rifles, something called "the medicine bag," and some baseball caps.

John resumed his fiddling with his new code while Siara and I got started on the scavenger hunt.

"Do you have all of this crap on hand?"

"I'm sure I do. I have to remember where I put it."

We sifted through drawers and cabinets until we'd collected everything but the guns and ammo. When I asked Siara where I could find them, she pointed me toward the garage and said she'd meet me there. I dumped my armload of supplies onto the floor of the RV and poked around until I'd explored every nook

The Rise of Lady Justice

and cranny and even tested the water pressure in the tiny bathroom. Thinking Siara had gotten side-tracked, I wandered back to the kitchen and saw that both the pantry door and the door to the secret basement were open.

Muffled voices floated up from the murkiness below. I couldn't make out the words, but the tone felt weighty as if they were discussing something of life and death importance. Before my foot hit the second stair downward, John appeared one step below me with Siara right behind him. Each shouldered two weapons and carried unmarked boxes of what I thought were bullets. Even though I was one step above him, John towered over me and dwarfed Siara. Neither he nor Siara moved to allow me to pass.

"Ready to go?" John asked.

I was starting to think of old horror movies where all the bad stuff lurked in the basement.

"What are you hiding down there?"

"We don't have time for this. We need to get going."

John occupied my step and my personal space, forcing me back up into the pantry.

Siara slammed the interior door shut and closed the pantry door behind her.

"Did anyone ever tell you that you ask too many questions?"

"All the time."

John meticulously reset each component of the security system when we exited, and after he'd satisfied himself that we'd dutifully fulfilled his supply list, he stuck baseball caps on our heads, donned one himself, and settled into the front passenger seat. Siara tuned the satellite radio to the 80s channel before angling the bulky RV out of the garage.

The plain little boxes stacked on the dinette set table were too small to house the rounds for the weapons we'd brought. I was curious to see what they were. Siara was concentrating on the road, and John was distracted by his inspection of the handheld remote- control unit for the drones.

I shifted in my seat so my body would block the view as I lifted the corner of the closest box to sneak a peek. Inside it were rows of stubby bullets capped with green, liquid-filled tips. I surreptitiously checked several additional boxes and found that the contents were identical.

I don't know why I did it, but I slipped a handful into my pocket and shuffled the boxes to hide the lighter one among the others. Depending on what was in those metal capsules, I might need them later. Sometime later, we pulled into the parking lot of the *SleepInnTime Motel* on the far, southeast end of downtown Dallas.

The plastic marquee was cracked in half, and all of the vowels were missing from the weather-beaten sign.

"Wtrbds & cbl t.v.," the decoded sign read.

It was a dilapidated, L-shaped structure where every front door opened out into the parking area to allow travelers to keep tabs on their vehicles and make quick exits. I couldn't imagine why the motel remained open considering that unlike the other sectors of the city, the southeast end been abandoned in the mid-1960s after a trainload of sulfuric acid derailed, causing millions of gallons of the caustic chemical to leach into the surrounding soil.

Thousands of people had evacuated, abandoning their homes and businesses and leaving them to the mercy of natural decay. Every mayoral candidate since President Johnson had vowed to restore the area to its former glory, but that was a promise none of the winners kept once they learned the cost of remediation.

Other than a few film crews who'd used the area as the backdrop for the post-apocalyptic worlds in movies that skipped the box office and went straight to rental, few came here, and even fewer put down roots. If the Pellico had a base here, they'd chosen wisely because it was unlikely that anything they did, short of causing explosions or fires, would garner any attention from the public or the media.

Siara visited the manager's office and returned with a set of old-fashioned keys for the last two rooms on the west side of the building. Not expecting any other guests, she parked the RV horizontally across several parking spaces so that its main door was just feet away from the motel doors to give us privacy for our operations.

John hopped out, told us to stay put, and performed a safety sweep of the rooms. He returned minutes later with a mischievous look on his face.

"The rooms are, uh, um…. *adequate,*" he said, with a particular emphasis on the last word.

We collected the weapons and some miscellaneous gear and ducked into the end room. Siara and I fell into a fit of giggles before John could shut and bolt the door.

Yellow shag carpet in pristine condition stretched across the room and stopped at the door to the bathroom. A television set with knobs and topped with rabbit-ear antennae sat on the dresser facing the waterbed covered with blue satin sheets. A rotary phone and a phonebook dating back to 1963 sat on the nightstand, and the only other reading material in the room was a copy of the Bible in the nightstand drawer.

Except for the white floor tiles, everything in the bathroom, including the toilet, sink, and tub, was an olive-green shade popular in the 1960s.

"Groovy," Siara said as she fell backward onto the waterbed and bobbed like a buoy until the water settled.

"This is our room," John said. "Siara is next door."

I peeked through the adjoining door and saw that the second room was similarly appointed although its carpet was a nauseating shade of orange. Before she could get up, I flopped onto the waterbed causing a ripple strong enough to pitch her over the side and onto the floor where she shook with laughter until John gave her a look signaling that playtime was over. Siara took her bag of personal items into the next room.

"How did I get lucky enough to bunk with you?"

"Siara needs sleep and privacy. You and I don't," John said. "And it's easier to keep an eye on you when we're in the same room."

Had I been alive, I would've debated him on those points. Instead, I silently disagreed to avoid picking a fight. He chose the brown plaid recliner over the waterbed as his makeshift command post and began loading the modified weapons with the liquid-tipped ammunition. It grew quiet next door, and when I peered around the doorjamb, I saw that Siara was curled up in a ball on the bed, already fast asleep.

When I asked John what I could do to help, he told me to relax and let him work. With nothing else to do, I turned my attention to the antique television set.

"Pull the big knob on the left to turn it on," he said without looking up.

I did, and the picture on the analog television screen faded in. With each successive click of the second knob, I scanned all twelve channels until I selected a news station. Around midnight, John checked on Siara, closed the adjoining room door to just a crack, and told me it was time for the first fly-by. After checking to see if the parking lot was clear, we slipped behind the motel and across a vacant lot to an old gas station.

Rusted shells of abandoned vehicles missing windows, tires, mufflers, and anything else that could easily be stripped and salvaged provided the perfect cover for the drone surveillance. During its two, pre-programmed flights, the tiny helicopter provided us with enough information to narrow down the target to a building complex just a few blocks away.

The Pellico's nest was hidden within a shuttered hospital complex that once housed those deemed by either the state or by their wealthy families to be mentally or criminally insane, which solved many an inheritance dispute. From the outside, the structure looked innocuous enough with its red brick façade and tree-lined driveway. Inside, it was, as reported by former employees, a sadist's playground where the games included lobotomies, live dissections, and amputations.

How the three of us could apprehend anyone in a space that large presented a logistical problem, but we had a Seer on our team. We hadn't been back in the motel room for five minutes when Siara emitted a yowl that had John by her side, weapon in hand before she closed her mouth.

"Get in here," John said in a low voice.

When I did, I saw that Siara was sitting up in bed, but she wasn't awake.

I put my hands on her arm and shook her gently.

"Siara, Siara, wake up."

Her blank face and now black eyes registered nothing.

I thought she'd had a seizure until her fingers started tapping on the bed as if she were typing out Morse code. She blinked and grabbed me hard.

"Something awful just happened. Whatever they tried was a catastrophic failure. I saw where it happened."

"Can you guide us there?" John asked.

"Yes, but you won't like what you'll find."

"We need to go," John replied, slinging a rifle around his shoulder.

I helped Siara shake off the cobwebs before we fitted our earpieces and checked the audio.

Siara propped herself up on her tiptoes to place the baseball cap on my head, pausing to tuck the wayward wisps of hair behind my ears.

"Prepare yourself," she whispered.

It seemed darker outside than it had been, even though I knew the sun was already making its way to the horizon. Directed by instructions from Siara's soft voice in my ear, I led our raiding party through the sketchy side streets until we popped out near the multi-level parking garage connected to the main hospital building by a steel and glass skywalk.

The thrum of electrical equipment, probably HVAC units or generators hidden somewhere above us in the parking garage, belied the lack of light. John, who'd now taken point, gave us the hand signal to proceed around the building. We flattened ourselves against the outside wall and followed him.

Each door we encountered along the perimeter was locked, and we lacked the equipment to break through the plate glass windows on the first floor, which left us with three, equally unpalatable choices. We could scale the walls and break into one of the many, smaller windows above, cross the skywalk, where we'd be nothing more than fish in a barrel, or force ourselves through the old, revolving door at the entryway.

☦

John made the call. The front door it would be.

Using his shoulder for strength and leverage, John dislodged the locking mechanism causing the door to swing freely within its confined circle. Siara gave us a quick and dirty set of directions through the building to the Pellico's main operations hub on the top floor. John told Siara to double back for the RV and wait for further orders. She left through the revolving door and disappeared into the early dawn.

John readied one of his rifles and followed the map Siara's words had created in his head.

I kept pace with him as he sprinted up the first flight of the service staircase headed for the top floor. When I rounded the first landing, I was knocked backward by an unseen punch to my gut.

"Help me."

I didn't hear the plea. I *felt* it.

The sound of static interference filled my earpiece. I looked up and saw John two dozen stairs ahead of me, dodging and weaving to avoid the bright streaks of tracer rounds raining down the stairwell. He never looked back to see if I was behind him.

I lunged at the door on the landing and stumbled into the main artery leading to several surgical suites. Bright light spilled into the corridor from an open doorway down the hall.

Déjà vu struck hard.

You've been here before, Sixth Sense said, although I had no memory of ever having visited the complex that reminded me of a more sinister version of Evergreen.

This floor was deserted. No one challenged my presence or guarded this area which meant that whatever was here was now disposable, dead or both. The compulsion to follow the light overwhelmed my other senses, but despite Siara's warning, nothing could've prepared me for what I found.

A hydraulic platform encased in a transparent shell took up a considerable amount of space in the large room. Electrical wires and tubes of different diameters and colors ran from a dozen or so machines into the shell, which appeared to be locked and airtight.

Something was anchored onto the platform.

When I eased close enough to the enclosure, I realized it was a man, or more aptly, the remains of a man. He was a large, Native American, whose rust-colored skin was fading before my eyes into a pinkish hue. His head had been shaven bald, and he was naked except for the elaborate carcanet of silver, turquoise beads, and stones that hung around his neck. His face was slack, and his eye sockets were empty holes without lids.

His arms, knotted with muscles, had been spread away from his body, palms up, and pinned to the table with metal clasps at the wrists. As were his arms, his legs were spread apart and fastened to the table with manacles. Stiff rods had either formed from or replaced all of the major veins and arteries that ran the length of his body and now poked through his skin like the piping on a garment.

His chest didn't move. He was dead.

Retreating from the *tableau vivant* of barbarism, I clasped my hand together hoping this small act could contain the destructive light mobilizing in my itchy palms. It worked until I backed into a mobile console table and lost my balance scattering paper, metal bowls, glass containers, dirty scalpels, and other detritus around the room.

My hands broke my fall. Their contact with the floor sent ribbons of flames across the room, up the walls, and around the ceiling melting the paint, plaster, and drywall. Thankfully, due to the Pellico's flagrant disregard for human life, the fire suppression system was deactivated and wouldn't trigger the sprinklers and a building-wide alarm.

With the flames once again in check, my tactile sensations returned, and my skin was greeted by a cold, wet liquid spreading across my fingertips. I recoiled when I saw the two eyeballs fixed in the oily serum that coated my hands.

I forced myself up and scoured the area for a container to collect the dead man's eyes. I found something that would work under a toppled medical tray covered with handwritten pages of medical notes in a script I knew well. I scooped the organs into it and added as much of the liquid as I could to keep them moist.

Guerrera was the master of this unpardonable massacre he referred to as "research." I gathered all of the notes I could find and stuffed them, along with the vial of eyes, down the front of my shirt. Even though I'd never met the wrecked individual who'd been the target of Guerrera's wrath, I couldn't leave him here.

I foraged through boxes and under sinks until I found several sheets in which to wrap him.

I had no plan and no contact from John. All I could do was hope he'd fulfilled his part of the operation while I figured out mine. The fire I'd sent through the walls had fried all of the electrical outlets, which prevented me from quickly freeing the wreck of the man from his cage. Without any apparent options, I took a leap of faith and used my barely controllable and as-of-yet singularly destructive light as a cutting torch.

I pressed my left palm against the platform cover and implored the light to do nothing more than cut through the material.

My hand warmed, but the prickling didn't follow. A thin line shot out and around the covering and retracted when it had come full circle. With the joints broken, I'd intended to pry a corner loose and topple the cover, but it cracked like an eggshell and fell onto the floor when I touched it. Standing just inches from the destroyed shell of a man, I saw how rigid his body had become with the rods and worried he'd crumble if I tried to move him.

I easily dispensed with the metal that confined his arms and legs, taking great care not to subject his limbs to any movement. I placed my hands over his and was mystified that when the Xs on our palms made contact, the rods poking through his body melted back into a liquid state, causing his body to soften.

I used one sheet as a cocoon for his body. With the other two, I fashioned a shoulder sling to assist me with getting him downstairs to the rendezvous point. I felt the weight of his body as I hoisted him up but had no difficulty shouldering him. As I exited the torture chamber, Sixth Sense nagged at me.

You're forgetting something.

Nothing stood out when I scanned the eye-level surfaces, but the flash of red appeared when I spun around in a circle for a panoptic view. I leaned over and nabbed the long, black braid, secured with a red band of cloth, from beneath shards of the discarded cover and added it to the collection inside my shirt.

The smoke-filled staircase was quiet as was my journey to the ground floor. After I confirmed the lobby was free from other Pellico members, I stepped into it with my precious cargo and was relieved to see Siara sitting in the driver's seat of the RV she'd pulled right up to the revolving door.

She disappeared momentarily into the back and reappeared outside the vehicle's side door clutching a tire iron, realizing before I did that the width of the spinning door couldn't accommodate two grown bodies, one of which was much bigger than my own.

It took her a dozen tries, but she finally cracked the glass and cleared an opening. I stepped through it and met her face-to-face. She placed her hand on the shroud and looked at me. I bowed my head and struggled to get the words out.

"He was dead when I found him."

Siara unleashed a torrent of expletives that included every swear word I knew and a few I didn't. Her rant completed, she opened the RV door and helped me get the body into the small bedroom in the back of the vehicle. I heard the timbre of John's voice in her earpiece.

"He'll be down shortly," she said, once again answering the question I was about to ask.

"Was he successful?"

"Yes."

"Why did he cut my communication line?" I asked.

"I can't answer that question, but you need to take the necklace and keep it out of sight before John gets here."

"Steal the dead man's necklace? Are you freaking crazy? I don't know this man, but I'm no thief."

"Redeem it," she corrected. "I can only tell you I think it will be of value to you in the future."

"She'd better hope she's right about this," I said to the dead man when I unfastened the dense ornament from around his neck.

As I'd done with everything else I'd already collected from the raid that morning, I slid it down the front of my shirt for safe-keeping. Displaced by the other curios resting against the skin of my chest, the bulk of the necklace settled at my waist, forming a noticeable bulge.

"That won't do. John will see it," Siara said, taking off her windbreaker and handing it to me.

The warmth that emanated from the rocks, stones, and silver spread through my torso, transmitting an energy different from the light from my palms.

It wasn't long before John appeared shouldering a limp figure. John's tactical vest was torn in half, and the shirt beneath it was missing the sleeves. His knuckles were black, and his face was bruised. Pieces of unidentifiable gunk were stuck in his hair.

Before I could lay eyes on our captive, John dropped his bounty, face first, onto the floor of the RV close to the back of the front passenger seat. The man's hands and feet were zip-tied, and he was blindfolded and gagged with the sleeves from John's shirt. John's pockets were empty, indicating he'd used his entire stash of the liquid-tipped ammunition.

"He'll be out for a few hours," John said. "I didn't find any survivors."

The bruises gradually diminished and vanished from his face.

"Aren't you going to ask me what I found after you ditched me in the stairwell?"

"I didn't ditch you," he said with his back to me. "I'm also aware of what you found."

I brushed past him and opened the door to the bedroom to give him a view of the sheet-wrapped body. I exposed the Indian's face, which was now as white as I was.

"I don't think you are."

John's face was expressionless.

"You should've checked with me before retrieving him. He could be booby-trapped or have a tracking device embedded somewhere."

What I wanted to do was unload a firestorm on him for keeping me in the dark and then questioning my choices. Lawyer Brain, which hadn't weighed in on anything for quite some time, cautioned me to hold my tongue and search for answers.

I slammed the bedroom door and took the window seat behind Siara. John jumped into the shotgun seat and told Siara to get moving.

Sunrise had given way to the light of day. Human and automobile traffic increased once we crossed the physically indiscernible boundary that separated the void of far, southeast Dallas from the southern sector of the city. Typical of most workdays in downtown

Dallas, motorists and pedestrians filled the sidewalks, scurrying to get their coffee and arrive at work.

An accident near my former law office had us inching toward the next traffic signal. Impatient with our snail's pace, I shifted to the seat behind John and stared out the window. It had to have been a coincidence that the little hand in the car next to us was waving energetically at me.

When I didn't respond, the small figure pressed his hands and face against the car window and mouthed words I couldn't understand. No one from my past was supposed to recognize me in this form, but Jackson did. He abruptly sat back in his seat, most likely due to a sharp rebuke from Ray, but continued to stare at me as the RV lumbered past them.

Ray was a scientist, which also meant he was a natural skeptic who would balk at the notion that someone who'd died could return to earth in a recognizable form. I felt sorry for Jackson because I knew that whatever he'd said about seeing me would alarm Ray and result in a series of new appointments with Jackson's therapist.

We drove in silence to Siara's. Just as John said he would, our prisoner remained incapacitated during the trip. A glimpse of his face would've been nice, but I wasn't prepared to risk a skirmish with John in the confined space of the RV. Once safely back in Siara's garage, John yanked the Pellico member off of the floor, shouldered him so the prisoner remained face down, and told me to follow him to the basement.

"Bring the body with you," he instructed.

Siara went ahead of us to unlock the doors and open up the pantry passageway to the chamber below and then made a beeline for the central control room. The basement stairs were narrower and longer than I'd expected and revealed a subterranean footprint that was larger than the surface structure above.

The walls were also thicker down here and reinforced with rebar to fend off the pressure of the omnipresent clay. Despite the existence of a painted concrete floor, everything smelled like dank, wet earth. With tightly controlled access, without windows, and without cameras to record interrogations and confessions, this was *terra nullius — no man's land*.

John positioned our guest in a contraption that looked like a medieval dentist chair with multiple sets of restraints from forehead to feet, which gave me an unobstructed view of his face. I laid the Indian on the only table in the room and sneaked a glimpse at the locking mechanism on the door at the top of the stairs.

"I left some documents in the RV that I collected from the area where I found him. They may contain useful evidence. Would you mind getting them for me?"

Satisfied that the other occupants in the room wouldn't pose a threat to me, John disappeared up the stairs on a fool's errand to retrieve nothing because everything I'd taken was still inside my shirt. I wanted time to ask my own questions, and I was going to have it. I closed the door and used a few strokes of the silver light to weld it shut.

Then I turned to Mateo.

"You don't have to pretend you're out. I know you're awake," I said as I removed John's shirtsleeves from around his eyes and from inside his mouth, careful not to allow my skin to touch his.

I pulled up a chair just a few feet in front of him and sat backward in it. I crossed my arms over the back of the chair and tipped it forward.

"Do you know what I am?"

"Better than you do."

When he lifted his head, I could see that John had gotten in his licks during their struggle. The still-fresh bruises on his otherwise flawless face told me that if Pellico members healed, the process took longer than it did for someone like John.

"What the hell does that mean?

His smirk accentuated the dimples in his cheeks.

"Carlos was right. For someone as bright and inquisitive as you are, you're clueless. Think, Adeleine. Has anyone told you where you came from and why you're here now?"

My defenses went up, and I glanced down at my palms before looking back at him. "I know what happened to me and why I'm here."

"They've been spoon-feeding you with crumbs of information, restricting your mobility, and withholding information. Don't you want to know your past and purpose?"

"What makes you think I don't?"

"We'd be having a different conversation if you did."

"Then why don't you enlighten me?" My palms tingled the way they used to when I banged my funny bone.

"You weren't like the others of your kind. Carlos sensed something was different the night you revealed yourselves to one another. He developed a damned brilliant plan, but we all know how that ended."

Mateo's voice trailed off as if he knew he'd said too much.

"Did you kill Katherine?"

"Me? That's not my style. I would've sent a more direct message by killing your dead-weight boyfriend and that interloper, Ray. You have Carlos to thank for the latest casualty of his jealous rage. He's always been temperamental, but something about you draws it out. Magnifies it. Makes him irrational, almost feral. And with the approaching *Gyratus*..."

Mateo stopped mid-sentence when the shadow of a silhouette appeared on the far wall and grew larger until it evolved into Marcus's substantial body, which he positioned between us, facing Mateo.

"*Finis,*" Marcus bellowed.

Mateo's mouth closed.

With a loud *pop,* the seal I'd welded on the door above broke, and John flew down the stairs with a battering ram in hand.

Who kept a battering ram in their home?

Reading Marcus's nonverbal cues, John stuffed a sleeve back into Mateo's mouth, secured a bandana from his pocket around Mateo's eyes, and placed a firm grip on my shoulders. Marcus and John spent several minutes debating something in a language I didn't understand until it sounded like they'd come to an agreement.

John increased the pressure on my shoulders while Marcus, ignoring my presence, threw Mateo over one shoulder, the Indian over the other, kissed his gold seal ring and disappeared.

I shoved John's arms off of my shoulders.

"I'm leaving."

I found my hiking boots on the floor of Siara's bathroom and began the lacing process. She watched me from her perch on the closed toilet lid.

"You did the right thing today by bringing him back. Qaletaqa was the *X Triplici* we've been trying to find. He didn't deserve this kind of end. Had the roles been reversed, he would've done the same thing for you."

"The secrets stop here. What's the *Gyratus*?"

"Why do you ask me all the questions you know I can't answer? Find the meaning."

I fastened the knot on the second boot and climbed the staircase home. Chunks of Texas-sized balls of sand-covered hail carried by the gale-force wind stung my face as I ran the short distance from the spot where I'd emerged to the front door of the Cabin. Even with my enhanced eyesight, I had trouble distinguishing where the sky stopped and the water started. We were in for a hell of a storm.

I slammed the front door, kicked off the boots, and joined Peter in front of the low fire. I threw a few more questions on the probe pyre.

What about my past did I not know? And what was Mateo trying to warn me about?

Peter's voice floated through my ears.

"A lot is going on in that brain of yours. Want to talk about it?"

I reached into my shirt to withdraw the contraband. The ponytail hair was shiny and jet-black like Siara's and measured twice the length of my forearm. I placed it on the floor in front of me and pulled out the glass container. The severed optic nerves trailed from the two balls in the viscous fluid. One of them turned slowly with the motion of the jar, and the brown iris dilated in response to my gaze.

As if summoned, the second eye turned in the same direction, and I nearly dropped the jar from surprise when they moved in unison and stared at me.

The pupils in the eyes without a face narrowed. At the point where the color seemed to disappear into the whiteness is when it happened.

The dead man's eyes became my own. Through them, my body processed all of his sensory perceptions as if the Great Chief himself and I were one.

Qaletaqa sat motionless and cross-legged atop Clagett Butte, marveling as he often did at the drastic changes in the sacred land below. Animal trails, created by and once crowded with bison as far as the eye could see, were now paved and packed with long trains of vehicles that backed up for miles when a wayward bear wandered too close to the blacktop. The hot springs not far from the river where he'd bathed as a boy were crowded with tourists who took for granted Mother Earth's gift.

The spirits that assigned his tasks came in many shapes. Today, they appeared in the forms of a glossy, black Raven and a smaller but equally regal Gray Jay. Qaletaqa recognized the vibrations from their wings and turned to greet them before they landed, side-by-side, on a pine branch several feet away from him. The birds tapped their beaks together before dipping their heads in greeting to Qaletaqa.

"Tell me, Great Ones, what I must know to decide the fate of this tortured Soul?" Qaletaqa held out his left hand, palm up, and closed his eyes. The Gray Jay landed in the middle of the three, intersecting Xs embedded in the Great Chief's palm and began his whisper song of soft clicks and quiet notes. The Gray Jay spared no details, and without the need to look at him, Qaletaqa could both see and feel the sorrow in the dark eyes that peered from the snowy-white plumage of the bird's face.

With a final click, the Gray Jay finished the story and used his beak to trace over the Xs on Qaletaqa's palm. As he did, each line glowed like a silver thread until all of the lines were connected. Qaletaqa opened his eyes, thanked the Spirit for his wisdom, and waited until the bird returned to the pine branch where its companion remained.

The Raven hopped onto the ground, walked toward Qaletaqa, and stopped directly in front of him. Qaletaqa closed his eyes again, acknowledged the arrival of the second Spirit, and held out his right hand, palm up, which was embedded with a matching set of three, intersecting Xs.

The Raven used Qaletaqa's right palm as a stepping stone to hop onto Qaletaqa's right shoulder. She pressed the gleaming feathers of her head to the opening of Qaletaqa's right ear and began to speak to him in the Great Chief's native tongue. Unlike the Gray Jay, who had provided Qaletaqa with the Soul's life story, the Raven provided the details of the Soul's impending death.

As usual, the gossip on the wind was right. Qaletaqa understood that this passing would be gruesome and tragic and test the limits of Qaletaqa's Grace.

With her story complete, the Raven hopped back onto Qaletaqa's right palm, outlined the intersecting Xs with her beak until they glowed, and bid Qaletaqa open his eyes and look upon her.

"A storm approaches Great Chief, and this Soul is connected to it in ways I cannot see. Be careful, for I cannot separate your fate from his."

The Raven rejoined the Gray Jay, and together they departed in silence. Qaletaqa had encountered many lost and seemingly faithless Souls. Never before though had the Spirits warned that Qaletaqa's fate was linked to that of a Soul whose fate he was charged with deciding.

Despite the number of moons since his death, Qaletaqa remained hopeful and even optimistic that humankind was capable of inner reflection and self-improvement. He held fast to his belief that people understood the difference between universal rights and wrongs and desired a pure and honest life.

"The Soul's name is Carlos Guerrera," floated the Raven's voice on the wind.

The brown color of Qaletaqa's irises returned, first as a pinprick in each eyeball and then as full circles marking the break of our connection.

I heard what Qaletaqa had heard, and based on the Gray Jay's account, Guerrera shared more with Rynner than I'd ever imagined. Both were orphans whose father figures had abused them, and both had worked hard to rise above their circumstances and cultivate their innate talents. Despite these similarities, the challenges in their lives caused two distinct outcomes. Rynner overcame his obstacles. Guerrera, on the other hand, succumbed to his and allowed them to break him.

†

"What just happened there?" Peter asked.

What I'd learned about Guerrera's life and death was both heartbreaking and revulsive.

"I was able to connect to Qaletaqa through his eyes. He shared information about himself and Guerrera's past and showed me that he was the one who decided Guerrera's fate. I think those eyes were trying to help me."

I set the container on the floor next to the tress and pulled out the stack of notes I'd also swiped from the hospital. I'd need to study them but now wasn't the time.

It took both hands to dig the carcanet, which felt heavier and warmer than it had when I took it from its owner, from my shirt. Interspersed between the silver strands were rough-cut turquoise beads and semi-precious stones of aquamarine, peridot, amethyst, citrine, malachite, and others I couldn't identify.

"That's interesting," Peter commented, turning his head from the floor to me.

Both eyes in the jar had pivoted and were locked onto the necklace.

"Put it on, keep it out of view, and stash the other stuff until you learn more about it and figure out whether it can help you," Peter suggested.

The eyeballs rolled up and down nodding in agreement.

"All of these belonged to the dead *X Triplici* I recovered," I said to Peter when I donned the necklace.

As for where to hide the other items, I chose the last place I thought anyone would look—inside a pot under the stove. I assured the curious eyes I'd keep them safe as I clamped the lid down over them.

Now I needed to figure out what Mateo said was coming.

"You've been here for over fifteen years now, Peter. Have you heard any unusual gossip lately?"

"Unusual is in the ears of the beholder. The Souls are more nervous than I've seen since I arrived. John's been in debriefing with Marcus and others since you returned. Whatever it is, it's serious."

A dictionary was what I needed. The laptop device was what I had. I pulled up the same search screen I'd used on the day I arrived at the Cabin and typed in my new search query.

"What does *Gyratus* mean?"

A dialog box popped up and told me there were no search results. I opened a new tab, pulled up a dictionary page, and type in *"Gyr!"* as a Boolean search. The closest thing I could find was an entry for the word *gyrari*, a verb tense for the Latin word for *flip* or *rotate*. After a few more searches, I gave up. Asking Acorn or John for help was out of the question. Peter and I were on our own.

Balls of ice battered my walls of glass. I knew the windows wouldn't break, but out of instinct, I moved closer to the middle of the room, where an unexpected change in barometric pressure caused my ears to plug until it felt as if my head would explode.

"Enough," I snapped out loud to no one.

The pressure in my ears subsided, and the hail turned to rain. With a run out of the question due to the current weather conditions, I settled on a decent backup plan. I closed the tub stopper, opened up the hot water spigot, and dumped an entire box of bath salts into the rapidly rising water. Once I'd shucked my clothes, I purposefully avoided a glance in the mirror at the wound in my chest and slid into the steamy bath.

With my head resting comfortably on the back edge of the bathtub, I took a moment to admire the glistening stones in Qaletaqa's necklace. The longer I doted on it, the more confident I was that the rocks were shining in a repeating pattern. I closed my eyes to reset them in case this was just a trick of the mind.

✝

Something landed on my face with a *thwack*. I batted it away and starting flailing until I realized no one was after me. Based on the smells of leather and dry cleaner fluid, I realized I was still in my closet where I'd been searching for a pair of shoes to flee from a naked and smoldering Guerrera. I didn't make it to the light switch before throwing up in the boot box that had struck me when Maverick knocked it off the closet's top shelf. He wasn't happy that we'd both been locked inside and rushed out the minute I opened the door.

It no longer mattered to me if Guerrera or anyone else was waiting for me on the other side of the closet door. I felt like crap, didn't know what time it was, and was worried about how long I'd been out.

The only thing I could see in the bedroom was the pale-blue light of the alarm clock registering 3:32 a.m. Today was the first day of jury selection scheduled to begin in just under six hours. That my gun was missing didn't register until I was out of the shower and scrounging around on my vanity for the toothpaste tube cap I'd misplaced. I checked the closet and my nightstand but couldn't find it. The next time I encountered Guerrera, I'd demand its return.

Rynner always teased me for complaining when I felt puffy, which was often.

"You're mental, it's all in your head," he'd say.

I knew I was bloated when I couldn't zip either the first or the second skirt I pulled on. The third one zipped all the way, and I shifted around in it to make sure I wouldn't rip the back seam while walking, bending, or sitting in court. The last thing I needed was for the jury to see my delicates.

I shuddered in disgust at the rumpled sheets I passed on my way to the kitchen. There wasn't enough space in my head to process how and why I started out naked on top of Guerrera and ended up partially dressed on the floor of the closet with an acute case of memory loss.

Liz would stage an intervention if I told her what had happened. My father would try to kill Guerrera, and Ray would call the police. I decided that after the trial concluded, I'd suck it up and ask Wiley to intervene on my behalf. Until that time, I had a case to win.

I stopped by the office to collect my jury chart and take a final pass through the notes I'd made during the meetings with the jury consultants. I planned to arrive at the courthouse early enough to beat any potential juror who might judge my client by the car I drove.

Everything I'd do from the time the bailiff called court into session to the judge's dismissal of the panel following the reading of the verdict was meticulously crafted to present a specific image to the people who would decide the case.

I'd trade my designer power suits and high heels for more modest attire and average dress shoes to avoid drawing any attention away from the case. Except for during closing argument, I'd wear my hair up to keep it away from my face and would keep my jewelry to a minimum.

Aside from smiling at the jury and making eye contact with them when appropriate, I'd avoid bathroom breaks and elevator rides with them, as well as steer clear of the cafeteria where most of them would take their lunch breaks. They needed to listen to me, not scrutinize my fashion choices. Most importantly, they needed to trust me.

The courthouse library was the logical choice for the morning hideaway because it's a restricted access area for attorneys carrying a valid bar card. My legal assistant had already staged the boxes of pleading binders, rule books, exhibits, motion notebooks, and other supplies for trial inside the currently locked courtroom. My trial bag was crammed with my jury notes and *voir dire* questions, a few extra notepads, a large bottle of water, and half a dozen protein bars. The last thing I did before exiting the library was to silence my cell phone.

Frantsen and his football team of bootlickers were already spread out at their counsel table conferring in exaggerated whispers. Sitting directly behind Frantsen was his lead jury consultant, Dr. Gabby Gomez. Dr. Gomez grew up in a family of lawyers and bucked tradition by snubbing her nose at law school and earning a doctorate in behavioral psychology.

I knew she could read people and pick a jury because I'd used her, with great success, in other cases. In terms of skill, she was well-matched with my consultant, Kip Maister, who'd worked as a trial lawyer for a decade before switching careers. As good as Dr. Gomez's team was, they would, although they didn't know it yet, be outmaneuvered by the intelligence gathered from Gator's data mining.

With reporters watching and at Reyna's direction for public relations purposes, I loudly greeted Frantsen with flamboyant kindness and introduced myself to his helpers. Wiley walked in to witness the display and huddled with Kip until I finished my show of good sportsmanship.

Judge Cordan had requested a jury pool of one hundred-twenty lucky souls and advised us that she'd seat a jury of twelve with three alternates. We'd had the completed jury questionnaires for a week and knew exactly how we'd use our jury strikes. Today, our benevolent ruler was twenty minutes late to the bench and was visibly annoyed when I requested a jury shuffle before the start of *voir dire*. By law, she was required to grant my request, which entailed the random reordering of the names on the jury list provided to the parties.

My team didn't like the first dozen names on the list but didn't have cause to strike them. With a limited number of peremptory strikes, meaning strikes for jurors we knew we didn't want but couldn't strike for cause, we agreed to gamble that a shuffle would reorder the list in a manner that would be more favorable to our strategy. The shuffle worked better than expected, and once the reordered group filed back into court, the parties began the whittling process.

Frantsen's questioning of the panel started with a well-rehearsed story of a small town devastated by greedy corporate America. Frantsen droned on and asked more than enough questions to uncover any biases. At noon, the judge ordered a thirty-minute lunch break and called us up to the bench for a sidebar conference.

"You'll have until 1:30 p.m. to finish your questioning," she told Frantsen.

Our panel was already visibly bored, restless, and ready to go home. Several had been warned by the court to turn off and put away their cell phones or face contempt charges.

Judge Cordan flipped her reading glasses on top of her head and looked at me.

"How much time will you need?"

"I can be done by 5:00."

She warned that she'd hold us to the timeframes and released us for lunch. Wiley and Kip had recorded every answer and studied the body language and demeanor of each person questioned. Frantsen had asked many questions on my list, so I was able to pare down what I had and focus on tailored questions for key individuals. As promised, I finished my questioning in the time allotted.

Court recessed by 5:30 p.m. with the judge's instructions to the panel to refrain from speaking or reading about the case, instructions we all knew they would disregard. In the morning, we'd provide the court with our strike lists, seat the jury and the alternates, and begin with opening statements.

Gator joined Wiley, Kip and I for a marathon meeting at my office to scrutinize the answers Frantsen and I had elicited during the day, as well as the nonverbal intelligence we'd acquired. Shortly before dawn, we finalized our strike lists and ranked the remaining individuals from most to least wanted. We'd reconvene at 8:30 a.m. at the courthouse.

Gator, Wiley, and Kip were picked up by a chauffeured limousine. I drove home alone, not because I could or would sleep, but because I had to shower, change clothes, and pay some attention to my neurotic cat. I also planned a visit to Evergreen, the last I'd make until I got a verdict.

†

My house appeared undisturbed, and the front door was locked when I arrived. I checked my personal e-mail and sent updates to my family, Liz, and Ray before grabbing a piping hot shower. It took minutes to apply the understated make-up and pin my hair into a bun.

I'd chosen a navy suit with a pencil skirt to wear for my opening statement. Only one pair of shoes matched the outfit, and when I didn't see them on the shoe rack, I knew they were buried in the nether-region of the closet. I crawled around on the floor until I found one hiding beneath an old dry-cleaning bag and the other wedged under Rynner's favorite sweatshirt and threw them on the bed while I finished getting ready in the bathroom.

Maverick was sitting on the shoes when I was ready to go. I pulled them out from under him and slipped on the left shoe first. I couldn't get my right foot into the other pump because something, probably a cat toy, was stuck in the toe. Nothing came out when I shook the shoe, so I reached into it to dig out the obstruction.

The little object in my hand didn't belong to Maverick.

It was the flash drive Rynner had asked me to keep safe on the night of the accident, the one I'd completely forgotten about. The hospital staff must've put it in the clothing bag I brought home with me following my discharge. I never saw it again after I threw it into the back of the closet but remembered that a few months ago, Maverick had left pieces of plastic strewn around the house. He must've shredded the bag, found the drive, and dropped it into the shoe where he was unable to retrieve it.

I pulled my laptop out of my briefcase and plugged in the drive to confirm that it was the one that contained a back-up of all of Rynner's research. When the password protection screen appeared, I typed in the last password I knew Rynner used and saw a screen full of file names, including "Ownership," "Test

Results," "Mapping," "Chemical Signatures," "Leases," "Notes," and "Preliminary Conclusions." Even though I doubted much of the information would make sense to me, I couldn't keep myself from skimming through the work that had consumed years of his life.

I opened the first file and scrolled through a busy, multi-page diagram of the ownership history of the contaminated site Rynner had been researching in Louisiana. The names in the boxes revealed that the dozens of companies with any ownership interest in the land begat other companies, changed names, changed hands, and were renamed. The name in a box on the last page stopped me in my tracks.

"TSC."

I didn't have much time left to dally but opened the file called "Preliminary Conclusions" to see if Rynner had reached any that implicated my biggest client. The blood drained from my head when I saw what he'd written.

"Based on the review to date of the property and corporate records, the site has been owned by TSC through a complicated network of shell companies. Drilling and other permits confirm dates and types of operations and when cross-referenced with the list of chemicals from sample testing, establish a direct connection between TSC's operations and the massive contamination."

Rynner knew I was representing TSC and understood the importance of the case to my career. I knew that based on his professional and ethical obligations, he wouldn't have shared anything with me about his findings related to TSC unless he'd confirmed them and was ready to go public. I stashed the flash drive in the coin pouch in my wallet and hustled out to Evergreen to find Rynner on the third floor, peacefully unconscious in his bed.

The bed Katherine once occupied was still empty, and someone had removed the curtain that separated the two sides of the room. In the months he'd been here, he'd lost a considerable amount of muscle mass and looked much smaller than I remembered. His complexion was waxy, and I slathered balm on his dry lips.

"I know why you didn't share what you'd found with me," I said, pulling the drive out of my wallet to show him. "Now that I know, I'm more than a little scared."

I told him my theory of how it ended up in my shoe and asked him what I should do with it.

He didn't move.

"I'll protect it until I have the time to figure out where it should go," I promised as I stuffed it back into the pouch full of loose change.

I asked him to wish me luck at trial, kissed the tip of his nose, and drove across town to meet Wiley and Kip at the courthouse. Onlookers, press, gawkers, and lawyers filled the courtroom gallery by the time we entered and took our seats. I searched the crowd and noticed that Wiley was the only TSC representative who'd shown up. Frantsen arrived, dressed in a pinstriped suit with a bow tie, just minutes before the judge took the bench.

To keep the jury pool's wait time to a minimum, Judge Cordan wasted no time, ruled on our respective strike lists, and ordered the bailiff to seat the jury and the alternates. Fifteen unhappy-looking individuals straggled in and took their seats.

Now it was time for the real show to begin. Due to the length of time taken mostly by Frantsen during the jury selection process, the court had allotted each side no more than one hour to present our opening statements.

Frantsen's opening was a repackaging of what he'd said during *voir dire* and amounted to nothing more than unapologetic pandering to the jury's emotions. I wore a poker face and made sure I didn't stare at the jury for reactions. That was Kip's job.

He passed me several notes during the hour to let me know how many jurors had lost interest.

Judge Cordan ordered an early lunch break and told me I'd start my opening statement when we reconvened. I spent the lunch hour alone in a corner of the law library enjoying the smell of musty old books and channeling my nervous energy by doodling on the back cover of my legal pad. Today, the library was crowded with attorneys preparing for hearings and making last-minute copies of cases. I recognized a few familiar faces but observed the unspoken etiquette that attorneys in the room didn't hold conversations with one another.

I hadn't filled half of the back cover with drawings when it was time to head back to the courtroom to get started. Notepad in hand, I took my place at the podium and watched the bailiff usher the jurors to their seats. Kip told me Wiley was held up by business, but I had his permission to proceed without him to avoid a rebuke from the judge.

A knock on the door behind the bench signaled the judge was ready to enter, and the bailiff gave the familiar instruction for the attorneys, jurors, and spectators to rise. I opened my notepad to the page where I'd scribbled the first line of my opening statement as the judge took the bench. I'd planned to start with an introduction of Wiley as the face of TSC, but he hadn't made it back yet.

Judge Cordan told me to proceed. The wooden benches in the gallery creaked in protest from the weight of the bodies that shifted forward to hear TSC's theory of the case. I rested my hands on the sides of the podium, inhaled, exhaled, and looked at the judge.

"Thank you, your Honor."

I turned to face the jury.

"Ladies and gentlemen, you, the jury, are the sole decision-makers regarding the facts of this case, and must decide…"

I felt a sting. And then nothing at all.

✝

I wanted to stay in the tub until my body had absorbed all of the heat. The song my mother used to sing to me at bath time, in Peter's voice, brought me back to consciousness.

"Oh, my goodness, oh, my soul, there goes Addie down the hole. Addie, where are you going? Upstairs, to take a bath. Addie, with legs like tree trunks, and a neck like a giraffe, raff, raff raff, raff..."

"I didn't know you knew that song. I haven't heard it in years. Mom sang it to me, and when Christopher was born, she and I sang it to him." I'd planned to sing it to my child when that time came.

I stepped out of the tub, threw on my robe, and wandered back into the living room. The bath had helped settle my mind, but my body remained jittery. The monsoon outside continued with no sunrise in sight. A good, long run was what I needed, and the need was strong enough to make an exception to my dry-sock rule in exchange for the endorphins I craved.

My running clothes and shoes were easy to find, as was the rain slicker I used for hiking.

"What should I say if anyone comes looking for you?" Peter asked.

"Tell them I'll be a while."

There was only one direction I hadn't traveled, and that was away from Her house and mine. Not knowing the condition of the beach, I trudged up the sand dune and started loping down the road. The wind at my back propelled me forward, and with each stride, I felt Qaletaqa's necklace beat against my chest like the metronome app.

It wasn't long before I started seeing people moving through the different dimensions, all of which were plagued by the same tempest. In one plane of reality, a child splashed through puddles in a pair of yellow, plastic rain boots. In another, a gust blew a man's umbrella upward to form a bowl above his head.

Judging by the curious looks I was getting, including a strange nod from a blind man who walked with a seeing-eye dog that was more wolf than dog, along with the occasional greeting, I was visible to everyone. When my legs, shoes, and socks were soaked, I decided to find shelter and take a break.

I took refuge under a thicket of pine trees, making myself comfortable among a pile of dried needles. Without a GPS device, I didn't know how far I'd gone or how far I could go. Away from the Cabin and the chance that John would interrupt me at an inopportune time, now was as good a time as any for another Skip.

This one, like the others, would be troubling and unpleasant but was a necessary evil to stitch together the past and future. With a sturdy tree trunk for a backrest, I bent my knees and tucked them under the rain slicker to keep them warm. I turned the Kairometer's bezel backward a few clicks and conjured the memory of the scalding shower.

I needed to know what happened to me before I awoke on the floor of my closet with no memory of what had happened.

The journey back to the night I assaulted Guerrera with my handgun was rougher than the previous two Skips. Instead of the gentle sensation of falling backward, I felt as if I were being thrust back into the memory. My entry point was the front door of my house, where I noticed for the first time that the porch light was out.

A dark car with its lights off cruised by and parked two doors down. Guerrera emerged from the vehicle with a leather satchel around his shoulder and hurried down the sidewalk to my front porch, where he made short work of the deadbolt. Inside the kitchen, Maverick was waiting, flat-eared and bushy-tailed. Guerrera swatted at him but missed.

"Salir, gato." Scram, cat.

Maverick hissed and spit at Guerrera before running down the hallway. Guerrera must've known I was in the shower because he walked around the house inspecting light fixtures and other objects before entering the bedroom. He pulled out his phone, checked the screen, which I saw included multiple live views from inside my bathroom and bedroom, and then began fidgeting with the tiny cameras hidden throughout both rooms.

He was turning them off.

In hindsight, it was easy to see how he was able to step into the bathroom, disable the cameras, and take my gun off the vanity without drawing any attention to himself. My human head was immersed in the cascade from the rain shower head, which allowed him to stand in the doorway watching me until I shrieked from the loss of hot water.

He stepped back into the bedroom, confirmed the gun was loaded and stashed his bag under the bed. Opting for Rynner's side, he made himself comfortable on top of the covers, unbuttoned most of his shirt, and twirled the gun around on his finger while he waited for me to leave the bathroom.

I'd forgotten how shaken I'd been by his appearance that night. Except for the narrowing of my eyes, an expression of distaste Rynner understood better than anyone else, my human face had remained unreadable.

As the spectator in the memory, I walked to the side of the bed where Guerrera had made himself comfortable.

What on earth were you thinking? I asked the former version of myself when she dropped the towel and stood naked in front of Guerrera. It was no different from screaming at characters on a movie screen. They couldn't hear you and nothing you said would change the predetermined outcome.

I cringed when I watched myself undress Guerrera but perked up when I saw myself bash his temple with the butt of the gun. When my terror-stricken, former self ran into the closet, I leaned over the bed to examine Guerrera. My human self had knocked him out but not for long. I didn't know that at the time because I never looked back at him.

He swore under his breath and rubbed his forehead. He pulled on his slacks, rolled over, and reached down to retrieve his bag from under the bed. He removed a pre-filled syringe from an outside pocket and flicked off the safety cap. I walked beside him to the closet door and stopped.

In no more than two steps, he was behind the crazy woman in the closet digging for a shoe and had the needle in her, or my, neck. He left my body on the floor of the closet while he finished dressing. He returned, zipped up my dress, and carried me to the couch in the living room. In his final trip throughout the bedroom, he reactivated all of the hidden cameras he'd previously turned off.

Honeymoon-style, he carried me out the front door and folded me into the back of his two-door sports car. Future me took the passenger seat and waited to see what happened next. Guerrera put his phone in the glove box and drove south toward downtown, passing through the city center and veering east. Our destination became apparent when we cruised past the *SleepInnTime* motel, its vowel-challenged sign now blinking like a beacon from the short circuit in the wiring.

With the memories of Guerrera's unsuccessful turkey doctor experiments still raw and knowing that whatever happened there hadn't killed me before I was murdered in the courtroom, I couldn't fathom his motive for bringing me to the hospital where I'd found Qaletaqa.

He parked on the second floor of the garage and used a key card to access the building. We were on the same floor where he'd destroyed Qaletaqa, only now, he walked past the surgical suite with the encased chamber and deposited my dead weight on a surgical table with stirrups.

In my current form, I could examine the smallest, grisly details in this room which was prepped for use in a fully functioning hospital. The buffed, clean floors emitted the same smell of bleach as Rynner's room at Evergreen. A surgical dressing gown and mask were draped across a chair. The surgical tray was stocked with a catheter, speculum, glass dishes, medical scissors, sponges, and a container of cloudy liquid.

Guerrera retrieved a journal from a drawer and spent several minutes reviewing his notes. When he finished reading, he donned the gown and mask, positioned a headlamp on his head, and snapped on a pair of rubber gloves.

His now-obscured face couldn't hide the tenseness in his body. He approached the table where he'd deposited me and then stopped.

The Skip had frozen.

I circled the room and even touched Guerrera's form, which was nothing more than an asomatous projection, but nothing happened. I walked out of the room and paced the hallway to see if there was another explanation for why the complete memory was on pause.

The only explanation was that there was something I wasn't supposed to see. Someone else knew about it and had the power to stop the replay. That I wasn't privy to my own diary irritated me and hardened my resolve to get to the bottom of the pile of questions. Based on the short snippet I did see, Guerrera, who'd been a doctor in his former life, was about to perform a procedure on me in a room prepped for a gynecologist or an obstetrician.

Mateo was right. Someone powerful was keeping information from me.

I messed around with the Kairometer to no avail, got frustrated, and returned to my pine burrow. Nothing there had changed. The rainstorm continued, sending streams of water down the street in front of me. I wasn't ready to return to the Cabin, so I left the sanctuary of the trees and kept on running.

†

A steady red light in the distance became my next destination. I hadn't seen anything like it since I'd arrived Here, whenever that was. I got close enough to see an illuminated cherry on top of a sign in the window of an ice cream parlor.

The bells on the front door of *The Devine Ice Cream Parlor* jingled when I entered. The interior resembled an ice cream shop I loved as a child, where patrons could choose between traditional seating and soda fountain seating on round, vinyl-covered stools at a long, marble countertop.

Racks of sugar cones dipped in chocolate and sprinkles lined the wall behind the counter. Ripe bananas hung from a wooden stand, and further down the bar were stainless steel shake mixers, containers of syrups and malt, and sundae flutes and cups. I took a seat on one of the stools in the middle of the counter and studied the menu on the wall while I waited for a server to appear.

The bells on the door jingled again. I'd just started chewing on a fat red straw I pulled from the glass jar on the counter when a woman with an unruly head of frizzy hair, hard to miss in my peripheral vision, sat down next to me. She pushed away from the counter to gain momentum and spun around in circles on her stool until it stopped on its own.

"I wonder why adults don't do this more often. It's so much fun."

"I used to love doing that when I was younger," I replied without looking directly at her.

She slid off her stool and stuck her face in mine.

"Addie, is that you? It sure sounds like you."

I twirled around and saw Katherine smiling at me. She'd never seen me before because, like Rynner, she'd been in a coma the entire time I'd known her. Here, she looked more like the brash and confident young woman I'd seen in the photo on Ray's bedroom nightstand. With some difficulty, Katherine ran her fingers through her hair and secured a pile of it on top of her head with a clip she'd dug out of her pocket.

"Damned humidity. I would've thought I'd be free from bad hair days now. What's a girl gotta do to get a root beer float?"

An older gentleman looking dapper in his white ensemble and red bow tie came through a swinging door to the side of the counter. He tied his white apron, inscribed with the words, "*Ice Cream is Heaven*," around his waist.

"What can I get you lovely ladies?"

"Root beer float with whipped cream," Katherine said.

"Chocolate malt with chocolate ice cream," I added.

"Excellent choices. Coming right up."

He began scooping vanilla ice cream into a stainless-steel container and added root beer with the expertise of an alchemist. A quick whirl in the blender finished the first order which he slid down the counter toward Katherine. She snagged the passing float and dug a straw out of the jar in front of me.

"Thanks, Henry."

Henry measured a heaping scoop of malt powder and dumped it into another blender. Bittersweet was the emotion I felt seeing Katherine Here. I was happy she hadn't landed in Purgatory or worse but sad that she'd never get to see Jackson grow up or her brother find his own happiness.

"Katherine, what did you mean when you said you recognized my voice? Could you hear me at Evergreen?"

"Yes, we heard everything. We just weren't able to respond."

I was so flustered by her answer that I didn't catch the finished malted milkshake Henry sent sliding down the slick counter. It rocketed past me and fell off the far end sending ice cream flying all over the floors and the walls. I apologized to Henry, but he laughed it off and began making a replacement.

"Rynner was worried sick that the TSC trial would kill you. There's some irony for you," Katherine joked.

I found out that while she and Rynner were unable to communicate with the outside world, they were able to communicate with one another and often spoke during their overlapping stays at Evergreen. She also told me how tough it was to hear Ray talk about his crush on me when she knew my fiancé-to-be heard it all.

"We shared a lot to pass the hours, but my favorite story was the one he told about how you met. Rynner called it your *crash encounter.*

I wondered if the version he'd told Katherine was the same one he told me.

"I'd love to hear what he told you. Would you share it with me?"

Katherine set her float on the counter and faced me.

"Rynner said that on the day he clipped you with his road bike, he was so focused on his mental review of his research that he didn't notice when he'd drifted from the bike lane into the pedestrian lane at the lake. He didn't see you until it was too late, and he couldn't react fast enough to avoid sideswiping you. The impact knocked you backward at least ten feet, and other than a heavy thud, you didn't make a sound when you landed on the pavement. He thought he might've killed you. When he tried to help you, he said you opened your lapis lazuli eyes and told him you thought he'd broken your iPod."

It wasn't funny then, but it sounded humorous coming from someone else, and Katherine laughed so hard she started coughing.

"That's not even the best part of the story. Rynner told me you refused to give him your number so he could confirm you didn't die during the night from a brain bleed. Although he never told you because he knew you wouldn't have believed him, he thought that no amount of make-up or fancy clothes would've made you look as beautiful as you did on that day."

Everything she'd told me to that point I'd heard before, but the last part was new. Rynner must've liked and trusted Katherine enough to divulge something that personal to her. I'd shared a fair amount of information about Ray and Guerrera with Rynner, thinking he couldn't hear me, or if he could hear me, he couldn't comprehend anything I said. Knowing what I'd told him then, I now felt as if I'd thrown salt on the wounds. I'd selfishly wanted to offload my guilt to Rynner but not have him *know* about it.

Henry noticed my distracted expression. To avoid another over-the-cliff incident, he placed the new glass of malty goodness directly into my hands. I'd tied the first straw into as many knots as I could and had to dig another one out of the glass jar to enjoy my treat.

"How does this work?" I asked Henry.

"How does what work?"

"How do we pay you?"

He looked at Katherine and then back at me.

"You're kidding, right?"

He nodded with understanding when I told him this was the first public space I'd been to since I'd arrived Here.

"We have no currency. Just come to see me once in a while for your favorite."

I liked this man who loved ice cream as much as I did.

There was only one answer I could give when Katherine invited me back to her house to catch up. The opportunity to share intel was serendipitous. I'd never known her when she was alive, but I knew and liked her brother, and would tell her anything she wanted to know about him and her son. We sucked our glasses dry and thanked Henry for his hospitality.

Katherine took a few more whirls around on her stool, hopped off, and extended her hand to me.

✝

Hand-in-hand like schoolgirls, we dashed out the door allowing the jingle from the bells to ride the wind behind us. We skipped down the muddy road to a modest house on the mountainside, much like the one Ray had purchased for her before her death. Inside her foyer, I shed my soggy running shoes and windbreaker and waited for a further invite. She ushered me into her living room, where she relaxed on an oversized couch and invited me to do the same.

"Auntie, we've got company," Katherine yelled.

A woman in her mid-sixties, looking comfortable in her purple velvet tracksuit and white tennis shoes, joined us in the living room. I could see the role genetics played in Katherine's nest of hair, which looked very much like the frizzy beehive on Aunt Alvinia's head. Katherine rubbed my arm.

"You'll never guess who I found. She's the one who held my hand and stayed with me through the end, Auntie," Katherine said by way of introduction. "She used her hairbrush to fix my hair before Ray and Jackson arrived, and she didn't even know me."

The day she died seemed so long ago now. I can't remember what I thought when I pulled the brush through her hair until I smoothed out the tangles. Aunt Alvinia wrapped her arms around me in a genuine embrace.

"We're sure grateful you were there for KitCat, and Ray and Jackson too. How are my boys doing?"

"They're doing well under the circumstances. Ray attracted some of Katherine's friends at the post-funeral gathering, and I doubt he'll have any trouble finding a date when he's ready to jump back into it."

"Ray was a looker like his daddy, but Ray had the common sense and intelligence my brother never had," Aunt Alvinia guffawed.

I agreed that Ray was both handsome and intelligent but stopped short of letting on that I was personally attracted to him. I didn't know what Katherine had told her aunt about our *Coma Club* at Evergreen and didn't want to divulge more than she needed to know.

"And Jackson, what a sweet, precocious boy. He loves books and animals and has a knack for drawing with a keen eye for his age."

"That must be because he's got the gift."

"What do you mean, Auntie? What gift?"

"KitCat, you were too young and unruly when I left you to understand it, and your brother was too full of his science to hear about it. It usually skips a generation or two, but it's been in the family as long as I can remember."

The gift, according to Aunt Alvinia, was one of clairvoyance, including the ability to see both the future and the supernatural. Aunt Alvinia's grandmother, who'd lived more than two decades past the century mark, had it, and it skipped several generations to land in Jackson's DNA. Without revealing why I'd gone back to the world of the living or what I was doing while I was there, I shared with them the story of how Jackson had recognized me in Siara's RV.

"If that's true, it means the power is increasing in strength," Aunt Alvinia concluded.

My thoughts turned to Siara. She shared a similar gift but had never, to my knowledge, met Jackson. He needed a nurturing teacher to help him develop his abilities and stay safe. Siara was the perfect candidate.

"How'd you pass?" Aunt Alvinia asked directly.

"Auntie, that's not polite," Katherine protested.

"KitKat, it's a question everyone here will ask her at some point. She might as well get used to it."

"I don't mind. You're the first person who's asked. A sniper shot me at the start of a career-defining trial. The funny thing is, I don't know who did it or why, but I'm working on finding that out."

Aunt Alvinia raised her eyebrows.

"Did Jackson foresee your death?"

I thought about the question and remembered the picture he'd drawn for me of the boxes with the star in the middle. At the time, I'd thought it was abstract art. I now realized that the box in that picture was the window in the courtroom. The star was the bullet hole.

"He did, but I didn't understand it at the time."

Jackson's young age limited his ability to communicate adult themes but didn't affect the subject matter of his visions or their potency. It was heavy stuff for a five-year-old. Katherine opened the next door for me.

"You must have questions about this place. Auntie's a long-term resident. I'll bet she can answer most of them."

I told them I'd be grateful for anything they could tell me about two subjects. The first was Qaletaqa and the role he played Here.

Aunt Alvinia bowed her head.

"He was a wise and honored *X Triplici* who for centuries mentored his kind. He was compassionate and loved humans despite their flaws."

"What happens when an *X Triplici* ceases to exist?" I asked.

Aunt Alvinia said he'd be reborn in another form, but she wasn't sure whether he'd retain the knowledge he'd learned and collected through the ages. His strength and longevity had made him the top target on the Pellico's hit list, and after years of trying, they'd finally succeeded in capturing and extinguishing him.

I brushed my hand across my sternum and felt his necklace resting against it. I'd guard it with my life, whatever that now meant, if faced with that choice.

"My next question is about the *Gyratus*."

"Honey, you might want a drink for this one," Aunt Alvinia said, pulling a bottle of bourbon from under the couch.

"Auntie, now you're embarrassing me."

"Old habits die hard, KitCat. You and your brother were a handful when you were younger, and this was my outlet."

Aunt Alvinia rested her feet on the coffee table and handed me the bottle. I'd never been a bourbon drinker and coughed hard from the fiery aftertaste that burned down my throat. Katherine released her tumbleweed of hair from the clip and tucked her legs underneath her as she settled in for storytime.

"I'm too young to know the nitty-gritty of when and how it all started, but I'll tell you what I know," the older woman began.

As cockamamie and absurd as the story was, it was the most rational explanation I'd ever heard to make sense of how and why historical events unfolded as they did. Aunt Alvinia explained that since the earliest of days, there have always been four levels of existence—life on earth, life after death Above, life after death Below, and life after death in Purgatory.

For millennia, the inhabitants of the afterlives fought physical wars, with cataclysmic results, over whether and how the balance should be maintained.

To prevent the destruction of the world, they formed a Council composed of eight representatives to help the Powers maintain equilibrium. It wasn't long before the Council deadlocked, requiring a creative workaround.

Risky as it was and to prevent the same thing from happening in the future, the Council members agreed to choose at random three humans to serve along with them.

"Since its inception, the Council has decided how long each of the three otherworldly constituent groups is allowed to be of primary influence on humankind. There are rules, but they've continued to loosen over time. The twentieth century, which included the Great War, the Spanish Flu, the Second World War, the Holocaust, the wars in Korea and Vietnam, AIDS, and a host of other catastrophes and maladies, was controlled by the Underlord. The Almighty regained control in the early twenty-first century, but in an unexpected move, the Council recently voted to reverse course and cede the power of influence to those in Purgatory. Most believe the Pellico found a way to sway the human members to gain their votes. The *Gyratus* is the name for the cycle of change."

"The Pellico's unrest and the annihilation of two of your own have caused some on the Council to worry there's a bigger plan afoot," Katherine added.

"Sounds like you've got an inside source."

"Does she ever. She won't tell me who it is, but she's got a secret beau on the Council," Aunt Alvinia interjected.

Katherine covered her eyes with her hands.

The Gyratus and the Pellico's plan are important. Find the connection, Sixth Sense told me.

"When is the *Gyratus*?" I asked.

"A week from now in earth time," Katherine answered in a muffled voice.

"There's one constant in all of this," Aunt Alvinia assured me. "Regardless of what group wields the influence, the *X Triplici* retain the power to administer justice by determining what happens to humans when they pass."

My new friends had been generous with their information, but I had one more question to ask. It was one of those instances where I needed to corroborate what Mateo had told me in Siara's basement.

I shifted on the couch to face Katherine.

"I confess I know little about how things work here, and I don't know if my experience was like everyone else's. Do you know if you passed from natural causes or something else?"

Katherine lowered her hands from her face and looked up at me.

"Tell her baby," Aunt Alvinia encouraged.

"I died from an overdose of a drug cocktail made up of lethal doses of adenosine and lidocaine, the same drugs that doctors use to stop a heartbeat during cardiac surgeries. I didn't see who gave it to me."

"Tell her the rest, KitCat."

"Other memories of that day stayed with me. The first was the smell of an intriguing cologne like nothing I'd smelled before. No one who cared for me at Evergreen ever smelled like that, and I knew it wasn't Ray's. The second memory was the voice of the man who put the concoction into my IV port. He was definitely a foreigner."

"Did he say anything to you?"

"He said goodbye in Spanish. Rynner heard it too and asked me if everything was okay on my side of the curtain. The drugs worked faster than I thought, and I died before I could tell him anything."

I will make Guerrera answer, and I will make him pay, I promised myself. That I almost surrendered to him, willingly, made my stomach flip.

"You look pale. Have another drink."

I took one last sip and stood up to leave.

"I can't thank you enough for the hospitality. You're welcome to visit me and my rabbit, Peter, anytime. I live that way. Just look for the house with the glass walls," I said, pointing in the general direction from which we'd come.

Both hugged me at the door before I stepped back into the drenching rain for the run home. On my way past my new favorite ice cream parlor, I saw that all of the window seats were filled with people enjoying their heavenly treats. The blind man with the wolf-dog waved to me as I ran past him.

Did they know the *Gyratus* was coming?

✝

A steady plume of smoke was exiting the chimney back at the Cabin. Inside, the blazing fire beckoned for marshmallows on sticks to toast into their altered state of gooey cement for graham crackers. The warmth was a welcome change from the dampness outside that had once again soaked my shoes and socks.

I found Peter burrowed under the covers on my bed, unapologetic about the pile of hair he'd deposited on my sheets. I shed my wet clothes, crawled under the covers with him, and placed him on my chest. When he asked about the run, I told him about my unexpected encounter with Katherine at the ice cream parlor and the subsequent visit with her and Aunt Alvinia.

"You're holding out on me. What did you learn?"

I massaged the length of his ears and used my palms to flatten the silky stalks against his head, a gesture I knew he loved.

"Nice try, but I'm not that distracted. Tell me."

Even with Peter, sharing the details of the last Skip was harder than I thought it would be because there was something uncomfortably intimate and perplexing about the setting and the inability to see everything Guerrera did in the lost gap of time.

"The more I learn, the more I feel I don't know who I was," I said aloud. "I mean, I know I'm my parent's daughter, but—"

"You are, and you're not," Peter said.

I sat up in bed and placed Peter in my lap. I'd already learned more than I knew how to process in the last few hours. But, as was my nature, I opened the door anyway.

"I have a feeling I'm going to regret this, but what do you mean I am and am not their daughter?"

"You were so excited on the first day of kindergarten that you'd forgotten to lock the door on my cage. Your parents took you to school that day, and while they were out of the house, I escaped from your bedroom and found a cozy spot under the living room couch for my nap. Not long after

your folks returned home, they had a visitor who asked how you'd been doing and whether your parents noticed any unusual behaviors or traits."

"How did my parents respond?"

"They said that other than your stubbornness and annoying habit of asking too many questions, they hadn't noticed anything out of the ordinary. The visitor told them to report anything suspicious to him and continue nurturing your interests. Your mother asked if he could share anything about your real parents, but he refused and said he would when they needed to know." Peter had assumed my parents had told me I was adopted. They hadn't, and between the rain outside and the everything I'd learned today, I felt as if I were being waterboarded with secrets.

Peter's revelation explained some of the little inconsistencies in my life I'd chosen to ignore, such as why I looked nothing like my parents and why there weren't any pictures of me as a newborn. I'd been at the hospital when my brother was born but never heard there were any family members present for my birth.

My parents told stories about Christopher's baby years, including the time he escaped from his crib by crawling over the bars, and the time they had to take him to the Emergency Room when he stuffed his peas up his nose to avoid having to eat them, but they never told similar stories about my earlier years. Come to think of it, I'd never seen my original birth certificate.

My parents' fraud by omission stung. Now that I was gone, I had no way to confront them, tell them how I felt, and ask them what they knew about my birth parents. To Peter's dismay, my hands had moved from caressing his ears to absentmindedly twirling beads from Qaletaqa's necklace around my fingers. I couldn't help myself at this point, but I could help someone else. The movement sparked a new plan.

"Cover for me," I told Peter.

I turned the Kairometer a click forward and told it where I wanted to go.

†

The door to Siara's pantry was closed, but I knew its contents wouldn't disappoint. Bags of chocolate chips, jars of salsa, snack chips, and a large container of peanut butter filled the shelves. I grabbed a spoon from the utensil drawer, unscrewed the top from the peanut butter jar, scooped out a heap of it, and rolled it around inside the bag of chocolate chips until I'd coated the glob with dark chocolate. Into my mouth, the ball of goo went, spoon and all. Before I could extract the spoon for a double-dip, Siara waltzed into the kitchen as if she'd expected me to be there.

"For someone who doesn't need sustenance, you sure have an insatiable appetite for chocolate."

Siara swiped the peanut butter jar off of the counter, slapped the lid back onto it, and folded the bag of chocolate chips. It took me a minute and a glass of milk to clear the gumminess from my mouth.

"Someone needs your help, only this time it's not me."

She leaned against the granite island with folded arms and waited for the ask.

"I'm fairly certain I've identified a very young Seer who could use a tutor."

Her body shifted forward.

"I'm listening."

In the *Before*, I had a friend who adopted his nephew when his sister—aw fuck it—when Guerrera killed his sister."

Siara pushed me onto a kitchen chair. "Continue," she said, falling back into the chair next to me.

I told her how I'd met Katherine and her aunt in the Afterlife and learned that Jackson was one of her kind.

"It apparently runs in their family. Jackson's not six yet, and he's already exhibiting the signs."

"What kind of signs?" The Eye of Horus tattoos on her wrists widened.

"He predicted my death."

Siara clasped her hands behind her head.

"And his father? Is he an ally?"

"Doesn't know it, wouldn't believe it," I said, sharing what Aunt Alvinia had told me about Ray's science-mindedness.

"I need to see the boy. Do you know how to find him?"

I did, and within minutes, we headed out to the pre-school Jackson attended in Richardson. For this trip, Siara had chosen a Maserati with windows tinted so darkly that they had to be illegal. Julie, Jackson's nanny whom I'd met at Katherine's funeral, would be picking him up at 12:30 when school ended. We parked across the street from the already forming line of cars outside the school entrance and waited for the kids to emerge.

The school bell rang at precisely 12:30, and within minutes, teachers shepherded squealing girls and squirming boys outside to match them up with their parents, guardians, and nannies. Jackson's curly hair and green book bag distinguished him from the rest of the pack. I identified him, and Siara pulled out and around to park behind Julie's car.

"Crack your window so I can get a better look," she said, crawling over me to stick her head out the passenger-side window.

Jackson trotted toward Julie's car but stopped in front of the open window of the Maserati. He looked at Siara, stood on his tiptoes, and peeped inside the vehicle.

"I can still see you," he said directly to me. "You're still shiny. Oh, and Rose told me to thank you."

Alarmed that Jackson was talking to strangers, Julie jumped out of her car and whisked him away with a good scolding. Siara rolled up the window before Julie could get a good look inside, pulled out of the pick-up lane, and gunned it as soon as we cleared the school zone.

"He's much further along than I was at that age."

She asked me about Rose, and I told her about the little tombstone I'd discovered at the cemetery.

"He needs a teacher, a Seer who can help him understand and harness his gifts. Will you do that for me?"

"I agree, and I will. I even have a plan."

Siara said she'd get a job as a teaching assistant at Jackson's school to get closer to him. When I asked if she could clear the state-mandated background check for teachers, Siara assured me she could get the highest level of clearance from the CIA if she needed it. I knew from what I'd already seen that she wasn't blowing smoke up my skirt. Before she parked the Maserati back in the stable, Siara asked me how John was doing.

"I don't know. Ever since our last foray he's been on my shit list," I told her. She dropped the subject while I took one last stroll through her pantry before saying goodbye.

✝

"Was your trip a success?" Peter asked when I returned to my spot on the bed at the Cabin.

"It was."

"John came by looking for you. I told him you'd gone out for some air, but I don't think he believed me. He told me to tell you not to stray too far."

Fat fucking chance, I said to myself. It was time, and I knew I was ready to Skip again, this time back to the day of my death and confirm my suspicions that the Pellico murdered me in connection with the *Gyratus.* I told Peter my intended destination.

"Are you sure you want to do that? They'll know you left," Peter reminded me.

"Let them. I'll return when I'm ready."

The Kairometer's face showed white static until I turned it counter-clockwise several ticks and visualized the image of my yellow note pad resting on top of the podium. My body felt heavy as time-pressed against me in protest of my return to the past.

I landed at the back of the gallery inside the courtroom in time to watch the jury parade in through the side door after lunch. My human form stood rooted like an oak tree at the podium, hands lightly gripping its sides, waiting for Judge Cordan to give me the signal to proceed. I'd been right that all eyes in that room were boring into my back, waiting to hear the theme of the defense I'd pitch to the jury. The judge arrived on the bench and told me to proceed.

I need this memory to pause, I told myself. And it did.

In an act of post-life defiance, I hopped over the bar and stood just to the side of the window where the bullet had entered. I peered out and was able to make out the block of buildings across the street, one of which toward the middle was covered in make-over scaffolding.

Start, I commanded to no one.

It took a fraction of a second for the bullet to penetrate the glass and find its mark. Considering the podium's location near the middle of the courtroom and the angle of the window, it was nothing short of the perfect shot.

Chaos erupted when the glass shattered.

The bailiff jumped up onto the bench and threw his body across the judge, causing her to yelp as her reading glasses flew off of her face. Frantsen's helpers scrambled under their counsel table toppling chairs and leaving the big man exposed as an even bigger bullseye. Spectators flung themselves over the wooden benches in the gallery and stampeded toward the exit. My former self crumpled to the floor, dead on arrival.

I looked out from the broken glass and saw movement on an upper floor of the building under renovation. I paused the Skip again and left the courthouse without giving myself a final farewell. I'd never liked the sight of blood, especially my own, and didn't need to see the river of it flowing from my human chest.

Multiple voices called to me from the Afterlife, beckoning me to return. I ignored them all and made it to the ground floor of the courthouse courtesy of the emergency stairs. Once outside, I scurried across the street and into the building under renovation. I found the service elevator and punched the button for the floor from which I thought the shot was fired.

The doors opened, and I stepped out onto the fifth floor. The interior walls had been gutted, leaving an ample, open space with exposed wiring and ductwork. The external offices were framed, and unpainted doors were mounted.

Rewind, I told the invisible force that controlled the Kairometer.

The service elevator door opened with a *ding,* startling me.

Out rushed Guerrera, looking unhinged in a sweat-stained shirt with his hair glued to his forehead. His arms were empty. He carried no weapon. I told myself that meant nothing because he'd probably stashed it at an earlier time.

He burst into one of the offices and started arguing with some-one. I moved in for a better view.

What I saw confused the hell out of me. Tomás was in a prone position on top of a plastic-wrapped desk staring into the scope of the McMillan CS5 rifle set up in front of him.

"Stop. Stand down," Guerrera ordered.

Tomás glanced over his shoulder and gave Guerrera a quizzi-cal look.

"What are you doing here? You know the directive. She found and opened the flash drive. She knows."

"She's a lawyer, not a scientist. She doesn't understand what's on it," Guerrera countered. "I can retrieve it tonight. Besides, you know how far I've gone to achieve our other objective."

"It's not my call to make. You knew the risks when you started your little experiment, and you should've taken it up with Tessa, although we both know that would've gotten you nowhere."

Tomás repositioned himself and adjusted the scope.

"Almost got a clean shot," he mumbled.

Before Tomás could make his final correction, Guerrera closed the gap between them and tackled Tomás, knocking the weapon out of position. The two men rolled off of the desk and onto the dusty cement floor, cursing, grappling, and trying to beat the crap out of one another.

"I won't let you do this," Guerrera snarled as he used a com-bination of his legs and momentum to maneuver himself into a position where he straddled Tomás. Both stopped mid-punch when they heard the kill shot reverberate off the walls of the con-crete jungle outside.

Guerrera grabbed the rifle and peered into the scope.

"No, no, no." He threw the rifle at Tomás's head and charged toward the elevator.

I'd gotten it wrong. Guerrera wasn't the trigger man. But if he wasn't, who was?

It was time for one last pause and rewind.

I walked from office to office and opened every door with a view to the courthouse. All of them were empty. Then it dawned on me that the shooter had chosen the same spot as Tomás, only he'd chosen the floor above us.

The ride up to the sixth floor was painfully slow. The doors opened to reveal a space that was much further along in the remodeling process than the level below. Internal walls and mouse-maze cubicles filled most of the area, which smelled like fresh paint. Pallets of shrink-wrapped furniture were stacked in the hallways creating a fire hazard.

I started at the far end of the floor and methodically opened each office door to reassure myself that the killer was alone. I counted doors as I went so I'd know when I reached the right place.

I hesitated at *the* door. Inside that room was the person who changed my fate, but because I was no more than an eavesdropper on my own memory, I wouldn't be able to extract the truth or alter my destiny. The identity of the assassin had to fill in a large, missing piece of the puzzle.

I grabbed the doorknob and stuck my head inside the room.

The hard hat-covered figure, dressed like a foreman in faded jeans with a Western-style belt buckle, a long-sleeved shirt, and steel-toed boots, was in a kneeling position facing a hole in the window. He had both hands on the Steyr SSG sniper rifle he'd just fired.

Without changing his footing, he reached down with his right hand to collect the ejected casing from the floor, exposing the hard-not-to-notice gold seal ring on his right index finger.

Seconds later, Guerrera erupted from the elevator and headed straight for the same spot. Unlike me, he didn't stop at the doorway and tore into the room just as Marcus had completed disassembling the rifle and packing it into its carrying case.

"Marcus? You goddamned son of a bitch. Why?"

"That's one hell of a pair of balls you've got to ask me that question, Carlos, considering that your actions forced our hand on this one. We thought your interest in her was superficial and related to the litigation but realized it went much further when you figured out she was an *X Triplici*. What you didn't know was although she was designed to function as a human being, she was never human, and when your genetic-altering in vitro experiment succeeded, no one, and I mean *no one*, could foretell the result."

Lawyer Brain worked on fitting the puzzle pieces together while Sixth Sense debated whether I'd been sucker-punched or bushwhacked.

"You're a depraved prick too smart for your own good. You should've known the risk was too high to allow this to go any further. Besides, if I hadn't done it, Tomás would've for an entirely different reason, so in the end, even though I pulled the trigger, you were the common denominator who gave her the death sentence," Marcus continued.

With the kiss of his ring, Marcus disappeared. Speechless, Guerrera sank to the floor, buried his face in his hands, and sobbed.

I didn't know how to interpret Guerrera's soul-bearing response and didn't have time to waste pondering its meaning. When I was damned good and ready, Guerrera would experience my version of justice.

I had one week to figure out how the Pellico planned to use the *Gyratus* to unleash chaos and assume the balance of other-worldly power in their favor.

I thought about the statue of Lady Justice in Judge Katzenburg's courtroom.

I might've been blind up until that point, but now I was armed, and I sure as hell wasn't stupid.

†††

Made in the USA
San Bernardino, CA
11 December 2019